MW01224681

DOMINION OF MERCY

Library and Archives Canada Cataloguing in Publication

Title: Dominion of mercy : a novel / Danial Neil.

Names: Neil, Danial, author.

Identifiers: Canadiana (print) 20200263609 | Canadiana (ebook) 20200267205 | ISBN 9781774390207 (softcover) | ISBN 9781774390214 (EPUB) | ISBN 9781774390221 (Kindle)

Classification: LCC PS8627.E48 D66 2021 | DDC C813/.6—dc23

Editor for the Press: Leslie Vermeer
Cover and interior design: Michel Vrana
Cover image: *The Martyr of the Solway*, John Everett Millais (1829–1896), Wikimedia Commons / Google Art Project.
Author photo: Danial Neil

 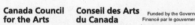

NeWest Press acknowledges the Canada Council for the Arts, the Alberta Foundation for the Arts, and the Edmonton Arts Council for support of our publishing program. We acknowledge the financial support of the Government of Canada through the Canada Book Fund for our publishing activities.

NeWest Press wishes to acknowledge that the land on which we operate is Treaty 6 territory and a traditional meeting ground and home for many Indigenous Peoples, including Cree, Saulteaux, Niitsitapi (Blackfoot), Métis, and Nakota Sioux.

NeWest Press
#201, 8540-109 Street
Edmonton, Alberta T6G 1E6
NeWest Press www.newestpress.com

No bison were harmed in the making of this book.

Printed and bound in Canada

1 2 3 4 5 23 22 21

For Rod and Kathy

To wake from low ambition's splendid dream,
Its gauds, its pomps, its toys, to feel how vain,
Like glitt'ring foam upon the turbid stream,
Or Iris' tints, upon the falling rain
— Joanna Baillie

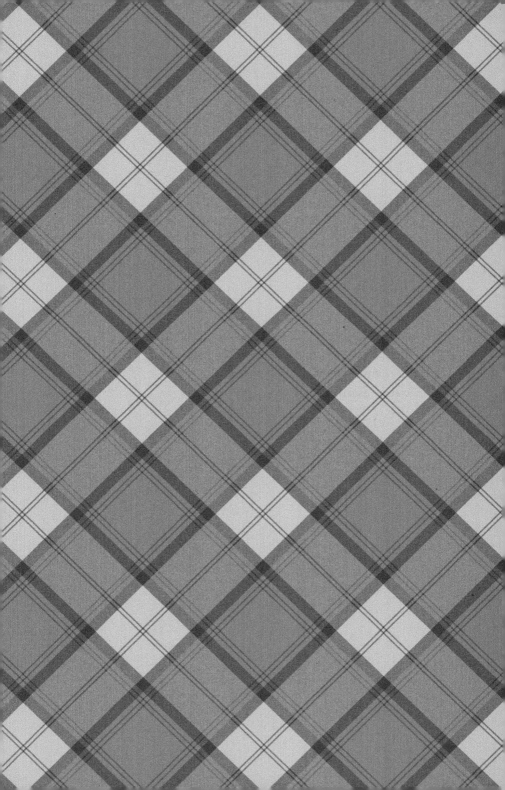

DOMINION of MERCY

A NOVEL

DANIAL NEIL

NeWest Press

PART ONE

CITY OF GHOSTS

CHAPTER

ONE

THEY HAD SEATED ME IN A CHAIR. THEY LOOKED AT ME from across the table as if I were some spectacle, an Old Town abomination. The smell of tobacco and starch, and a certain mustiness that I did not recognize as my own. I had been kept in the jail overnight. Now outside the window, tongues of Edinburgh fog in the street. I knew what they were going to say. Such looks always proceeded a lecture. They had seemed more like sermons, truth be told, with their dire warning if I continued with my immoral ways. Such grim mouths: Chief Constable Ross of the Edinburgh Police, a matron from Magdalen Asylum, and my uncle, a solicitor for the Crown with a *sudden* sympathy for the wretched of Scotland. Finely dressed in his frock coat, and his bowler on the table with a fashionable cane. I was surprised to see him, an absent man most of my life. Perhaps I misjudged my circumstance there in the Torphichen Street police station. There had been the cautions. How many? I wondered now.

"Now, Miss Stewart," the chief constable began with what I was sure was the answer, "I must inform you that you have now received three cautions. And I am most certain you know what that means."

"I wasn't counting, sir," I told him. He was a large man in a uniform that cramped his neck like a stovepipe, and I was certain that his twirling moustache consumed far too much of his time. In fact, they were all imposing figures with their loom of fat faces, my uncle included. I believed they only wished to frighten me.

"Well, our constables fortunately can count. And that deems you a *common prostitute*. Do you know what *that* means for an eighteen-year-old girl in nineteen seventeen, Miss Stewart?"

"I suppose it means you would rather I be an uncommon prostitute, sir."

"I would rather you were not a prostitute at all. You are new to all this, I know, but you don't seem interested in changing the fortunes of your life. It is puzzling indeed why you would choose such a profession, if one could call it that. It seems you think all this rather amusing. Well, I can tell you, Miss Stewart, your options are limited. There is a war on, as you know. It has been a year since the Zeppelins dropped their bombs on our city. There were casualties, buildings damaged. I'm sure, like us all, you will never forget that night, a *bomber's moon* the newspapers called it. And so, the brave young men of Scotland are rushing to the ports. Now, these boys cannot be subjected to venereal disease. The *khaki fever* has to end. They have a war to win. The stakes are high, Miss Stewart. I feel I must be blunt with you. You leave me no choice. Mrs. McFater will speak to you now."

The chief constable turned to the matron as my uncle sat silently, his hands folded on the table. I noticed that he hadn't looked at me squarely; instead, he merely turned slightly to the matron. She was an ill-faced woman, stout and bulging horridly in a much-too-tight suit with a rather military look to it. She wore an undersized rolled-brim hat that seemed to amplify a red face that gleamed like a September apple. She had been staring at me. Her eyes scalded me somehow. I didn't like her from the start, but it didn't seem to matter as I was about to hear my first option.

"First of all," she said, "we'll look after you proper in Glasgow. It's the least we can do. Do you know what we're about?"

I felt at such a disadvantage sitting there. I could feel it all escalate, a worsening of temperament, a mood against me, the authority that wanted to punish. But I wasn't a dafty girl at all. I knew when to speak plain and when to be shrewd. "I've heard of the Magdalen Asylum," I answered. "It's a female college of sort. Some of the girls were taken there. I haven't heard from them since, though I'm sure it's grand."

"You will get your industrial training, my dear. You will work in the laundries. You must submit to the discipline. It'll be hard work, but you will be fed. You're a rather scrawny thing now, but you'll have some flesh soon enough. And that plain 'hoore' dress ..."

A smart girl can lose command of her tongue when the winds change and mockery rises in the throats of witches. "This is your good deed, Mrs. McFater," I said, "putting me to work as cheap labour?"

"We like to think of it as a responsibility to our country," she retorted rather sharply. "But there are certain measures that must be undertaken, Miss Stewart, an *examination*, before the wayward girls receive the training."

"An initiation, you say?" My hands lifted before her emphasis. She knew how to be cruel, that one.

"You can call it what you will with your smart mouth. But first of all, you will be checked over by the men, constables with their cold hands. You have a sweet mouth and a fine figure with your brown eyes and ginger hair. And not big-boned like some of the country ladies we get. You will undergo a genital examination. They will inspect your woman parts for disease, and if you have the signs, you will be sent to hospital. And if you are free of disease you will be kept in solitary confinement for three months to be rid of the *moral* contagion. We'll save you from a life of shame, Miss Stewart, and at the same time restore the moral values of Scotland. That's what we'll do. Now tell me without your cheek, how does that suit you?"

"I don't have the disease, Mrs. McFater. I tell the boys to put on the rubber boots. I'm no fool. And I don't think I like you. You are here to scare me. But I will answer your question. It doesn't suit me at all. I have no interest in leaving Edinburgh. You see, my father and my sister are in need of my income. That's what it is, you know. I'm making a living. And my mother is lost at sea. How can I leave her? It will never be for the likes of you!"

"Your mouth ...!" the matron said. She reared back.

"My greatest asset, Mrs. McFater!" I said glaring at her. I wanted to set upon her, claw and fang. I felt the muscles in my neck tighten and my heart quicken, but I stopped myself. There was something about her, how she wanted to intimidate, strike fear in those she thought beneath her.

"Please control your outbursts, Miss Stewart," the chief constable said. "This is a serious matter. Now can we continue?"

I sat back. "Yes, sir." The chief constable stroked his moustache disconcertedly. Oh, I was more than a nuisance to him. But I knew he didn't want to send me to prison. He had daughters of his own, and he knew my story. The matron knew nothing. She was a cow. I feared her. I wanted her out of the room.

"Now, perhaps you wish to reconsider Mrs. McFater's offer."

"No, I would not, sir," I said. I glanced to my uncle. He sat gravely, no doubt shaken by the assertions of his unmanageable niece. "I understand that the good solicitor here has possession of my last option? And if that is so, I ask that you excuse Mrs. McFater as I have declined her offer, and perhaps anything else you wish to impose upon me."

"I'm sorry to say, Miss Stewart," he said, "but you are sadly mistaken. You are not in control of this meeting or its eventual outcome. I must inform you that you will be sent to the Magdalen Asylum, if not by an injunction from the court, by your cooperation. That will be your fate, unless ..."

"Unless?"

"The solicitor, Mr. Calvin Stewart, your uncle, has a proposition for you."

"Oh, Lord, I believe I'm about to faint, sir."

"Miss Stewart, please. I strongly suggest you listen with a clear head. Your impertinence will be your undoing. It is perhaps what provoked the bruises on your face. I can only imagine the injuries you have suffered. Perhaps it was due to drunkenness, or both. If you wish to see your nineteenth birthday, then consider his corrective solution to your circumstance."

"That's plenty of words, sir. But you confuse me. You cannot see the *corrective solution* for yourself."

"Please, solicitor," he said turning to my uncle and appearing somewhat exasperated, "if you could explain to your niece, the possibilities that might sway her. I know you have given this subject considerable thought."

"The matron ...," I interjected without giving her a look, scowl, or otherwise. The chief constable gave her a nod and she left the room. The great huff of her.

"Yes, Chief Constable," my uncle said, "I do have a remedy of sort." And now he looked right at me, but he couldn't hold it. I could see that it was difficult for him. His eyes jumped here and there. It was rather humorous, ruffled he was to be in my presence. "But first, Mary," he went on, "I am curious. I would like to hear what *corrective solution* that you think the chief constable cannot see."

"The poverty," I said. "If the city wishes to reduce prostitution on the streets of Edinburgh, then redirect the attention you give it on jobs and better wages for the poor folks. That's all they want, to make a living for themselves."

"Yes, I understand. But still you must cease with your occupation. That would be the place to begin, would it not?"

"You can say it, Uncle. There's no need to squirm on my account. I know you find it hard to accept that your niece is involved in a most offensive trade, but it's only a word. The chief constable has no trouble with it at all. You heard him say so. I am a *common prostitute*. Oh, yes, I would cease the business in a minute if I knew a better way. Did you ever consider how awful it might be to have some love-starved minger stick his crusty knob up your fanny, then punch you with his fist for your trouble? I know of such a man."

"Mary Stewart ...!"

"Tell me, sir," I said leaning over the table now, defiant and desperate to shock him as if my world would never be known to him otherwise, "why men have a need to rent my body at all? It seems the city is preoccupied with the women. And tell me why the sudden interest. You know very well the state of the poor. Your own brother jobless in the tenements. There with my young sister Lizzy. You haven't been around since my mother passed on. Perhaps in your mind we were decent enough back then when we had a fine home in Portobello Beach. And then my father lost a leg when he was crushed at the Leith docks. You know the story, Uncle, a steel beam fell upon him and sliced him bad, but not clean through. They couldn't save it. A stump with a bit of knee now. Hobbles about on a crutch. I'm sure he would have appreciated your interest in his daughters' welfare then. And my brothers dead on the Quintinshill train wrecks, Paul and Robbie. Going to war for our country. Half the soldiers from the Leith battalion gone. Did you share your brother's pain, sir? Expelled to waste away in a wretched flat in *Old Town*. Tell me what has brought you out now. Tarnished the good family name? I suppose a solicitor cannot have his ambitions with a scandalous niece about. You must have thought we had all but disappeared into the shadows of Edinburgh. Sorry to have disappointed you. So, tell me, Uncle, what do you have in mind?"

He sat for moment, and it seemed the blood had drained from his face and pooled about his neck. But a seasoned solicitor will find his composure when it's needed. "Firstly," my uncle began, restored somewhat, "I regret, indeed, the circumstances of your father. He has fallen on hard times, to say the least. I may be of some assistance to him, of course, depending on a satisfactory outcome of these proceedings."

"You seem to think me on trial, Uncle. If guilty of your moral crimes, shall I be hanged in the Grassmarket?"

"Please restrain yourself, Mary. Such dramatics will not serve you. Try to understand that what I propose may benefit your father and sister as well. You will have time to protest my remedy if you wish. But know this: you will be leaving with Mrs. McFater before the day is through if you so choose to reject my offer. And then we will see what happens to headstrong and capricious women."

A dreadful pall settled over the room like the fog in the street. The chief constable tapped a finger like a metronome. "Very well, Uncle," I said, accommodating now. It was a sobering moment in that humourless room of authority. It seemed they all had their rules and laws. But I must confess that there was a moment when he at last threatened to surrender me to that awful cow, that I wouldn't be able to outsmart them with my satire. I could curse and sally with the best of them. I suppose it had its place when I had to outwit a rough man roused with his demons.

My uncle mopped his brow with a handkerchief, then removed a sheet of paper from his coat pocket. He studied it briefly and then continued. "A magistrate of the Scottish Courts," he said, "a man that I have known for some time, may have unwittingly provided the solution. I was in his chambers one afternoon a few months ago when he began to tell me of his nephew. He liked to speak on matters that didn't include the law at times. I suppose it gave him a certain balance, perhaps a broader perspective on life. It seems the young man was adventurous, and keeping to that spirit, found his way to a land in the *far colonies*, as the judge liked to call them. British Columbia, Canada. There is a city on the north coast of that province. It is called Anyox. A strange-sounding name, derived from the natives, he told me. It is a mining town, a copper smelter, a robust settlement in the coastal forest. There is a hospital there in need of nurses, as it turns out. The city has all the amenities of a good city, schools, churches, and a tennis court to keep one fit. And there is unbounded fresh air from the sea. You can have a good home of your own. It's a prosperous port, with fortunes to be had by the willing. It just takes forbearance — and willingness, which I am certain you have in untapped supply.

"You see, Mary, I have arranged and agreed to provide the necessary tuition at the Edinburgh Infirmary to give you a start at nursing, enough training at least for you to begin in the hospital at Anyox. I understand that you were doing well in school before your family's troubles."

"Before my family's troubles," I said. "That doesn't sound so bad, does it, Uncle?"

"It took considerable convincing, I must say, but I believe you can succeed, Mary. That's what I'm trying to say to you. You seem rather educated, apart from your tendency to quarrel."

"What is an education, Uncle? My father gave me a bible to read when I could no longer attend school. He thought that was what I needed. No, it was the *Encyclopedia Britannica* and the *Scottish Enlightenment*. An old volume handed down through generations of Stewarts. And the *Oxford Dictionary*, I read it like a disjointed novel. And every child of this country knows *Treasure Island*. I've read Sir Walter Scott's poems and his *Ivanhoe*. Then there was Joanna Baillie and her poems — a true woman of the Enlightenment. *Life*, you should all read it if you wish to learn a thing or two. The rest I learn every day on the street. Is that a proper education for our children? And quarrelling, Uncle, is my defence against those who wish to extinguish what I believe to be true."

"Mary, listen to me. I'm offering you something different. I have taken the liberty of reviewing the journey. It is not unlike the journey of the many Scots immigrating to Canada every year. The nephew claimed that half the population of Anyox is Scots. You will be right at home by the sea. And there are good wages to be found, enough to send a portion home to your family if you so wish. This is an opportunity, a chance to start over on a good foot, if you do your part, Mary. I don't want to see you perish in some dark tenement, and you surely will. You must leave it all behind, change your ways. No one will know your past. You will not get another chance in Edinburgh. I took the liberty of writing to the hospital when you received your first caution. I did it out of concern. The hospital will be expecting you."

"And my father and sister?"

"I will see that they are looked after."

"Speak their names, Uncle Calvin."

He looked at me with a sleepy eye, hesitated as if it were a struggle for him, as if he did not truly believe that we were kin at all. "My brother Donald, and niece Lizzy. There it is."

"And you have not spoken to him, then?"

"No, Mary. Your father will need to hear it from you. Go to your family now. Leave your old life in your wake. Report to the infirmary in a day's time. It's all for the best."

"I don't have a choice now, do I?"

"I believe you will choose this offer over Mrs. McFater's."

"Tell me, what if I do not succeed at the infirmary? What if they don't like me? What if I'm not up to it?"

"Then I'm afraid you will be dealt with accordingly. So, do all that you can to *succeed*. I suppose, I have some trust in you."

"Tell me one more thing, Uncle: how will you benefit from this offer? Let me guess. Your political ambitions will proceed unimpeded."

"Absurd."

"Of course that's it, Uncle, isn't it?"

"I don't think you are in any position to judge me, Mary."

"I have been in many positions, Uncle, but most, I'm sure, you wouldn't approve of. Nevertheless, your motives belong to you. I feel a certain resentment to your charity when it comes with a condition, the condition that I be banished to the far reaches of the Earth. How perfect for you. However, I see no alternative. I do not want that cow of a woman to set her dumb eyes upon me ever again. It would be ill-advised for her to pass by the butcher shop on High Street. There it is."

"Perhaps, Mary, there will be a time when you will remember this day. I pray, even if you do not wish to believe me, that good fortune will follow you, and if by chance you meet with difficulty, then may you have the strength to see it through."

I watched my uncle as he put on his coat and hat. And then he picked up his cane from the table. I watched the subtleties of cheek and jowl, the steady eye now, the resolute mouth, a nod to the chief constable. A game they played in the name of moral reform, or perhaps something more. Good riddance.

CHAPTER

TWO

THE STREETS WERE COLD AND HARD, AND EVEN IN MAY THE chill poured in from the North Sea. The wind gusted along the cobblestones, down the rows of tenements that seemed to have stood forever like sunless cliffs, shoulder to shoulder, medieval and smouldering. And there was evidence of the bombing still, piles of stone rubble, boarded windows. I was thin and I shook inside, as if ice were forming in my veins. I could never find enough clothes to wear, rarely a good coat. I would have given it to Lizzy if I came by one, anyway, bartered my flesh like livestock. She needed it more in that cold room tending to our father, emptying the slopping pails. That work fell to her, and though the youngest, she had the most to lose. How was she to have a future in Scotland? And now she would be alone without the few shillings I gave her. And how she would look when I placed the coins in her dirty hand. Her bright little face. My father would turn away, unable to wonder where the money came from, unable to look at me, unable to show me his shame. I wondered, as I walked home, if Uncle Calvin would be true to his word. I worried so.

I hugged the stony walls as I went along High Street, then Cow Gate, past the narrow lanes wary as a feral cat. I was far away from the trams and bustle on Princes Street, in New Town beyond the castle, far from the safer places. There were few motor cars, but now and then the clop of horses. Traders with their wagons moved listlessly in the grey light. I didn't want to be seen. Jimmy would be about looking for me. I rented a flat in a tenement from one of the other girls, Josie, when I needed to. It was nearby. Jimmy wouldn't be happy with the plans for me, the exportation of his merchandise, my money-making bones. How quickly the bullies think they own you, think you're nothing at all but a body for sale. Do what you want with your animal needs. Farthest thing from love, I wanted to tell the chief constable. He knew Jimmy well enough, but never once arrested him. I would have paid dearly for fingering him so. And now I had the money I owed him but didn't want to give him. I kept the money in a pocket I stitched on the inside of my dress. I was done with him, but still he was out there. He was the shadow that steals up behind you, cold and lethal, the fright that seizes you like the sudden clap of thunder, the accursed wail that haunts the graves of the dead. I feared him more than anything, more than I feared Mrs. McFater's moral panic. More than leaving Scotland.

As I reached the tenements on Dumbiedykes Road, several women in the street saw me coming and gathered their children around their skirts. Perhaps they had watched me disappear into the many nights, hurrying like a thief in the same penny-plain dress. They could only think that it would never happen to them. It was a shameful thing to fall into, because it *was* like falling, life giving way under you, a trap door or a precipice that opens up and then tempts you with a way out — Jimmy willing to catch you. Just one time. A bit of money. But there would never be a time when our poverty would cease to be, would be supplanted with prosperity. Not even hope could find a foothold in the tenements. So what was it that my uncle had given me, my family? If it was hope, I couldn't feel it. That word, and all the imaginable things heaped upon it, had abandoned me at the very moment my mother's life left her drowned body.

I wouldn't give the ladies the benefit of looking me in the eye with their condemnation stalled on their tongues. They said nothing as I brushed passed them and hurried up to the door to our tenement, but then one spoke, emboldened, it seemed, with my back to her.

"Mary Stewart," she said loud enough to surely span the breadth of the street, "your poor mother will be rolling over in her grave!"

And I spun at the door because I couldn't let such a disparaging thing go unchecked. "You're no daft woman, Mrs. Drummond," I said, "but you are heartless, for you know very well my mother drowned. She was lost at sea and not a grave for her. May your children forgive my rebuke, and their mother's manners."

"You will go to hell!"

I quickly went inside. I stopped inside the door to gather myself. That's the way I was treated on our street most times. They would never come out with it and shout, "Whore!" But they didn't have to. I suppose they were afraid, afraid for their children. But wasn't I a child, too? They blamed me for it all, just like the chief constable, Mrs. McFater, and my uncle. They seemed to think that it was my bad character, some flaw that put me at odds with middle-class morality and the established conventions of femininity. At times I seemed to have arrived back at the bottom of a well, or a mountain, and looking up at the great height to be climbed, felt the not-too-subtle pull of giving up.

Our flat was on the second floor. The steep staircase was poorly lit except for the landings where light came in through a window. My father could manage the stairs on his one leg on the days he allowed Lizzy to help him, when the misery of idleness drove him nearly mad for an hour in the tavern down the street. If we had lived on the floor four stories above, I was certain he would have been confined to a prison-house with its lofty view, unenviable compensation. And when I arrived outside our door I stopped and looked down the long hallway. The smell of degradation, tainted air, fetid meat, the smells of a compressed humanity. I listened for a moment longer before going in, listened to the human sounds that lived in the building, each one connected to a soul, each one wanting something better. But I wondered if that was true, if they dared dream anymore. And I wondered if Lizzy still had dreams, for she was a prisoner of a kind and had done nothing wrong at all. And when I went in, she was standing at the door, as if she had known I was on the other side. She was in tears.

"What is it, Lizzy?"

"Oh, Mary, he was here," she said, sobbing.

"Who was here, Lizzy?"

"That awful man who makes you do things for him. He was here. He pounded on the door with his fists. I had to let him in. I had to." She dried her eyes with a knuckle.

"Get in now!" my father called out. He was sitting at the table with his stump pushed out toward the stove, his hand over a bible. "You've brought trouble to this house. And you didn't come home last night, Mary. You can't leave us alone like this. Lizzy can't keep the bullies away!"

We went to the table and sat with him in the dim light of a lamp, a shadow with his beard and dark eyes. The stove glowed red but the light was scant, though warm enough to soothe a stump. They both looked at me now as if I had to explain my life once again, to my own family who had witnessed it all but could not accept the consequences that I had accepted myself. I turned to hide the bruise on my cheek. It wasn't so difficult in the muted light.

"I was in the jail," I said, "locked up for the night. I'm sorry, Da, but you see —"

"No, I don't see. That man was but a boy who was looking for the money he says is owing him. Can that be true, Mary?"

And Lizzy with her mouth open, wondering, I knew, what I would say. She possessed a loveliness even with her threadbare clothes and soot-smeared cheeks. A golden-haired girl with a sheep of curls. Her eyes were blue in the shadows as if in spite of it. Would they ever grow dim? It made me doubt that I had done anything at all for them. Where was the progress, the furtherance, the gain I had often told myself of? What words would keep them safe, fed, and reassured that it would always be so? How could I leave them now, with their brittleness, their profound vulnerability? And what would happen to them if my uncle's proposition was not gallantry, but betrayal?

"It was Jimmy McDuff, and he may be a man, but still a dreadful boy. He is ..."

"Mary, tell me why you are beholden to him," my father insisted.

"Say it, Mary," Lizzy said, her hands folded on her lap, curious to know, perhaps, a little bit of the outside world beyond the sooty walls.

She had questions about life, I knew, things a mother imparts to a daughter in timely and proper ways. She was my biggest worry. I could hear our mother's sorrow at times, her lament in the screech of wind, in the petitioning peal of church bells, and in the common voices of the street, as if restless in death, unable to depart the world entirely until her children were safe. *Oh, Lizzy.*

"How do I tell you where the money comes from?" I said. "How do I tell you about the shame that I had to swallow, or a world that measures a woman's worth based on the compulsive appetites of men?" I removed the coins from my inside pocket and handed them to Lizzy.

"Then don't say where it comes from, Mary," our father said. He watched Lizzy place the coins in a tobacco tin. "It is all going to end badly. I can feel it. Lizzy tries to tell me what you do, but I don't want to hear it. No father wants to hear what his child must do because he cannot earn a living. Yes, Lizzy tells me, a girl not yet a woman. It was she who chased the boy off. Oh, you should have seen her. I would have been proud if not so ashamed. I am useless in my own home. I cannot defend my girls. I don't want him around this house. So, if that is his money, then you shall give it. Let it be done with."

"It is the money meant for this family, Da. There is no other money if I give it away."

"Please, Mary, you must stop it."

"He will not leave me alone. He wants more and more from me."

"Surely, he's a man by age and can be arrested."

"But he never is."

"And you were?" my father said, outrage and impotence thick in his throat. "There is no justice in that. This cannot go on, child. It will be your death!"

It all seemed to converge, a family, our diminished family hanging on to the threads of its fragile existence. Everything in that room, the bare and the plain, minimal necessities in an inequitable world. All shades of incessant dimness that demoralized the most intrepid of spirit. A window with sacking. Hanging sheets for privacy. A single shelf with two photographs, one of my mother and the other of Paul and Robbie in uniform. My father couldn't speak of the boys, but I saw how he would stare, perhaps still in shock, not wanting to believe that they were gone. And my mother with a perplexing grin, and the laughing ladies with her. I had often wondered what was behind it, what private joy they had. All of it, our depressing circumstance. I would take the tough line when pressed, but truth be told my shame was more than I could bear at times, that I could do such a thing, lie on my back in a filthy room to please a man, relieve him of his pent-up desires, his desperation, take his rough love without complaint, all for a few coins that we may eat. And the solution to it all was untried, so far away, and unreachable.

"The chief constable does not wish me to go to prison, Da," I said. I had to tell him now. "And there are industrial schools for women who are exploited for their labour. Exploited one way or the other, it seems to me. But there is one thing that I can do."

He turned to me with his urgent dark eyes. "Tell me, girl, what is it?"

"Uncle Calvin has a plan for me."

"My brother Calvin, you say?"

"Yes, Da."

"Tell me, Mary. What in God's name has he done?"

I couldn't answer without proper reflection, an inventory of costs. And of course, the greatest cost of all would be to Lizzy.

I could see it so clearly, the sacrifice of a child who never had a choice with anything in her young life. She knitted and sewed a bit for the ladies in the nearby tenements, bartered for coal that she carried in buckets up the stairs. I couldn't allow her to follow in my footsteps. I had to stop it, as they all would surely agree. I would leave, perhaps for a little while. They would be looked after. I had to believe in that. I had to believe that Lizzy would be all right, that she would find some small thing to hope for, that the glimmer of light would remain in her eyes. I had to believe that the Zeppelins wouldn't return.

"Uncle Calvin wants me to go to Canada," I said at last.

"Canada?"

"British Columbia, Da. There is a mining town on the coast. It is in need of nurses. I'm to start my training at the Edinburgh Infirmary in the morning."

"Impossible, Mary. How will we manage without you?"

"Uncle Calvin. He said he would help. You see, Da, there are good wages in the hospital in Anyox. I will send money home. It's best, Da. If I don't go, the chief constable will send me to the Magdalen Asylum in Glasgow. They will put me to work in the laundries for their own purse. That won't help us at all. Uncle says that the land in British Columbia is full of Scotsmen wanting a better life. There's land. There's opportunity. So I must go. Don't you see?" How quickly I affirmed my arrangement, as if it were born out of my own enterprise.

"A man can have no pride in one good leg. I am afraid that it has come to this. It is not what I wanted. I had a good job on the Leith docks, and your mother chasing the herring down the coast in the summer. Two sweet girls and two devil-making boys. It was all we ever wanted, a good life in Portobello. In my dreams I can find that life, but only to awaken to my wasting days. Know this: my life is as good as gone. The both of you deserve a better life than I can give you now. It will break my heart to see you go, child, but I can see why you must. Nothing remains for you in Edinburgh.

No man will want your hand in marriage, and no children to tug on your skirts. A woman will be ruined by this business. But there is one thing I want you to do, Mary, after you settle in that new land. Now, it may take a while, but you send for Lizzy. She'll be fifteen years old in a year and you send for her. You promise me."

"Yes, Da."

"And my younger brother Calvin, well, we had a falling out. I can say it to you now; it was my fault. He was the brightest of the Stewarts. I have envied him all my life, to be so smart and sure. I believe now that I was jealous of his success. I could have done better. Aye. He came to me with plans to go to university. Well, he wanted a loan of twenty pounds for his tuition, but I wouldn't give it. We were doing well, a young family at the time. We had the money, but I turned him down. But it didn't stop him. He managed to find a loan and paid it back in full after he graduated. And there he was, a proud young man ready for the Scottish Bar. I didn't lift a finger to help him. Now he wishes to help my family. I will never understand how a man's brain works. I am a mystery to myself."

He slumped in the dark, and we watched him. His hand hadn't left his bible. I could see that Lizzy was afraid of such talk, the family shrinking one body at a time, the dwindling constellation until there was only her, a lone star in the blue-black sky. I didn't want to say anything about Uncle Calvin's motive, his political aims. Perhaps it was only the suspicions of a cynical girl in a cynical world, and he truly wished to help us. But what was his motive after all, but inspiration to alter the course of a life for its greater good. Perhaps. And there my faith would rest.

In the early evening we set the plates on the table. A supper of boiled potatoes and tinned meat. We were all very quiet. The stove made a sound like breathing, a sound of hunger and its endless demands. It always wanted the coal, the fire, and the sound of its own existence. And then the great drumming of fists on the door.

CHAPTER

THREE

MY FATHER CURSED WHEN I OPENED THE DOOR AND JIMMY
burst in. "You leave us be now, boy!" he shouted out, a war cry
from a lionhearted man forsaken by a limb. He thrashed about
for his crutch.

"I have no quarrel with you, old man," Jimmy railed, his voice
freakish and shrill. "The girl here owes me money and I've come
to collect." He stood there with his shaved head and his lips glis-
tening with sores. Not a tall boy, he had an unhinged look in his
eyes, as if he had been born malevolent and motherless.

"I'll kill you with my bare hands if you hurt her," my father
threatened. "Do you hear me?" He scrabbled toward the door.

"Da, please." I turned and put my hand up to stop him.

"Out!" His eyes blistered black.

"It's just a misunderstanding, Da."

"Is it?" Jimmy said, showing no concern for my father, dismiss-
ing him as he were a half a man. Nothing at all.

"I don't have it, Jimmy. I have no money to give you."

"Then you'll come with me now. There's a customer."

"Have you no shame, Jimmy? You must never come to my
house."

"It seems you've left me little choice, now, doesn't it, Mary?"

"There's no money, Jimmy. I have nothing."

"Come, you have an appointment with some dumb soldier.
He wants a young one. Then you'll have money. And you'll be
getting none for yourself. And where were you last night? There's
got to be an accounting. If you're holding out on me, well, that's
a dangerous thing. You know what I'll do."

"Leave Mary alone!" Lizzy commanded all at once. She had been standing with our father, holding his arm as he simmered with an impotent rage. She stepped forward, a brave girl with her scalding face.

"Lizzy, get back!" I implored. I held her shoulders with both my hands and looked into her eyes. I had to shake her, and I was sorry for it, sorry for her and my father, for I truly had brought trouble to our home. "Now leave this to me."

"I'm going for the constable, Mary," she persisted, unable to comprehend why I would leave with such a terrible boy.

"No, Lizzy. It'll all be fine. I promise. You need to trust me now."

"She's a fiery one," Jimmy said. "I can say that." Then he took hold of my arm and pulled me out into the hallway, reclaiming his property, so brazen and confident.

"Close the door, Lizzy," I said turning back, his fingers digging into my arm. "I'll be back in no time at all. A misunderstanding, that's all it is. I'll make it right."

And then as he jerked me down the hallway, heads poked out of the flats one by one, then quickly retreated. I was alone. I didn't have the physical strength to get away from him. There was no help. I had to decide how it was all going to be. I had to use my wits. I had to keep Jimmy away from Lizzy, the way he looked at her. She was a pretty girl and he could see what she could do for him, a girl ripe with her latent sexuality. How could I leave her now? I had to go with him. I had to find a way to end his evil governance over me.

Jimmy pulled me down the stairs. He twisted my arm and I called out in pain, but he ignored me. He said little as we went but made sounds under his breath like laughing and derision, a compassionless boy, unfit to be a soldier, his nature without mercy or kindness. There was something broken in his head, a dangerous business contrived out of his depravity. I was hauled down the street in the coming dusk. The lamplights would not be turned on with the German Zeppelins threatening to return to Edinburgh, and the streets would remain clogged with shadow. Patrons hurried along the cobbled street toward the taverns in temporary sobriety, paid us little mind, a girl in distress, a bully having his way, as if we were non-existent, the unremembered, out of phase with their world. Everything that had transpired that day, my unexpected plans, the Edinburgh Infirmary where I would begin something I had never imagined for myself, all of it in motion toward some redeeming end, seemed in doubt now.

We neared the tenement and several soldiers gathered near the shadows, laughing, shoving one another playfully. Some joke among them. Jimmy noticed my distraction and jerked me away like a tethered animal, into the building and up the stairs. Josie was coming down, and she stopped as we came up to her. Jimmy let go of my arm, but I could see how she looked, noticed the fingerprints like brands on my arm, and perhaps the anguish pulling at my mouth. I tried to convey that very thing to her for she knew him as I knew him. Josie was much older than I was, had known the bullies one by one, but none as mean as Jimmy. It was always wise to just do what he asked, what we needed to do in order to protect ourselves as best we could. And I knew I couldn't tell her of my plans, and never Jimmy, for he was unpredictable and I feared what angry and malicious thing he might do. There was a story how he killed a girl, strangled her for nothing at all, perhaps only keeping money from him.

"I let him in," Josie said. "He's just a laddie. But I suppose if he's old enough to kill Germans, then he's old enough to use his banger on a girl."

"Off you go now," Jimmy said, jerking his head impatiently.

I followed him up to the flat. I had to go through with it. The tortuous fretting, how I was going to end it with Jimmy. It was all so orderly, the way he was, pulling me here and there, as if I had surrendered my soul to him. But I knew that I was more, could feel it inside me, caged and wanting out, wanting to make my own way in the world. It was a torment at times, for the societal mores said it plain, that women were of a certain character and purpose, nothing more. And I wondered why we allowed it, why *I* allowed the scabby Jimmy to appropriate my life, his wedge of promises, his pretense of prosperity and resurrection. The promise of emancipation from poverty had been a sweet temptation, but a cruel and remorseless lie.

I had heard of the suffragettes scandalizing the men and their dominions. My mother would have stood with them, I was certain. She was strong-minded, and my father a better man because of it. She made him thankful for the world she had forged for us all, out of nothing but a fervent love. And I felt her loss more than ever now, felt the absence of her guiding hand as my father mourned his missing leg.

At the door Jimmy turned to me and pushed up against me, his nose nearly touching my own. Then his hand came up to my throat, and his breath was foul, and he seethed.

"Now, you do your business, Mary. Get your fee for the service. I'll be nearby, so don't think you can take the money. You'll be getting none of it. You crossed me once, but not a second time. Think of that. I'll be fair when you've paid me in full. I think you've been holding out on me for a while. Do you think I'm daft? I don't want to hurt one of my own girls. But you can't be stealing from your employer. I can't allow it. I won't allow it. Now, if you want to keep that pretty face, you best do what I say. Do we have an understanding, Mary?"

My throat was squeezed by his thumb, and I couldn't speak. In my ears, my pulsing heart, its perilous meter. I tried to swallow, and then managed to, but painfully. "Yes, Jimmy," I said. I opened the door to the flat, then half-turned back to him. He was walking away. I waited until I could hear him going down the stairs; then I went in.

I drew a deep breath and my racing heart slowed. Danger subsided, ebbed. A room with nothing at all but the compulsory bed. He was sitting on it, sandy-haired and freckled, a lean *farm* boy, I guessed. He watched me walk in, a young soldier in uniform, kilt and hose, spat-covered shoes. He held his Glengarry cap in his hand. I strangely felt safe with him, as if I believed in what he stood for, without question. He had the look of astonishment, his mouth open in that way men do when they are overcome with bewildering feelings of sensuality, the way their bodies change in miraculous ways. It was his first time, I surmised, by the way he sat, unsure. Then I noticed that his looking was more like confusion now. I sat beside him.

"What is your name?" I asked him. My voice was thin, painful. I sensed right away that he was no danger. The harmless had a way.

"Allan," he said.

"Is this new for you, Allan?"

"Yes, I suppose it is."

"Suppose?" I wanted to know, more so to get Jimmy out of my head. One to the other like different horizons in the span of moments.

"They teased me, you know, the lads in my unit. They said I had to become a man. They said I could leave God at the door. But I don't know."

The soldiers in the street, their observance. "Will it make you a man?"

"I don't know."

He kept looking at me, studying me, then turning away, then back, then sitting with his head down. He didn't seem to know what to do. He was nothing like the other men.

"You're nervous," I said. "You don't have to be."

He made no suggestion of anything, no movement toward me. His hands remained tightly clasped to his cap. "I'm thinking about the war," he said as if to explain himself. "That's where I'm going. I'm leaving on a ship in two days. They say I'll be fighting the Huns in a month. Private McGinnis said that if I didn't lay with a girl now, I could be killed in France, I could die never having done it. I suppose I'm nervous about that, and something ..."

"Something else?"

"Well, to be honest, you look like someone."

"I do?"

"Yes, my sister Katherine. You look just like her, everything. It makes me feel strange. I don't mean to offend you. But I just can't ..."

"I take no offence, Allan. You must like her, then."

"She's my twin. She cried the day I left on the train in Stirling, more than my own mother. She ran alongside the train but couldn't catch it, you know. I watched her from the window until she just stopped. It was the saddest I've ever felt. Now I'm sitting here with you and I'm wondering about things."

That young soldier was such a sweet boy, with such a simple and essential understanding of himself. Allan gave me hope, sitting with him, the space between us more sacred than carnal. I decided that I would not influence him, his decisions, and his sexuality that could be roused with a small measure of playful stimulation. The consideration seemed appalling somehow, that I would manipulate him for a few shillings. But he needed to tell me, for I knew that life was a fleeting affair, something he was just learning.

"Then what would you have me do, Allan?" I said. I reached for the buttons on my dress, hesitated, and then withdrew my hands.

"I don't know."

"We don't have to do anything, you know."

"You're not what I thought you would be."

"What did you think I'd be like?"

"An older woman, perhaps not too pretty. All business, you know, like the other ..."

"Like Josie? This is her flat."

34

"I didn't mean that. She seemed nice. She said your name was Mary."

"Yes."

"You're so young, Mary."

"It's not easy being so young."

"So, why do you do it, with all the men?"

"Money."

"That's so important?"

"It is when you have none. It is when you have a family to look after, a sister and father. He can't work. It's not so simple, Allan."

"There was someone with the other lady, Josie, a rough-looking lad. What does he do?"

"He has girls who work for him, in the flats. They won't let him near the brothels. He is a broken man with the mind of a horrid little boy. Simple in some ways, and lethal in most others."

"He did that to your cheek, then?"

I brought my hand up to touch it. No one had cared that much before, a rare kindness from a young man leaving for war. I felt the need to rest my hand on his. It was most peculiar, a kind of answer to the yearning that I had buried deep inside me, that I could be something for a man. It seemed that I had paid a very dear price for what I had to do, my own estrangement from intimacy and the beauty of lasting love. I suppose I had given up on that possibility. And then I took his hand in mine and held it to my breast. He watched me. He was curious, but not in the way I had expected. I lowered my hand, still holding his.

"How old are you, Mary?" he asked. He looked at me now, perhaps forgetting his sister Katherine for a moment.

"I am eighteen years old. I must seem older to you."

"No, you're just a girl who has to do things that a girl shouldn't have to do. I don't mind holding hands. That's something I've never done. I don't mind it a bit, if it's all right with you. I'll pay you just the same."

Allan was more comfortable now, his words loosening from his lips. For a moment I did not feel like a prostitute, nor did he seem like a stranger behind a wall of concealed truths. "No, I cannot take money from you," I said. "Where you are going is dangerous. I can't imagine it. Scotland's boys. I won't take money from a brave lad for a moment's comfort."

"I'm not so brave," he said. "Some of the Royal Scots are excited and can barely contain themselves. They can see, I think, their own glory. It seems they have accepted their fate. Well, I suppose I do, but I am still afraid. So many have died in terrible ways. I feel ashamed of my fear. I shouldn't be speaking like this. I don't know why I'm telling you. I'm no talker. Perhaps you wish to let go of my hand. I won't blame you. I'm not such a good customer."

Allan's easy nature was lost for a moment. What he had been asked to do was not an uncommon thing with Scot history of clans battling for lands and honour. But now the warring tribes of old had gathered under the banner of the Royal Scots. It seemed the world was in need of our young to protect the lives and history of free people. It made me wonder about freedom, my own captivity, and the tyrant that lived in Jimmy's foul heart.

"You're not a customer, Allan."

He must have noticed the way my head slumped with my troubles. He placed his hand under my chin, and then he lifted it and looked at me. "I don't know you, Mary," he said, "and I may never see you again, but you mustn't let anyone harm you."

I just looked into his eyes. He was hiding nothing. It was so easy to be with him. He was shy, but I believed that honesty had a certain vulnerability. Did we each feel safe in the other's company? "Perhaps, Allan," I said, "those who harm will feel the same pain for themselves. It will end, as all things will."

"Your talk is as dreamy as the poets."

"I'm more apt to be sharp-tongued," I said. I laughed, but he didn't, for he knew nothing of my survival strategy.

"I must go now. Thank you, Mary." He stood up, placed his cap on his head, and straightened it. He started for the door.

"And what are you thanking me for?" I got up and followed him. I didn't want him to go so soon. I would forget his tenderness, how he looked at me, how it felt to be moved by a man's incorruptibility. And I didn't want to face what would come next.

"You listened. No one wants to hear sad stories." Then he reached into his pocket and withdrew several coins. "Open your hand," he said.

"No, I don't want to take it."

"You must, Mary. It is for you." He placed the coins in my hand and closed my fingers around them.

"What will you tell the others?"

"I will tell them nothing. I don't want to share the time I had with you. It wouldn't be right. I want it all to myself."

"Well, then. Stay safe, Allan."

"And you."

"Do you have a last name?"

"Private Allan Rose."

"Pleased to make your acquaintance, Private Allan Rose." I stood on my toes and kissed his cheek without thinking. It felt that I was losing something, an incomprehensible friendship. It was if I suddenly felt his future death, and that some part of me grieved as if he belonged to me now.

He touched his cheek with his fingertips, smiled boyishly, then went out the door.

CHAPTER

FOUR

I SAT ON THE BED AND WAITED FOR HIM. I PLACED THE coins in my inside pocket, wrapped in cloth to keep them still. I could have fled into the night, but that wouldn't have solved a thing, wouldn't end what I needed ending. I felt the shaking of my limbs, my insides, all of me, feeling my fear in its full measure now after having sat in the presence of its absence. I had no plan for him, something that I could do to walk away, to rid him from my life without endangering all that I held dear. But still it had to end on that night. There would be no other time. I could never speak to Jimmy like I did the others, no words to cut him like knives, to reduce him, unarm him, and render him impotent in the way that I knew he was. I waited. I waited as the flies crept over the lampshades, inched toward the brightest thing. I waited as the memory of Allan Rose faded from my thoughts. I couldn't hold it, the soft measure of his words, the benevolent intonation. Then the turn of the doorknob, and he rushed in like the unclean, the embodied gloom, so singular and possessed with one thing on his mind.

"Now then, out with it," he said, his hand outstretched, impatient for his money.

"I don't have the money, Jimmy," I said. "The young soldier changed his mind."

He stood over me. "That's nonsense," he said, his chiselling voice oddly composed. "I saw the lot of them in the street. The way they carried on with that boy. Now give it. I know you have it."

I sat immovable and determined. I needed time. Josie would return soon. Then perhaps he would grow weary and leave. But

39

then all at once he pushed me back on the bed, and in an instant, he was on top of me. He pinned my arms with his legs, and then began to pull up my dress, his fingers searching blindly like the noses of rats in the dark.

"Where is it?" he snarled. "If I find it, you won't live to regret it!"

I quickly realized that Josie might not return in time. And so many shouts in the tenements, arguments, every manner of quarrels and scuffles. There would be no notice. Jimmy was steadfast on that night, as if he had also made up his mind how it would all end. I knew I had to fight him now with everything I possessed. "You'll rot in hell, Jimmy," I screamed. "You're nothing but a wicked child. Not a man at all. Someday you'll make a grave mistake. You'll get what you deserve!"

"Shut up!" he said and then struck the side of my face with the back of his hand. The blow stunned me, laid waste to my only defence — my pathetic bluster.

He ripped at my dress and finally the inside pocket could no longer hold and released the cloth-bound coins onto the floor. There they spilled and one by one rolled across the room.

"You've done it now, haven't you?" he said. "I never believed you. You see, I cannot forgive you for this. You know I can't. I wouldn't be able to trust you ever again. Don't you see?"

He had his money now, and it seemed to appease his anger momentarily. And the way he held me down, my dress open to his lecherous regard, did something to him. I saw it in his small black eyes, the lust in them that he could never expose, that was undeveloped, or perhaps an illness, a deficiency. And it seemed that he wanted me to prove him a man. The grotesque twisting of his lips. He would kill me before the night was out, but not before he would assault me with his horrible secret. I had such sad and bitter regret that I had allowed it to come to that, as if I had conspired with him. And as he began to unbutton himself I closed my eyes. I wouldn't look. And then I remembered what Josie told me one time, how she had an answer for the vicious and cruel. She kept a knife under her mattress, the right side where her good hand could find it. But my arms were held fast by the weight of him. In that despairing moment, I prayed for the return of my wit to save my life, something that he wouldn't expect, something to free my arms.

I opened my eyes and looked up at him, his lips greasy with his animal slaver. I tried to smile, something of submission, and then I spoke his name, my horrible affection, my guile that he could not understand. He tilted his head like a curious dog, deviant but amenable. He began to lower himself, freeing my arms. And at once I searched with my hand, along the bottom of the mattress, along the springs, but I couldn't find it. It startled me to think that it wasn't there. It could have fallen onto the floor, under the bed, unreachable, or perhaps it was no longer there at all. I was trapped with Jimmy. He mouthed my neck, my throat, then lower and lower, making pitiful sounds of gratification, some heinous pleasure. I searched desperately, my arm reaching, and then at last I felt it. My fingers crept along the knife until I held the handle firmly in my hand. I slipped it out from the mattress. I had only one opportunity, one daring attempt to stop him. He was pre-occupied with my rigid body, and I had to be quick, decisive. And then with all my strength, I let out a primal scream and thrust the blade of the knife deep into the flank of his belly.

He rolled off of me like a barrel onto the floor, his blood spurting darkly through his fingers where he held his wound. He howled like a dying thing, looking down at the puncture and the pooling blood to see what I had done to him. He looked up at me with such shock and horror, the knife still in my hand, shaking, dripping with his blood. His rage boiled in him now, boiled in his eyes. He was dangerous still and I waited to see if he was done, waited to see if he would bleed to death there on the floor. I slipped off of the bed. I was ready for him. I would stick him again if I had to.

"What have you done to me?" Jimmy said. His face softened, slowly melted like candle wax, and his hard mouth reformed into

a kind of terrible pout. He began to cry, but his tears seemed outrageous, out of place. He had inflicted so much pain onto others.

I didn't feel sorry for him. I didn't feel a thing, only that
I wanted him to die, to be gone from the world. All at once Jimmy
managed to get up on his knees, then slowly onto his feet. He
wobbled awkwardly, then turned to me. He held his wound with
his hand and the blood ran down his trousers to the floor. I waited
with the knife, brought it out in front of me. He wasn't done, it
seemed. But he didn't lunge at me, made no gesture toward me
at all, only a look of unthinkable betrayal. He simply turned away
and limped for the door and was gone.

I knew I had to leave. I couldn't wait for Josie. I had to get out
of that room. It was a frightful scene, blood on the sheets, on the
floor, crimson drops out to the door and most certainly beyond.
It seemed someone had been murdered, and perhaps Jimmy was
already dead, but it wasn't murder at all. I had fought for my life.
And my dress was stained with his blood and ripped apart at the
seams. I found a length of string and made a belt from it. It would
hold my dress together until I got home. I cleaned up the room
the best I could with some rags and a bucket of water. I cleaned
the knife and set it on the bed so Josie would know what hell had
taken place. And the blood lingered still in spite of the scrubbing,
and the metal smell of it I could taste on my tongue. And then
I gathered up the spilled coins and left two shillings for Josie's
trouble.

I left the flat with the full knowledge of what I had done, a
thing that settles in the brain like a stranger. I was cautious for
the streets would be unlit and treacherous. If Jimmy were waiting
for me, I would never know. I moved down the stairs and then out
the door to the street. I stopped and listened. The air was cool and
I shivered, but more so from the fright of the pitch-black night. It
was difficult to keep my bearings, but I continued on, and then in
the distance I could see a square of light in the street. There was
an amber light from a window and shapes inside passed before

it. It was the tavern. I hurried past it and still there was no sign of Jimmy, no blood trails in the dark, no huddled shapes prone and wounded.

I began to conjure up all manner of frightful thoughts. Perhaps he had crawled under a carriage or motor car. He could have been anywhere, dead in a lane, a gutter. And if he lived still, then he surely would be going home, but that was something unknown, only rumours and hearsay. Some said he lived with his mother on St. Leonard's Street. Perhaps she was a good mother in spite of a wretched son. She would nurse him back to health, back to the way he was, back into my life. And then he would surely kill me like the other girl, strangled with a cord and dumped into the River Forth.

I made it to our Dumbiedykes tenement, up to the second floor, and to Lizzy standing stiffly and aghast at the sight of my bloodied dress. Our father was asleep in a chair by the stove, warming his stump, as if it were not a blunted appendage but a good dog. We went to our sheet-partitioned rooms where Lizzy helped me out of my dress.

"We need to burn it, Lizzy," I whispered. We crouched behind the curtain as I removed the coins from the pocket, and then the buttons. I handed her the ruined dress.

"Now whose blood is this, Mary?" she said in return. "I know you left with that bully Jimmy. Could it be his blood, or perhaps the young soldier's? Tell me, Mary."

"Don't say a word to Da, Lizzy, but it's Jimmy's blood. In the morning they'll find his cold, stiff body in a lane. I'm sure of it. Oh, Lizzy, I killed a man who was more a boy."

"You won't be blamed, Mary. He would have killed you. I saw his face. If he's dead, then surely it is for the best."

"You're a good sister, Lizzy. I am truly blessed. Now go put the dress in the stove. Do it quickly while Da sleeps."

I put on my nightdress and waited for the stove to flare through the sheets. Then I heard my father's voice. He had been awakened.

He was calling my name. I parted the sheet and walked across our little room like something breakable, flimsy as air. He had his head turned toward me, looking at me from the corner of his eye as if to say, *I know what the night has brought you.*

"Sit down, Mary," he said.

We sat before the stove, the three of us a family torn. It was late and the weight of the night pressed against me, a presence of what I had done, an entity that had followed me home to Dumbiedykes.

"Now, a father is never still," he began. "I suppose I had left such things to your mother who had a way with knowing the goings-on of her children and, I'm sure, her husband. I heard the talk behind the sheets. It is only a thin barrier to a worrying father's ear. So you must tell me, Mary, and be very clear about it, how Jimmy fared. I couldn't get all of your whispering but enough to know that the bloodied dress was fouled with his blood."

I was saddened that I continued to bring such trouble to our flat, even as I planned to leave Scotland for some distant city in an unknown country. But I was certain Jimmy was dead. "Jimmy was bleeding badly, Da," I said. "He won't last through the cold night. It's not possible."

"I won't ask about the circumstances, Mary," he said, "how a young woman comes to kill a man. But if you say that Jimmy is soon to be dead, then so he is." Then he lowered his head in the dim light, his thick fingers laced together as to affirm some careful consideration. "Now, Mary, you will be going to the infirmary in the morning. There you will begin your training. You mustn't say a word about this. They'll find the boy's body and that will be the end of it. There will be no suspicions. He'll be known to the police. They will surely see it as a crime among the criminals. Nothing more. Carry on with your duties. It's done now. You can make a clean break of it. Not all bad news, you see. And, Mary, stand on your tongue."

"Yes, Da."

I turned to Lizzy in the flickering light, the warm wafting of the stove casting a mood calamitous and grim. Her eyes were the size of saucers, as if she had been the recipient of an impossible tale, some bedtime fiction worthy of a haunting. And we sat without speaking and the night settled inside me. The soldier Allan Rose perhaps another fiction. He could not survive alongside Jimmy in my head, the forces that drive madness or sanctuary. Oh, why must disorder and affliction triumph over the right and the proper?

CHAPTER

FIVE

THE ROYAL INFIRMARY OF EDINBURGH WAS A GRAND BUILD-
ing with its grey-stone wings, clock tower, and spires. The open
space of the splendid grounds it occupied on Lauriston Place
revealed the sky at last with its drift of clouds and gulls that circled
over the rooftops and streets, never far from the sea. They heralded
the new day with their staccato proclamations. The city opened
up like a spring bloom, in stark contrast to the sandstone escarp-
ments of Dumbiedykes where it seemed I had been lost in the
drudgery of my life, without trees, blades of grass, or the sweeter
air of affluence. Motor cars with their modernist presage veered
and sped. Always the sense of a new world beyond the tenements.

My father had given me one of my mother's dresses to wear.
He wanted me to look smart and confident on my first day, but
as I walked up to the big front doors I was far from self-assured.
I felt discomposed by a cloud of apprehension. I couldn't stop
thinking about Jimmy, where he had died, how he would have
been found, perhaps by the dairy man with his horse and cart as
the first rays of the sun found the dark lanes of Old Town. I didn't
feel the approach of something favourable, something that could
change my life for the better. There was something to dread, but
I didn't know what. I had killed Jimmy, stuck Josie's knife deep
inside him. I had watched him bleed. I had seen the fear in his
eyes. I wanted him dead, and I should have been happy about it,
but truth be told, I wasn't.

Inside the infirmary I was overwhelmed at once by the industry
of activity, of gentlemen with their stiff sophistication and the
nurses like a white-uniformed mob, rushing here and there. And

one noticed me standing idle, perhaps because I stood out against the rush. It seemed she had been expecting me.

"Miss Stewart, I presume," she said, marching up to me, chin up.

"Yes."

"Well, then, you must call me Nurse Hare. I receive the new girls, get them started. I set the tone, you might say. Now come with me. You'll need specific orientation, given your circumstance. I'm sure you know what I mean. I must say that your arrival here defies belief."

The nurse angered me at once — must this, must that. She was well seasoned, I could tell, thick bodied with an inflexible mouth. How quickly she wanted to make me wrong, imperfect, something well below par, and not a minute inside the infirmary. And I did know what she meant, but I resented her tone, the insinuation. I wanted to say so. But my father chimed in just in time. *Mary, stand on your tongue.*

I followed her down a hallway to what appeared to be a small meeting room. She led me inside and we took our seats at a table. There was a folded uniform and bonnet on the table, and she pushed it toward me. She started at once, as delicate as a hammer.

"Look at this uniform," she said. "Think on it, what it represents. You will report to the men's ward on the second floor. Then you will carry out the duties as prescribed by the senior nurse. That is Nurse Monck. You will follow her orders without complaint. You must show a willingness to learn. You must show respect to your superiors. You will do so with the utmost of self-discipline and restraint. There are classes for you to take. There is much to study. And I will not allow you to sully any of the young nurses with your vulgarity. When you are on the ward, the care of patients is your primary concern. You must show that care in all that you do. We have *Nightingale Nurses* here at the Royal Infirmary. Learn from them. Take some pride if you can find it." She paused to take a breath, then continued. "I will be blunt with you, Miss Stewart.

I don't want you here. This is no place for a streetwalker. Now, you may ask a question if you so choose to."

The law according to Nurse Hare. I felt stunned, as if she had jabbed me in the chest with her thick conjecture. Although I was cautioned by my father, having known that I was prone to speaking my mind in artful ways, I did have a question for her.

"Now that I am *here*, Nurse Hare," I said as diplomatically as I could, "and knowing that you do not wish me *here*, perhaps you would be so kind as to tell me who it is that wishes me *here*?"

"You will not bait me, Miss Stewart. I have heard about your sponsor and your clever riddles. I expect all of our nurses to conform to the highest standards of work performance and conduct."

"I do believe my past work performance has exceeded expectations. I come highly recommended. I see no reason to change now."

Nurse Hare sat back and regarded me, her arms folded and her head shaking slightly from side to side. "You seem to have great difficulty with authority, Miss Stewart," she said. She was not speaking from her rule book now, it seemed, but rather from her own opinions. "You will never be a nurse with such a brazen display of insubordination. It is highly unlikely that you will amount to much. I've seen your kind over the years. Not fit for marriage and destined to be a withered spinster. And not fit to serve in the war. They don't want you touching the wounded young Scots and Brits in France, but they'll send you far away, out of sight. Think about that when you feel the need to sting with your snappish tongue. You are here to clean the debris of illness and death. That will be your first duty on the ward. Soldiers are coming in fast. It's all part of your training. I doubt you will last. That is my compensation. So I suggest you get on with it. There's a shower room. A good inspection and cleaning is in order." She motioned with her head to a door at the back of the room.

Then Nurse Hare stood up from the table and looked down at me appraisingly. I detected an odd smile, sly perhaps in a way I didn't quite understand. Then she placed a hand on what I thought was my uniform, and with one sweep snatched it away from me and left the room.

She had censured me with her superiority, and a clever way to cut me to the quick. It seemed that I was thwarted by the woman. It was clear that she hated everything about me. And she may have been correct relative to her own experience, but it did not give her a right to erase the rest of my life and relegate me to the scrap heap of impoverished women. I felt a strong need to prove her wrong. And as I looked to the door at the back of the room, I wasn't sure what awaited me. *A good inspection* ...

I stood before the door and listened. There were voices. I opened the door and slowly looked inside, and standing rather grimly were two nurses. They wore the same uniform that Nurse Hare had mocked me with. I suddenly realized why they were there. It seemed that Mrs. McFater's warning had come to pass.

"Now then," one said, "remove your clothes and sit up on the table."

"I will not," I said. "If you have a proper uniform for me to wear, then give it. I can dress myself."

The one turned to the other, and she went to the door and closed it. "If you don't do as we ask," the one said, "then we will assist you. How would you like it to be, Miss?"

"I would like you to leave me alone," I said. "I can bathe myself. I do not want any trouble with the nurses."

"We will need a clean whore in good condition," the other said. "You won't get on the wards otherwise." She had one squinting eye, the other eye adrift in its orbit.

I took exception to her remark, like so many who took liberties with their tongues in my presence. How did I become less human? I watched her wandering eye. I could play the game of intolerance if need be. "Well," I said, "it seems to me that they let you on the ward with that loony eye."

Then all at once they took hold of my arms and began to undress me. I protested, put up a good fuss, but they were rough and practised women, and they easily overpowered me. It was a humiliating experience with them grabbing and prodding, and then in the shower with the water sloshed over my head until I nearly drowned. Their strength was impressive, thick arms like a man, short stumpy legs. It seemed Nurse Hare had sent the most able, if not brutish, to do the job. I was glad to see them leave.

The uniform was loose fitting, drab grey, a kind of apron affair with a simple cap. It made me feel like domestic help. I didn't like it. I stored my clothes in the locker. There was a mirror and I paused to look at myself, but I didn't recognize the reflection as me, not totally, at least. I suppose I couldn't see a nurse. When Nurse Hare pushed that white-starched uniform toward me, I will admit feeling a certain pride that she had spoken about. I felt like someone, however briefly, but I didn't know who. Perhaps I had glimpsed something that had seemed impossible, a thing of dreams. All that and I hadn't set foot on a hospital ward, nor seen a patient, for that matter.

Everything was moving so fast. The night before seemed like some distant memory, and the soldier Allan Rose a fading dream, and Jimmy's violence and blood a nightmare. Where was he?

I made my way through the hospital, found the stairs to the men's ward, feeling out of place, that I didn't belong there. It was so contrary to what I was used to, the things that poverty demanded of me, staying alive in the dismal streets. But I momentarily forgot my troubles as I pushed through the doors. I stopped and looked. The ward was immense, countless occupied beds in rows, tall windows evenly spaced down the corridor, all bright with white linens, shimmering floors, and an undeniable order that struck me at once. Nurses at bedsides tended to patients with sheets to their necks, and a doctor, so it appeared, looked on rather contentedly as if all was well in his fiefdom of medicine. He stood on a Persian carpet as if to be reminded of pattern and colour. The grand hall of healing at Lauriston Place.

And that order, it seemed, was more of an illusion. I had stood for a matter of seconds with the sense of the ward making its impression, a caring mood, as if time had stopped and I were the privileged witness. But I could not remain remote for long as a nurse saw me standing there as if resting on my oars. There was a sudden commotion at a bedside. She looked right at me. I surely felt her insistence.

"You there, come here quick," she said.

I noticed the doctor moving toward the bed, and the other nurses looking up from their work. I hurried up to assist her. She was an older nurse. It seemed the fellow in the bed had vomited on his sheets.

"Now, you get a pan of hot water and some cloths," she said. "He'll need a clean nightdress. You're new, and you will learn to do a proper cleaning."

I looked down at the gentleman. He was an old man, whiskered and gaunt. His eyes seemed to roll back in his head. The smell was bad, but I had smelt worse. And I suppose I looked too long as I felt a hand on my arm. One of the other nurses jerked me away, instructions spewing out of her mouth so fast that I wasn't sure what she was saying. I could only follow behind her through the doors and into another room where the supplies were kept. We loaded a wheeled cart and filled a basin with hot water and soon we were back at the bedside. The doctor was beside the gentleman now, tending him with his instruments, leaning over him gravely. I stood aside as he worked. The older nurse worked with him. There were murmurs between them, the nodding of heads. The other nurses looked on. It was all so dramatic and hushed, as if something beyond my comprehension were unfolding before my unacquainted eyes. And all around the ward the other patients lifted their heads to see. They seemed to know. And soon the doctor stood back. I saw the gentleman now, his head tilted back and his mouth jacked open in a muted bawl. He was clearly dead.

They all moved away now. The doctor left the ward, and soon two orderlies arrived and placed the body on a gurney and wheeled him away. The older nurse turned to me. "Clean him up," she said.

How was I to do that? I wondered. And she must have read my face, the look of confusion, the horror. She waited a minute until we were alone.

"I am Nurse Monck," she said, "and I know who you are. You are that girl. But I don't care where you've come from as long as you do the work. That's what I need, someone willing. If that is you, then we'll get along fine. It takes a special kind of woman to clean up after the sick and dying on their first day. But a nurse has to begin somewhere. We'll see. Now, you know where he's been taken."

"In that room beyond the doors."

"Yes, that's correct. You need to prepare him for the morgue."

She had sent me to that room. How did she know that I would see the sinks and towels, instructions for handling the deceased pinned to a cupboard? "What was his name?" I asked.

She looked at me in a measured way, her eyes narrowing as if considering the question, its merits. "His name was Mr. Graham," she said. "He had his long life. Now you get to it."

She was an unusual woman. She seemed to carry great importance, the way she held herself, a certain decency. The doctor's consultation. She was smallish, but broad shouldered. She had a mature face, perhaps wise. And she seemed *willing* to allow me to learn on my own. A test, perhaps. She was a woman to be feared, or perhaps respected.

I stared down at Mr. Graham on the gurney. He was so still. Oh, he was dead of course, but it was that, the utter stillness of him, unmoving, no breath, no rise and fall of his chest that made me fully realize the fact. I wondered where he went. I looked up at the ceiling. I wanted to see him ascend, go to heaven. I wanted it so that I would know that my mother was all right, and that Paul and Robbie were with her. I had never been with a dead body. My mother drowned and was never found, and my brothers were never recovered from the incineration of the train wreck.

I removed Mr. Graham's nightdress and cleaned him with a damp cloth, the drying vomit on his neck and chin. It was matted to his fine white hair. His skin was thin and translucent and had yellowed. I cleaned him carefully and thoughtfully. I wanted him to think that I was a good person, that what I had done in my life was not evil, that somehow it was necessary, and that it was over with. I told him so. I told him that his family would be sad, but they would be relieved that his suffering was over. That he had lived a long life and had seen many things. And then I remembered. It came rushing into my head, as if leaping out from a pitch-black lane. It chilled me to my very bones. How could I have forgotten? And as I stood alone with Mr. Graham, his death reminded me of what I had done. I had wanted Jimmy dead, and I surely killed him, but I prayed now that he had survived.

I finished cleaning Mr. Graham and placed a clean sheet over him. I turned and was surprised to see Nurse Monck at the door. She had been watching me. I felt self-conscious at once and stepped away from Mr. Graham. My face was hot, and I looked away from her.

"You were talking to him," she said.

"I suppose I might have been, Nurse Monck," I said. She must have thought me mad, talking to a dead body, wishing to see him illumined and blessed. I had these notions of the dead, where they go. Many did, but I wasn't particularly fond of sharing my views. I hadn't set foot in a kirkyard since my mother passed, not even for my brothers. The Stewarts of Dumbiedykes were rather godless now, though my father was rarely without his bible. And if there was a God, what would he say? He would have known what I had done.

The orderlies came and took Mr. Graham away, but still Nurse Monck remained. "You are a curious young girl, aren't you?" she said.

"In what way, Nurse Monck?"

"You have a way. I noticed it at once. But I can't say what it is, why it arises in you. Some have a quality of caring that can't be taught. There are many here that want to see you fail. They will give you all the jobs they don't want to do. I know we shouldn't talk about such things, but one cannot keep secrets for long in this world. Your secret is out, Nurse Stewart. I will call you that now. Your nursing career has begun, until you prove me wrong."

"I am not a nurse," I said rather modestly. "It is true that I'm willing to learn, but perhaps ..."

"You will be called upon," she said, "to assist the nurses and doctors in extreme circumstances, emergencies, all the while you are in training. And you will need to rise up to meet those challenges. You will become a nurse, for a minute, an hour. You will not be left unsupervised. That is my job. So leave it to me."

"What about the others?"

"Prove *them* wrong, of course," she said simply, and then went back to the ward.

I wondered why Nurse Monck had such trust in me while the others resented my presence and took advantage of me.

CHAPTER

SIX

THERE WAS WORK TO BE DONE ON THE WARD, AND THE nurses in turn reminded me of my primary duty: changing the bed linens and emptying the bedpans. The beds were fouled and they were calling for me. Bloodied bandages, some with rot from infected wounds, and soldiers home from the battles in France without their limbs, and always cleaning and scrubbing. Mopping the floors for all was blood and bodily functions. *You, more saline. You, get water for that parched man. Right away, now. Dispose of this. You, more bandages. You, hurry now. And you, I told you before. Come now, do I have to do it myself?* Never *Nurse Stewart*, of course, or *Mary*, or *Miss Stewart*, only *You*. They didn't want to know me.

As the day wore on I was aware that Nurse Monck was keeping an eye on me, not giving instructions but remaining on the periphery of the ward, as if better to assess the efficiency of her staff, of the new girl. I didn't know how I was doing, what I did right or wrong. And as the nurses needed me around the bedsides when changing bandages, I watched what they were doing, each step, each word exchanged between nurse and patient. Medicines and tinctures, the proper application of a bandage, the elevation of an arm, a leg. Some patients were ill from various afflictions, diseases, some minor, and some I was certain would kill them in the end like Mr. Graham. Patients left and patients were admitted. Patients were wheeled in from the operating theatre. And it was one such man that Nurse Monck had taken an interest in. I hadn't attended to all of the patients in the ward, and it seemed she wanted to teach me something, and I was pleased. She called me over to his bedside.

"Now," she said, "there's a dressing to be changed. Do you think you can do that?"

"Yes, Nurse Monck," I said eagerly, "I believe I can." I quickly retrieved a cart with medicine and supplies and moved it to the end of the bed.

The patient's eyes were closed. The bedridden men on the ward had a similar look, a certain grey mask they wore, their faces unshaven and flattened, hair dishevelled, all in their white nightdresses, as if they all belonged to one ailing clan. But as I looked closer, past the likeness shared by illness, to the patient, my heart suddenly began to race. There was a clipboard attached to the head of the bed. I dreaded what I might find. I looked up and it read *unknown*. But it was inescapable and horrifying. It was Jimmy. He had survived after all. I stepped back all at once. I felt faint.

"Come, Nurse, I need you here," Nurse Monck insisted. "You can do this. There must be a first in everything. The anatomy lessons can wait."

"Perhaps I'm not ready," I said. I spoke in a whisper. I was so afraid that Jimmy would awaken and see me looming over him. He would surely wail, and I didn't know what else. It seemed so impossible, but it was so. And I surely had prayed that he was alive, and I wanted to take it back, but I couldn't. It elicited such panic and contradiction in me. I didn't know what to do.

"Are you unwell?"

"Won't changing the bandage awaken him?"

"This one has had surgery and is sedated. He is in and out of sleep. Don't be alarmed if he rouses. He is our mystery man. Now, I was certain that you would be most able, and *willing*, to do this. Am I wrong?"

"No, Nurse Monck, I was merely thinking of the patient's comfort." I stepped up alongside her.

"Yes, of course," she said. She seemed favourably impressed and pulled down the sheet and exposed the bandaged wound. But then all at once a nurse called out to her. She was urgently needed as there was a patient in distress. "Carry on, Nurse Stewart," she said, and left me to my own devices, between the devil and the deep blue sea, it seemed to me.

The bandage was bloodied. And as I looked at Jimmy, he seemed harmless, like the infant he had once been. One can't imagine that assailants and saints were born as such. But his vulnerability disturbed me. And slowly I removed the bandage. His stitched belly where I slipped the knife. I noticed at once the colour. His skin was blue–black and his stomach distended. I didn't know what it meant, but it wasn't good. I looked in his bedpan. It had been emptied, but traces of blood remained. I could only guess. Jimmy was bleeding inside.

I slowly looked around the ward. Nurse Monck was occupied with several nurses while Jimmy perhaps was dying before me. Was it a mercy bestowed upon me, that he would die with his untold truth? Perhaps it was best that I did nothing. It seemed a perfect solution to my predicament. He would die in his sleep, just one last breath. I could feel myself willing it, willing him to draw one last inhalation upon this temporal world. And then like some deep abiding covenant that I had forgotten, I heard another voice. It came as a question. Was I a nurse or a killer? I believed that I was neither, but it seemed temptation was like a mirror, and one must accept the image of one's making. I called out to Nurse Monck — my urgent appeal to her now.

She hurried over to me, her eyes locked to mine, but not to measure the pressing nature of my call. Nurse Monck saw something else, the terror in my eyes that did not petition her help, but her forgiveness.

"What is it, Nurse Stewart?" she asked, true to her word, and then looked down at the heave of Jimmy's stomach that was tight as a drum. I feared it would explode.

"I don't know," I said, "but he may be bleeding inside his belly. There's blood in his bedpan."

"He's fevering, and he is surely hemorrhaging. He'll need to return to surgery. Get the doctor," she said, turning to one of the nurses. "Hurry now."

"Will he die?" I asked.

"He has lost a lot of his blood. A coal vendor found him in a lane. It seems he got the bad end of a knife. We will do all that we can for him. He's just a young man."

The doctor came and immediately called for the orderlies. His name was Dr. Munro. He placed a stethoscope on Jimmy's chest and listened. And then he touched his forehead. He looked up to Nurse Monck, a look of such doubt and futility. Jimmy's faint heart and mine wild and inconsolable.

"Still no name for this patient, Nurse Monck?"

"No, Doctor, he hasn't regained consciousness since his surgery."

"The chief constable has been duly notified," he said, "and we'll have to leave it to him. It's a shame, I must say. A mother should see her son."

Then the orderlies arrived and moved the bed with Jimmy, the doctor following behind. At that moment I recognized that there were things in life that were larger than I was, that the compassion of a doctor didn't require a person to be of a certain stature. He only wished to save a human life. And I knew I would never be able to carry on in that ward without some accounting of myself, some disclosure of what I knew. I didn't so much as owe it to Jimmy. I owed it to the faculty of truth and sanity. I had to uphold something in a world starved of love.

"His name is Jimmy McDuff," I said loud enough for the doctor to hear.

He stopped and turned to me, uncertain why I had said so just then. He cocked his head briefly, then turned to Nurse Monck. He seemed more surprised than needing an explanation. It didn't matter so much at that moment, for I knew it would come to me soon enough. And it did.

Nurse Monck quickly escorted me into the ward office. She dismissed a clerk and closed the door and pointed to a chair. She did not sit but stood before me with her hands on her hips. She was upset, and it was quite reasonable. But that look on her face was more than anger. She was disappointed in me, and in herself, perhaps.

"Nurse Stewart, why did you not tell me that you knew his name?"

"I was afraid to." I kept my head down, away from her scrutiny.

"Why were you afraid?"

A look between us that demanded the precise and true. "You see, Nurse Monck, I am the one who put the knife in him."

"Dear child, what have you done?" she said, her arms raised now, aghast.

"He was my bully. He was going to kill me."

"A pimp, you say?"

"It is a most agonizing thing to admit it, Nurse Monck. You've been most fair with me, but yes, it is all true."

"Now you mustn't say another word," she cautioned. "I will report this to the chief constable when he arrives. I'm sorry, but I must. I have a duty. Now please remain in this office."

"I understand."

I waited in silence. The muted voices of nurses on the ward. The door opening and closing. I was naïve, I knew, about the provisions of law, my rights as a woman, as a victim. And I knew that to be a prostitute and a victim might seem an outrageous notion to some. In fact, it would seem Jimmy was less a social liability than I was. Of course, we were the scourge, the gutter people, nightwalkers. The slut and the white slaver. Who will weep for the detestable? No one, perhaps. I kept thinking that I could have been something. I felt it, not every moment on the ward, but there was something there, something meaningful in a collective way, that life indeed had a purpose. But now every good intention of my uncle, and every wish of my father, seemed all but damned and dust.

It was a long and excruciating wait, when time stretched unbearable and punishing. There was a photograph of a woman on the wall. She watched me. I felt uncomfortable with her haughty scrutiny. I was sure that I would soon find out what that *hell* was like that our neighbour, Mrs. Drummond, so inelegantly had predicted for me. Then the door finally opened and it was all men now, Chief Constable Ross with one of his young policemen, and Dr. Munro. I was outnumbered to be sure. Their looks, as could be expected, were rather grave, but it was the chief constable who seemed most affected — *troubled* would be more accurate.

"Miss Stewart, we meet again," the chief constable said. "This will be a preliminary interview. The constable will take notes. But Dr. Munro has word, and it doesn't make the situation much easier."

"Yes, Nurse," the doctor said. "The patient that you identified as Jimmy McDuff has died in the operating theatre. He was beyond recovery, given his blood loss and complications from surgery. But we can contact the next of kin now. I wanted to thank you."

I didn't feel anything with the news. I was neither relieved nor sickened, but numb. And the doctor clearly didn't know a thing about me. I simply smiled, not wanting to risk a contradictory word.

"Thank you, Dr. Munro," the chief constable said. He waited for the doctor to leave. The constable intent with his notes. Then he turned to the young policeman. "That will be all for now, Constable," he said.

He pulled up a chair and sat opposite me. How the numbers had changed.

"Miss Stewart," he began, "do you understand the seriousness of this circumstance?"

"I believe that I do, Chief Constable."

"I inspected the body of the deceased, Mr. McDuff, and it appears that he had succumbed to a knife wound. Now, you must realize that the Edinburgh Police were fully aware of Mr. McDuff's activities, and also your association with him. Miss Stewart, I will ask you straight away, and you may choose not to answer. Do you know how Mr. McDuff came to suffer such a wound?"

I was so afraid now, muted was my mouth with its slings and arrows. I had to be meticulous. My answer required an equal amount of intelligence and wit, for I knew that a bully dead and a prostitute destined for prison would not be deemed a loss at all, but a moral victory. And it occurred to me that I had confessed to Nurse Monck, and it seemed an egregious error now, but how odd that the chief constable hadn't mentioned it.

"I imagine he had it coming," I answered. "The brothels despise him, and he was a cruel man. I can't even call him that. He was a boy with a devil's mind. Perhaps it was a settling of accounts."

He looked at me hard, the way policemen do when they don't believe a word of your prattle. I wondered if he was waiting to hear my confession for himself. It would most certainly save him a great deal of police work.

"It appears there may have been a murder, Miss Stewart," he said, "and I need to facilitate justice. Now, if you have nothing further to say ..."

"Am I a suspect, Chief Constable?"

"I have no grounds to include you as a suspect at this time. I would say that the evidence is lacking. Nurse Monck is going to join us now. There are a few more details I need from her. There is one point that requires clarification." The chief constable went to the door and soon Nurse Monck joined us, the young constable as well.

They all looked dour as they took their seats, an unfriendly gloom, full of dreadful news, I was sure. Perhaps it would all come out for the record. What I had experienced so far was, undoubtedly, the protocols of police work.

"Nurse Monck," Chief Constable Ross started, "I understand that Miss Stewart identified one of your patients who had been unknown since he was brought into the infirmary. However, Dr. Munro did say that she did not inform you right away."

"Yes, Chief Constable, but I quite understand. Patients in the ward who are incapacitated due to illness or injury are not themselves, to say the least. I have seen family members shocked by the appearance of loved ones who are ill and not at their best. They're not used to seeing them so. It's not unusual."

"She offered no explanation?"

"I didn't ask for one. She recognized him and that was that. I was happy she did."

"She said nothing more?" He turned to the young constable feverish with his notes.

"In fact, Chief Constable, it was Nurse Stewart who notified me that the patient had taken a turn for the worse. The doctor was called, and I know that Dr. Munro did everything that he could to save the boy's life. I would say that she did quite well."

The chief constable stood up. "Now, I believe that concludes my inquiry. I thank you for your time. Constable, come." He went to the door, but turned back all at once, as if he had forgotten some detail of his inquiry. "Miss Stewart, I understand that you will be leaving for Canada soon."

"Yes, sir."

"I believe that time has come."

"Sir?" But he didn't answer. He stood a moment, then left with the young constable without further formality. I was confused by the ambiguity of his statement. Then I understood. It wasn't unclear at all. It was a requisite condition of his inquiry.

Nurse Monck remained sitting with me. I suspected that she thought I needed an explanation. It was most unusual, something

I didn't expect from her, or from either of them, for that matter. Something between them, neat, rehearsed.

"You didn't tell him," I said.

"No, I did not."

"I don't understand."

"It seems the chief constable is rather relieved that you will be leaving Scotland. You somehow complicate his life. He could have pursued the investigation, Nurse Stewart. He said as much. It may have led right to you after all. But I think we had an understanding between us, what was the right thing to do. What would be accomplished by your incarceration? Another wasted life. He has seen enough sad stories in Edinburgh."

"And you?" I searched her grey eyes, how they softened now.

"You see, you and I are much alike. That must surprise you. I know what it's like to be you. I know what it is like to be poor. You may hear it in my voice, the dialect that is not purely Scot. I was born in Ireland. A poor family. And I found myself taking desperate measures, as I'm sure you have done. I will not speak much more on the matter, only that they called me a 'fallen woman,' though I was more like a child. I was sent to a Catholic convent, to the laundries where young women were treated cruelly, held against their will. Many died. My family managed to take me away. I was one of the lucky ones. We came to Edinburgh, you see. I know your story. I cannot judge you, Nurse Stewart. And I believe that Chief Constable Ross was sympathetic to your plight. And I can say that not many are. I will write you a letter of introduction for your new life, in the hope that it will be of some use to you. Do you see that photograph on the wall?"

"Yes, she's been watching me all afternoon."

"That's Dr. Elsie Inglis. A compassionate doctor who looked after the poor on High Street. You may have seen her in Old Town. She is a forward-thinking woman, founder of the Scottish Suffragette Federation. She is a champion for women's rights, you might say. And now she is committed to the war effort. But the vote for women will come. See what you can do, Nurse Stewart. See what your new country can do for you. It will always be difficult, but still we must try."

"You're a kind woman, Nurse Monck."

"The world is at war. If we can find a moment's kindness, then we should give it. It doesn't take much at all. What I offer you, Nurse Stewart, is not so much kindness as empathy."

"I understand, Nurse Monck."

"Chief Constable Ross wishes you haste on your departure. I am sorry that it is so, although I know that the loose tongues on the ward would not serve your or the chief constable's ... let me say ... amnesty."

It would take a long time to understand what was at play on that short but most difficult time at the Royal Edinburgh Infirmary. I could not reconcile the fact that I was given another chance. Perhaps it was the hand of providence that had considered the possibility of my death at Jimmy's hands to be of no compensation for the money I kept from him. I was a woman who had to fight for her life.

CHAPTER

SEVEN

LIZZY WALKED IN FRONT OF ME, UP THE GRASSY SLOPE OF Arthur's Seat below the Salisbury Crags. She moved like a girl still, a jaunty enthusiasm to be away from the city, out of the suffering tenements where astonishingly she carried on undeterred. It was all she knew, like the way water feels to a fish. She never complained about her responsibility to our father, always eager to please him, reading his bible to him until he fell asleep and coaxing the blood down into what remained of his severed leg as if she were kneading bread dough. But on that misty morning her arms and legs moved arbitrarily, a kind of anarchic locomotion that propelled her upward along the trail. And now that rare freedom to touch the sky above Edinburgh was such a welcomed pleasure for her. The gorse grew thick and yellow along the hill's flanks and the heather with its more reasonable tones hugged the ground like a soothing blanket. She picked dappled bunches and clutched them in her fists. Now and then she would spin in front of me, as if she could not account for her good fortune. I secretly wept on the trail when I thought about leaving her, her little strength that was glorious and triumphant.

The heather glistened with countless droplets of water as the mist drifted in from the sea and moved over the hillside. The rays of the sun slowly began to break through the soft wet veil of it. Lizzy stopped and turned to me. I knew what she wanted. She asked every time we climbed that hill, something our mother often told us on such spring days, and always in the colourful way of hers.

"Tell me, Mary," she said, "why the girls bathe their faces in the dew on May Day."

"To make themselves beautiful, Lizzy, of course," I said. "A long-standing tradition for the Edinburgh girls."

"Tell it, then."

"All right," I said, "but you continue on now. It'll be our marching song." As Lizzy bounded up the trail, I called it out to the ancients to be sure they knew we were about.

On May Day, in a fairy ring,
We've seen them round St. Anthon's spring,
Frae grass the cauler dew draps wring
To weet their een,
And water clear as crystal spring
To synd them clean

We reached the top of the slope and knelt in the damp grass with the rising sun warm on our backs. The mist slowly began to disperse and Edinburgh Castle appeared like polished stone above the city. There were things that I needed to tell Lizzy, serious things from an older sister. It wasn't a sudden reordering of morality that I could impart to her, nor were there demands that I could make that would alter what I had already patterned for her. Still she needed to hear me out.

"You must be watching the boys, Lizzy," I said. "Never let them take from you what you don't want to give them. There's plenty of time for you to meet a fine young man. I'm sure of it. But you see, I'll be far away and you won't be able to come to me for help and such. So you must write once I'm settled. Write to me every day if you so wish. I'll write to you as soon as I arrive in Canada. Remember that you are a strong girl who knows what she wants."

"How can you know that there will be someone for me, Mary? I see nothing but the tenements and ..." She knelt with her head down and her hands folded on her lap, their sudden containment.

"Oh, Lizzy, surely a day will come," I said, placing my arm around her shoulders. "You must not give up hope. And you'll be joining me soon enough, in no time at all. Dream a little. It's not a bad thing."

"Mary, you let Jimmy have his way. I've seen the way he treated you, and I saw how it couldn't be stopped. Why would it be different for me?"

"You don't know the half of it, sweet girl. You can't see what's inside of me. There are scars. Some days they burn, and other times I am sick with fever. I made a terrible mistake. And I will not make it again. And you have seen enough. You will not follow me. But remember, Lizzy, not every boy is like Jimmy. You must believe that."

"He is dead, then?"

"Yes," I said. "Jimmy was in the infirmary. His belly was bloated with blood. The doctor tried to save him. I suppose he paid for his sins."

"What made him bad, Mary?"

"I can't say for certain. They say the bad are born cursed in a way, that they inherit a fate of wickedness."

"You killed him, Mary. Is that not a sin?"

"I don't know, Lizzy. It is a question that needs to be answered. I carry both relief and regret about what I have done. We can justify most anything, but it won't always make a safer world. The Huns attacked Edinburgh and people were killed. Did they feel it justified? See the ship in the harbour? It is on its way to defend freedom, and many will die. We believe it to be justified."

"How will I know when I meet a good boy?"

"You won't be afraid of him," I said. Her eyes followed my lips. The things she yearned for. "You'll feel safe, Lizzy. You will know."

"Are you certain, Mary?"

I turned back to the harbour, to the ship leaving port. "There is a boy on that ship," I said. "His name is Private Allan Rose. I wasn't afraid of him. I believe he is a good young man." And then quite unexpectedly, I felt a tug on my heart, a suggestion of a different regret that made me remember. I had kissed his cheek.

It had all seemed so natural and unaffected. I felt the loss of it. I suppose it arose out of contrast, of virtue and vice. I knew the difference, of course, but I must have forgotten to hope. And to see the face of hope suddenly appear that night. I had to trust that it would happen for Lizzy, too.

Lizzy was quiet now. I watched her looking out over Edinburgh to the jammed multitudes, to the church spires piercing the sombre ash of countless coal fires. A smudge of smoke like a black stain. Edinburgh's mood. The sunbeams reached in vain to console the cobblestone lanes and alleyways. A melancholy beauty that seemed to reach back in time to King Arthur, to Camelot, to the very charms of an enduring Scots mythology. It was if the clouds of our history rose up from the kirkyards, not hauntings but out of some otherworldly liberation. Moving on. And I could feel it, too. Soon Edinburgh would be only memories, like all things that pass on. I wondered how it would be to leave it all, and to leave my unfound mother.

"Tell me about the *silver darlings*," Lizzy said all at once. "Tell me about Mother that day."

She had turned and looked back out to sea, and how strange that Lizzy had said that at the very moment I had thought of her, as if my thoughts had found their way inside her little head. But I wasn't so much thinking of our mother's herring-chasing days, but that she was out there still, *unfound*, drifting endlessly without a port to take her body. That was the hardest thing for me, not to feel the indisputable sense of her death, the close of her life the way a church so dramatically fulfills with its ceremony and ritual. Perhaps it was because I could not think of her as gone. And yet I could not argue that she was alive somewhere, nor could I say with certainty that she was dead. I often wondered about the photograph, our smiling mother with her *darlings*, and so far away from her children. Had she fancied that young fisherman so long ago and returned to him every season? Did she dance to "The Fish Gutter's Song" still?

The story was a connection to our mother. Lizzy's yearning for her was much like my own, and to keep the story alive was to give life to her when the fisher-girls followed the herring fleet from Shetland to Yarmouth. I told it whenever she asked, and when she didn't, it would often come to me as if I had lived it myself.

"Lizzy, you were just eight years old that season," I began, "when another thousand fish-gutter women were needed in the harbours and coves. They would follow the shoals from May to November. Mother had been gone for several months, as she was each year, gutting and packing fifty herring a minute when the boats came in with their catch. The women gathered around the *farlins*, long shallow vats where the herring were poured. Then they went to work slitting the bellies and taking out the guts with their sharp knives, then rousing the fish in salted tubs over and over until they could be packed in barrels. All day long they would gut and pack, and when the last fish were packed away, they would knit and sing their *gutters'* songs. It was a community of women, sisters really, sharing the same hard work, making a few bob a week. On Sunday the fishermen would come to have tea with the ladies. They were far from home themselves. So it was singing and having a fine time of it.

"But there were awful cuts from the knives, and the women would have painful sores on their hands and fingers. It was terrible working with the salt and brine. They would wrap their fingers with strips of flour sacking, *clooties* they called them. They were quite the sight with their leather boots, oilskin skirts, and knitted woollen scarves. They say they glistened from the slime and scales. Mother was fast in her work, and I suppose she sliced her fingers plenty. It was the day when the cuts on her hands festered badly and she couldn't work. They say that is why she went out with a young fisherman. The girls had told her to take a day off. Now the story is unclear, Lizzy. Da received a letter from one of the *silver darlings*, a friend in Yarmouth.

"She said the shoals were right off the coast and the boats were making great catches. The young fisherman was going out for more, a father and his two sons. The seas were rough, but the temptation was too much for caution. She called our mother *Maggie*, a pet name for Margaret, you know. She said Maggie wanted to see the herring shoals for herself. She said Mother thought it would be a wonderful adventure. They would make a grand catch and return. But they never returned. The other boats on the water were hauling in their heavy nets, staggering catches. One old mariner saw them pulling in their net, but the weather turned foul and the sea began to swell and the water, green as a bottle, frothed and boiled and poured over the stern of his boat. It was all he could do to pack his fish away and return to the harbour.

"They say the boat rolled over with its load of herring. No one saw it. One minute it was there and in another it was gone. No sign of those aboard. Swallowed by the black depths. It was a perilous business on the North Sea. So there it is, Lizzy. Now, why do you want to hear such a story over and over?"

"I like the way you tell it, Mary. That's all."

"It's a heartbreaking story, really."

"Why did she go?"

"The money, Lizzy. She wanted the best for us. We lived in Portobello Beach on High Street. Do you remember the donkey rides on the beach?"

She looked once again to the sea, perhaps remembering. "Yes."

She seemed rather morose all at once. "Perhaps I shouldn't tell it anymore, Lizzy."

"It doesn't make me sad, Mary," she said. "She was happy. I think she loved that life for a while, sharing it with the other ladies. I hear the song. She sings it to me."

"Ah, yes, a comfort in our dreams."

"No, Mary, not in my dreams. She comes to me when I'm heating water for the laundry. Other times when I'm alone in the streets. She's watching over me. I know it to be."

"That's a lovely thought, Lizzy."

"It's not that at all, Mary. I've heard many times that the dead watch over the ones they leave behind. Well, it's true. She's here now. Don't you feel her?"

I looked into her eyes. She was so earnest, so wanting to believe that our mother was with us just then. I didn't want to take it away from her, dismiss the fanciful world children can create. But I would admit that I had often wondered why I couldn't sense our mother's absolute demise. I reasoned that it was because she was lost at sea. What was I truly feeling? Had I lost my own divine connection?

"Yes, Lizzy," I said to accommodate her. "I think it's grand that she comes to you. I really do."

"She comes to help me. I think she wants me not to be afraid of death when it comes."

"Goodness, Lizzy, you're not going to die. You'll live to a fine old age."

She simply gave me a look. It was a queer little smile that made her seem old somehow. Then the wind caught her hair and blew it across her face. She held up her chin as if to feel the solace of her mystical world, and then closed her eyes and sang.

Haud the fishie
bi the gills
Rug the knife
alang its belly
Banes are staunin up
like quills
Haud yer heb,
it's affa smelly!

The Lizzy I didn't know.

73

CHAPTER

EIGHT

"HELP ME WITH THIS, MARY," MY FATHER SAID. "I WANT TO look my best."

"I'm not about to be married, Da," I said, snugging his tie.

"It's no small thing when a daughter leaves. I will send you off looking proper. Your mother would have surely set this old suit out for me. I aim to make her proud."

I felt a clutch in my stomach. She could never be proud of me. "What would she think, Da?"

He knew what I meant, the pursing of his lips as he considered my question. "She was a tolerant and loving mother," he said. "She would shout out to anyone who cared to listen: *Mary Stewart, off to save the world!* I am most sure of it."

"Oh, you're in a mood, aren't you?" I said. I was pleased with what he said. "But I have no aspirations to save the world. It will need a lot more than I can give. Can it be that you wish to make a statement to one whom you haven't seen in a long while?"

"Don't be absurd, Mary. Where do you get such notions?" He regarded me critically now.

"I don't blame you for it, Da," I said ignoring his displeasure. "Uncle Calvin will be duly impressed. And I am *most* sure of that."

"Now look, daughter," he said fervently, steadying himself on his good leg. "Something terrible has happened in Dumbiedykes. A boy is dead. It's all a dreadful thing. But it's over and you'll be on your way. I won't hide my gratitude for the opportunity your uncle has given you. And I don't particularly care why he is doing so. I can live in peace knowing you had a new start. It won't be long before Lizzy joins you. That's all I want now, to see that you have a better life. I wish to celebrate this day while I can. I am both sad and pleased. So, if you could keep your cheek to yourself, I would be grateful as well. I'm a little nervous, truth be told, as I had a part in our estrangement. Brothers don't cease to be because of one's success and the other's misfortune. I will eat my portion of humble pie if I must."

"Yes, Da," I said apologetically. I had been insensitive to him, and my cheeks burned with regret. I had only wanted to bring a measure of levity into our sombre flat as I was feeling apprehensive myself. My life in Edinburgh was quickly coming to an end.

"I do admire your spit and fire, Mary," he said, warmly now. "I always have. Your mother, too, had it in good measure. And I would encourage you to use it in that new land, albeit in moderate allotments suited to the circumstance. You'll be on your own and it may be an asset. I only caution you to stay on the *good* side of the law."

"Yes, of course, Da."

"How do I look, daughter?"

"Well, you are very handsome, I must say. A fine gentleman." He truly looked distinguished, his hair and beard with a striking dash of silver and his white collar raising a proud chin.

"Now if you go to my bed, you'll see something for you."

I left him for a moment and went to his room. A bright shawl lay on his quilt. It had belonged to my mother. It had been put away with the few things of her life, and to see it brought her back to me, however briefly. I picked it up and held it close to my cheek and breathed it in, and there she was as fleeting as her sweet essence. I brought it back to him. It was his treasure.

"Thank you, Da, but ..."

"No, not a word. You take the Stewart colours on your journey. It comes down from the Stewarts of Atholl. Your mother wore this shawl on special days, and this is a special day. The slogan will give you comfort and strength. *Courage grows strong at a wound.* Think of that. Now put it on, daughter."

I placed it around my shoulders. I looked down at it against the green coat and dress that I wore, an ordinary look that was simple and common, but now seemed bright with charm, a tartan of red and green in what felt at times to be a drab and colourless world. And the tam-o'-shanter that I wore had been wonderfully transformed by Lizzy's clever hands. A thoughtful girl who remembered what I had told her on Arthur's Seat. She had stitched a scarlet rose into the crown of it. All at once I felt quite fine for the first time in my life.

"Da," I said, "what would she say? Would she hate me for the things I've done?"

"No, Mary."

"How do you know?"

"Believe me, daughter, I know. Now, not another word on the matter."

I thought about what he said about my mother. I sensed there was something between them that I would never know, perhaps the answer lost at sea. Then the door suddenly opened and Lizzy burst through. "He's here," she said excitedly. "Uncle Calvin. He's waiting in his motor car!"

"All right then, Lizzy," my father said, "take Mary's suitcase down to the street. Mary will assist me down the stairs. Off you go now."

Lizzy went out the door with my suitcase and my father took up his crutch. "Here we go," he said, "into the unknown."

I knew he was speaking for the both of us. The journey facing me was no less than the challenge that he faced, seeing his brother for the first time in years, his soon-to-be benefactor. It was a mountain to him, an emotional height that I was sure he feared far more than he let on. Family grudges and wounds would keep brothers stubbornly apart for a lifetime. He would do it for me, and for Lizzy.

We went down the stairs arm in arm. It was the first time I had done so: supporting him had always fallen to Lizzy. But there was a certain ceremony in our descent to the street. I did not feel his shame. He seemed more tolerant, perhaps resigned to the choices I had to make, and all that I had done, the unimaginable and unthinkable. I knew he blamed himself. Perhaps he had lost too much in his life.

And I suppose he was relieved as well, for the worrying I had caused him. I wondered if he would ever be proud of me. He may have admired my tenacity, my creativity, but he wasn't proud of the fact. He did not expect much from me, a woman. No one did, really, except Nurse Monck. But when I had showed him my letter of introduction from her, it seemed to him that I had just received a most prestigious appointment. His finger slid across the page, stopping at the words *Nurse Mary Stewart*. Of course, I was far from it, a *nurse*, but I had done the very same thing. It seemed from the bottom of the social pile that every little thing upward was a triumph.

We walked out into the light of the new day. Still the coal ash and shadow. But the sun lit the tops of the tenements, and a motor car rattled in the street, animated and high-spirited like a living thing. And Uncle Calvin stepped out of it as regal as a royal, and heads popped out of the tenement windows above me as if certain of it, their mouths shaped in circles of astonishment. Lizzy was standing beside the motor car with a smile on her face. I knew she thought it was all great fun to see her uncle, and the anticipation of riding to the train station in such uncommon luxury. And then Uncle Calvin stepped forward to address me, before my father. It seemed that I was to be the buffer on that most auspicious but dubious occasion.

"Mary, you look lovely today," he said, removing his top hat and taking my hand like a gentleman. His eyes moved over the shawl in a rather bemused way. He didn't notice the mismatched buttons of my coat or Lizzy's stitched repairs. It seemed I no longer fit the portrait he had created for me. "I am pleased that this day has arrived for you."

"Thank you, Uncle," I said. But of course I knew that he was far more than pleased. And there was something else. I watched his eyes. He wouldn't look at my father. It was rather odd and uncomfortable, his aversion. It seemed that he was fearful himself. And when I turned to see what my father would do, I could feel his rigidity, the tightening grip on my arm. But then he did a most courageous thing. He reached out with his hand. Uncle Calvin just looked at it, the gesture that I had expected would come from him.

"Calvin," my father said, "take my hand. You are my brother and all that I have left beyond these two girls. And one going away and the other to follow. Take my hand and forgive me. I have no other means of compensation."

My father's hand was shaking, and I prayed that Uncle Calvin would take it. If he did not, I feared that my father would collapse there on the street, a man defeated once and for all. But Uncle looked up now, the narrowing of his eyes as if he confronted the same wall, a wall of grudges, a wall built out of the strata of class and social order. And yet he was an intelligent man and seemed to recognize the effort it took for his brother to reach out to him. He took my father's hand at last, and their grips seized the other like duellists who had each missed their mark, a measured respect without blame or explanation. The Stewart seal between brothers, it would seem, had been restored.

We drove like kings in Uncle Calvin's bright red Argyll motor car, through medieval Old Town and down into the narrow valley to Waverly Station and the steam-gushing trains. Lizzy howled the whole time, not out fear, but in pure delight. She waved to everyone we passed on the street. Never had she been treated to such extravagance and privilege. And I wondered, as my uncle unloaded my suitcase from the back of his motor car at the station, if he had done all that for us. He could have made arrangements, a taxi, perhaps, or a driver in his employ. His motivations were unimportant, if he would only stay true to his word. And I had to trust that he would. Did he feel what I felt, that something seemed to embrace us all on the platform? There was a sense of family, that we belonged to something larger than ourselves. The pitiable Stewarts of Dumbiedykes were no longer alone. But after all, I suppose it was only my deep-down wish. Nevertheless, I wouldn't sully it.

And in the station, crowds of people moved and surged, passengers, soldiers crippled from the war, and bunches of children milling about like stray cats. I waited with my father and Lizzy as Uncle Calvin bought my ticket to Liverpool. He handed it to me along with my passage to Canada in an envelope. I could see in his eyes his regret that he did not really know his nieces. I embraced them in turn, my father last. He could not find the words he wanted to say. But I understood them. His bearded face hid his own regrets. I believed that at such times our sorrows and failings come to the fore, out of contrition, out of love. Words were not essential and yielded to the unspoken gestures and emotions.

As I stepped up to the train to Liverpool with my ticket, I stopped and turned to them. Lizzy was standing with her shoulders bunched forward and her legs awkwardly apart like a broken bird, her face awash with tears. It seemed she had suddenly understood the enormity of the day, its meaning and its consequence. The agony wasn't lost to me. I felt a hole in my chest where my heart had been, and in its place a stone of ruth.

I boarded the train and found my seat. Through the window I looked out at them. The train moved, belched its hot smoke. Their waving arms, and Lizzy coming up the platform. She didn't want me to go. Why would she? She was just a girl. I thought of Allan Rose, what he had told me about his twin sister, how she ran after the train when he left Stirling for the war. The heartbreaking departures. And the train moved faster. Then Uncle Calvin left my father's side all at once and hurried after Lizzy. I could see only the vague shape of them now, how he stopped her and then leaned down and took her in his arms. Farewell, Edinburgh.

CHAPTER

NINE

IT WAS HARD FOR ME TO UNDERSTAND WHAT I WAS DOING and why I was leaving. It was all happening too fast. I was in a woeful state, unsure of everything. The ache under my ribs kept me from dozing, though the plush burgundy seats were comfortable enough. How does one go so far without submitting to the death of loneliness? I sat alone with my head against the window, overwhelmed with uncertainty and such grief. I watched my country over the muted clack of wheels. The heart of Scotland with its crofts and holdings rushed to meet the train. Farmers with their draught horses turned the stony earth and shepherds tended greening pastures of black-faced sheep. The plots were broken now and then by the purple haze of heather rising to meet the tumbling clouds, all blessed upon every child like a baptism.

Soon we crossed the road to Stirling and the River Forth in the distance, serpentine and slow. We passed quaint farmhouses contained by stone walls and hawthorn hedgerows. And of course I thought of Allan Rose. I imagined that he lived in one of them. Perhaps it is that one, I said silently to myself. And then a boy and girl running through the spring grass like new lambs. The girl tossed her red hair. Were they brother and sister? But the train moved on, away from them. I could no longer hold them in my imagination. It seemed that nothing waited now. I was moving away from everything I knew. I removed my tam and touched the rose with my fingertips, felt the loving threads. But all at once I felt the pain of it, and the bitterness that the past could bring. The rose seemed but a remembrance of one long dead. I knew right then that if I was to survive, I had to keep my eyes on the path ahead of me. I would not hold a candle for a man I scarcely knew. But then what of my poor *unfound* mother and the receding sea?

I had fallen asleep and when I awoke, the same glens and hills of Scotland. It seemed so immense to me, its great reach of land and sky. How big was Canada? I had seen the maps, the vast empty space of provinces and territories. Lakes like oceans. I reached in my coat pocket and removed the envelope Uncle Calvin had given me. There were bank notes from the Bank of Scotland. Paper money was new and strange. And there was a letter.

Dear Mary,

I will be brief with my instructions. The journey will be long, but you will reach your port of call. The ship awaiting you in Liverpool is the *SS Missanabie*. It also awaits Scottish orphans bound for Canada. You may encounter the women of the Salvation Army with their charge of young children on one of the coaches. It may serve you to travel with them, keeping them in your company during your voyage. I am uncertain of their ultimate goal; however, once the ship makes port in New Brunswick, you undoubtedly will be on your own. When in doubt, ask. Find someone you can trust for assistance. You will travel across the country by train until you reach Vancouver. A ship will carry you north to your new home. You will need to rely on your wits, which I know you have in ample supply. I cannot say with any certainty that obstacles will not occur. Nevertheless, anticipate that certain adjustments may be required. I wish you good luck with a more wholesome vocation. I will ensure the welfare of my brother and niece.

Sincerely,
Uncle Calvin

I suppose he couldn't resist it, one more disparaging footnote as if he couldn't quite comprehend poverty after all. And of course, I wouldn't be able counter him that time. He was safe. But I must admit a renewed admiration for him. He showed a measure of respect for my acumen. And he would honour his promise to me. My father and Lizzy would be looked after. He must have realized that if he did not, I would surely return to torment him. And he did it all at his own expense. I must say that I felt more at ease now.

I returned the envelope to my coat pocket. I surveyed the coach, assessing my company of travellers. It seemed they had all suddenly just appeared. A spectacled middle-aged gentleman reading a newspaper — news of the war. Several women with their spouses, no doubt. There were soldiers, too, bound for glory. And the children sitting at the front of the coach interested me. They must have been the orphans. They were accompanied by two women in Salvation Army frocks, all royal blue and red sashes. Broad stiff bonnets overwhelmed their pale faces. I considered approaching one of the *salvationists*, offering my assistance. We were bound for the same country, after all. And then all at once one of the children, a little boy, ran down the aisle in my direction and stumbled when the coach suddenly lurched on a bend. It was all so very ordinary, a boy running, falling, and of course he began to sob. It seemed he had skinned a bare knee. I felt an immediate impulse to get up from my seat and come to his assistance. But before I could, one of the escorts marched up to him. She seemed to have no sympathy for the boy's misfortune and hauled him to his feet by one of his large ears. He wailed, of course. I saw no need for such rough treatment. I left my seat.

"Excuse me, madam," I said, "but the boy only stumbled. Surely he shouldn't be punished." He looked up at me, his twisted mouth, his red-hot ear, and the pink scrape on his knee. He had a name pinned to his coat. Gulliver.

"You can mind your own business now," she said tersely and then took a cursory look around the coach. The fellow passengers were all watching. Heads up like pond ducks. She was a pasty-skinned woman without a grain of tenderness, her clamped hand squeezing the neck of the blubbering boy.

"You are entrusted to the care of these good Scots children!" I said, my voice rising uncontrollably now. "Do you know what that means, madam?"

"You have nerve speaking to me like that, young lady!"

And then the other escort came up behind her, all warm mouth and smiling grey eyes. "Please return Gulliver to his seat, Agnes," she said calmly. It seemed she was the overseer of the group. She waited until the boy was taken away by the huffing Agnes. "The children are very tired," she said to me. "They are beginning a long journey. Discipline is imperative for our home-less boys and girls. They must behave at all times. It is for their own good. But I imagine you are too young to know anything about children."

"I suppose the self-evident eludes you, madam, but I was one myself, you know."

"You may call me Isla," she said leaning toward me, her voice a mere whisper. "You are a tiresome girl, Miss."

"And you may call me Mary Stewart," I said. "Isla, then, did you ever think to console Gulliver with a kind word?" I noticed he looked back now and then from his seat, strained his sore neck to see what would happen next. It occurred to me just then that I may have inadvertently made things worse for him. But before I could concede my objections, I felt a heavy hand on my shoulder. I was spun around like a top. It was the man with the newspaper.

"Miss, the children are being properly supervised," he said. He pushed his moist lips uncomfortably close to me as if he wished not to be heard. His fat tongue lolled, and below his chin a ruddy flush of jowl like a rooster's wattle. "We cannot tolerate wretched foundlings on the loose. This is a civil society. And I am most certain that everyone on this coach will agree with me. Now if you will please take your seat."

I was stunned by his censure. It all seemed so unjust. "I see no reason for your rebuke, sir," I said. "I wanted only to help the child. Now, what is the harm in that?"

He didn't answer but strangely stepped back. I thought perhaps he couldn't counter such an incorruptible question. And then he began to inspect me in a rather shameless way. He seemed to be appraising me as if I were some commodity in a shop window. His fine clothes revealed a certain status, perhaps a wealthy business-man. But I didn't wait for whatever it was that distracted him so. I needed to get away from him, his dripping mouth, and returned to my seat. But to my dismay, he quickly took the seat beside me. He leaned toward me, unwanted and scheming now.

"This train is bound for Liverpool," he said in a low, duplici-tous voice. "There are destinations for each of us. The children are destined for Canada, as am I. And I will wager that you will be aboard that same passenger ship. Now, I can see by the buttons on your coat and the mends to the sleeve that you are without the necessary funds to keep you out of steerage. They call it third class now, but the lodging is insufferable. On the other hand, I have excellent accommodation that I am willing to share. And please accept my apologies for my uncharacteristic outburst." He placed a chubby hand on my knee.

"If you do not leave, sir, I will scream. Surely a soldier or porter will come to my aid."

"I have done nothing," he said, whisking his hand away. "I have only taken a seat. If you wish to scream, then you must. Certainly, the good boys will come to your aid. But as you can see, the pas-sengers suffer from a certain malaise. They are a sleepy lot wanting nothing but to be free from their misery. The train, they realize, takes them nowhere. They care not for your circumstance. I am only offering you an opportunity. I have unlimited money. I do this out of kindness."

"Now, that isn't kindness, sir. It is repellent. I know what you want from me. I do not wish to continue this conversation any longer." I wasn't so pure, I knew. Many times I had consented to the solicitations of such a man with his soft skin and money. That very thing repulsed me now. I sat with the contradiction and watched the green valleys come and go, and then Dumfriesshire where the trains collided and Paul and Robbie burned. I gasped as the train raced through without ceremony. I pushed away the tears. I wouldn't allow the man to intrude any further.

"I see the lovely rose on your cap," he said, "and I must say that you look very attractive." He seemed to sense my sudden vulnerability. "I suppose that is my shortcoming. I only want a companion, a bright young woman like yourself. What could be wrong with that?"

"I do not want your company, sir. I would like to be left alone. Please leave."

"You are travelling alone, Miss Stewart," he continued, relentless now. "I overheard you tell the salvationist your name."

"And you are unlikely to tell me your name, sir."

"Ah, it all depends now, doesn't it?"

"You are persistent and I do not appreciate any of it."

"I only want to be of some comfort to you."

"And what is your business, sir?" I asked, to move him away from me.

"Textiles. I am on my way to Montreal. Military uniforms are in great demand. I have several plants. Travel can be a lonely affair, you see, back and forth. So lonely."

"You insult me, solicit me with your wealth. Now you want my pity." I looked straight ahead, but felt the sudden rise of his bitterness, his discontent. I had clearly frustrated him with my unfaltering rejection.

"You are a dangerous woman, aren't you, Miss Stewart?" he said through his teeth now. "I know your type. Never knowing when to be silent, always wanting a better stake for yourselves. It's a nasty state of affairs, and that's the truth of it. It seems more and more that women have forgotten their place in the world."

"And I can see that you surely haven't."

"You may regret this."

"Are you threatening me now?" A sudden surge of alarm. It was the same sense of desperation I had felt that night in Josie's flat in Dumbiedykes, to escape from oppression, and now from the evil disguised in the man's unwanted attention.

"We will be aboard the same ship for several weeks, Miss. You may wish to reconsider."

I wanted a moment with my brothers, to remember them. That place where they took their last breaths. The businessman robbed me of my own will, my solitude. I was tired of him. And then I remembered what Nurse Monck had said about Dr. Elsie Inglis, how she campaigned on behalf of the women of Scotland. I had to dissuade him, get him away from me once and for all.

"And you may wish to think of this, sir," I said turning to him now. "There will be suffragettes aboard that ship. Do you know who they are?"

"Yes, of course. I've read extensively of their methods. I find them very disruptive and disturbing. Quite repugnant, I must say. Nothing but criminals."

"That's a mouthful, sir. But you will not be able to tell which ones they are. Some don't want to be found. They have plans for Canada. I shouldn't be telling you this at all. You may despise them, and they may seem dangerous to the likes of you, but to your point, sir, *you* have overstayed your place in the world."

Then a cruelly disguised smile. "Do you think a gaggle of discontented women could frighten me?"

"You underestimate them, sir. And it is true that most of the women have put their energy toward the war effort for now, but they will assist me if I ask them. They will come to my aid if I am in trouble. It is a sisterhood that will change the world. And it seems, sir, that I must report your solicitation to the proper ladies. I wouldn't be surprised if some had their ears bending our way at this very moment. They will do what they must, and believe me, they will. To answer your question, their aim will not be to frighten you. Sometime in the night they will come to your cabin. We'll be hundreds of miles from land. You will be gagged and bound and carried to the upper deck. Silent as mice. And they won't say a word to you, not a moment's hesitation before they pitch you over the rail into the cold, dark sea. They've done it before and will do it again."

Air rushed out of his sopping mouth. "This is an outrage!"

"Which part, sir, your vulgarity or the foretelling of your demise?"

"I shall have you arrested!"

"Then I hope you are a good swimmer, sir."

"You have no idea who you are dealing with, young lady. I made you a most honourable proposal."

"And I'll make you one. Never lay your hand on me again, and never say another word to me, nor look my way. I don't want trouble. I have a long journey ahead of me. Take your seat and read your newspaper, sir."

He just stared at me. It wasn't with hate or even fear. It was the kind of look that comes from seeing something for the first time, a sunset, a storm, or the divine, a look of bewilderment and profound wonder. Something encountered without explanation. He was struck dumb and sat agog. But after a moment he seemed to have found his decency at last, or perhaps it was only prudence on his part and, I would hope, an introduction to compromise and better conduct. He regarded some of the passengers on the coach skeptically, the women I was sure, then got up without further fuss and returned to his seat.

I couldn't sleep. I fought against the lull and rhythm of the train, the flutter of light and shadow through Carlisle and

Blackburn. There was only the strain in my limbs, my shoulders, a tightness in my jaw and a sickness in my belly. My vigilance was exhausting. Why did it have to be so? The man was rebuffed in the end. Was it my wit? It seemed a peculiar way to protect oneself. Why did I need it at all? And the anger I felt when pressed to despair was not a common anger. It was the rage that killed Jimmy McDuff.

CHAPTER
TEN

THE LOOM OF LIVERPOOL WITH ITS BUSTLE AND INDUSTRY, and soon our drift of steam and black smoke stalled at Lime Street Station and rose up like nightfall against the station's glass dome. Outside, the heaviness of centuries, of brickwork and stone. I would follow the orphans and the unmistakable blue ladies with their red ribbons and salvation. I heeded what Uncle Calvin advised in his letter. I would seek their company, insert myself among *the wretched*. But of course I knew better. Young Gulliver clung to me as we boarded the carriages with our luggage and moved through the crowds to the docks on the River Mersey. The escorts didn't seem to mind. I suppose he was less trouble when occupied so. I wondered sadly if my words had been the only kind offering he had seen in his short life.

We arrived at the Landing Stage dock and the gush of life met us like a storm of mortals, as it seemed the entire city of Liverpool was departing, every man, woman, and child. Every standing space was occupied: women in fashionable frocks and silk-plumed hats held umbrellas against the afternoon sun, and men outfitted in their suits and straw boaters gathered in groups and smoked and leaned back against the magnificence of the ship. It seemed like an iron world lifting from the river. People waved to departing loved ones from grandstands. There was a carnival atmosphere: something very important was playing out as far as I could see up and down the river. The working class, big boned and solemn, held to the periphery, Scots and Brits soon to be leaving their home behind. Then there were ranks of wounded soldiers returning home to Canada. The countless children hand in hand seemed lost in the shadows. I found myself unwittingly worried and turned to the orphan boys and girls in our group. They craned their little necks as they looked up at the *S.S. Missanabie* with its twin yellow funnels, their open mouths and popping tongues. I felt Gulliver squeeze my hand, so frightened by the scale and confusion of life before him. It seemed he wouldn't let go lest he be devoured. I knelt down to him as I waited in line with the others for our boarding passes.

"Now, Gulliver," I said, "soon we will be on that grand ship. There are many folks from Scotland leaving their homes, just like you. They will be starting a new life. All the other boys and girls are afraid, too, but in no time at all it will be nothing. Just an adventure. That's what it will be, Gulliver. Things to do. Things to see."

"I don't want to go, Miss," he said.

His twisted face. His uncombed hair. His lovely big ears. "How old are you, Gulliver?"

"I'm a six-year-old boy. I've heard them say so."

"Well, you are brave. I can see that. I'll be honest with you. I'm a little afraid myself."

"Will my mother come?"

"Your mother?"

"She cried when she sent us off."

"Us?"

"Me and Dougie."

"He is your brother?"

He nodded his head.

"Where is Dougie, Gulliver?"

"I don't know. They took him."

Something seemed terribly wrong. I hadn't seen Gulliver with any other child. He had always been under the close supervision of one of the escorts. And as I looked up, I could see the blue shadow of one of the salvationists. It was Isla. She had been listening.

"It seems that Gulliver is missing his brother," I said. "Surely you have seen him."

"Yes, Mary, I have seen him. He was placed on another ship. Likely he's in Canada by now. The older boys will be going to work on farms. Dougie is ten years old. He's a strong boy and will be fine."

"You separated them?" I stood up now, holding Gulliver's hand.

"The boys are destined for different parts of Canada. It is vast and will provide new opportunities. They will be housed with good farm families, good working families. It is all proper and official. Please do not concern yourself."

"Surely Gulliver and Dougie should be together. Can't you see how it distresses him? There is no good reason to keep brothers apart. There must be a mistake."

"We do not make the rules, Mary. We have done this many times. You seem to have a way with Gulliver. Perhaps he sees his mother in you, the mother he had to leave. She was dying, you see. I ask you to use your kindness where it will be needed. Your manner is somewhat exasperating, but I am willing to disregard your criticisms if you can provide the boy comfort for his ills. He is a rather contrary child. There are two dozen children in my charge. It is a long voyage and I confess that I lose my patience. I don't enjoy slapping an insolent child, but it is necessary at times."

She turned away, and that was that. And soon the gangway was lowered and the wounded soldiers were helped up the ramp. Then first class and the working class, and finally the orphans. It was late afternoon when we made our way up the gangway, trying not to peek down at the receding dock and black water, keeping the little ones looking straight ahead. But Gulliver had to see and stopped several times. Perhaps he was looking for Dougie. How difficult it was to leave the entirety of one's life behind. I thought of Lizzy at Waverly Station, her collapsing knees, the unbearable weight of a family's truncation. And Gulliver was younger still.

How could he make sense of his world — given away by a dying mother, then separated from his brother, alone and six years old, and then punished for his broken heart?

We were pushed and shoved along the decks by the stewards and then down a steep staircase, down, down into the cold dark belly of the ship where lightbulbs from the iron ceilings cast squat shadows onto the damp iron floor. It seemed an omen of confinement, of some unknown and inescapable future. I didn't like it at all, and the children whimpered like kittens. I looked around and there were people jammed from end to end. There were families with children, and older women in groups, perhaps travelling together without their husbands, and young women like myself standing uncertain and alone. And there were men, grown men who watched from the edges, from the margins of the third-class compartment like overseers. Perhaps they were too old for the war, or unfit. Their caps were drawn down low over their eyes, a shadowed scrutiny that made me feel uneasy and circumspect.

There were bunks, row on row, and families began to claim their beds. Isla was quick to keep the children together. "Come now," she said, "follow Mother Agnes. She'll see you through to your bunks." They used the title of *Mother* when addressing the children, not in the religious sense but as surrogates to a motherless tribe. And as we settled into our accommodation, I helped Gulliver with his fears that seemed to fester like an illness now, all the while keeping an eye to the unnerving attention from the men.

"Perhaps, Gulliver, you can make a friend with one of the boys and girls," I said to him. "Surely they will like that very much. You must keep busy on the voyage."

"Mother Isla doesn't like play very much," he said, his eyes open wide as saucers in the dimness.

"I suppose children can play quietly. Don't you agree?"

"Some said when we reach Canada, I won't see them again. Can you help me find Dougie?"

All he wanted was his brother. Nothing would appease him, it seemed. How could I say no to such a simple, but daunting question? "Yes, of course, Gulliver. I'll do what I can."

Later food was brought out to the dining room, where we sat at long tables. Stew was ladled from substantial pots into our bowls, loaves of bread sliced and stacked, and cheese in wheels cut by the kitchen stewards and passed among the passengers. A solemn lot on that first night as we left the River Mersey and slipped away from Liverpool into the setting sun. There was low talk among the ladies that told of German U-boats lying in wait for the *SS Missanabie*. Some of them had lost relatives two years before when the *RMS Lusitania* was torpedoed off of the coast of Ireland.

"There was a great loss of life, nearly twelve hundred souls," one said. "She sank in eighteen minutes. The Cunard line offered the local fisherman and merchants cash rewards for the recovery of bodies floating on the Irish Sea. Americans, Canadians, and Brits. An awful day. The Germans claimed there were munitions aboard."

"Surely they won't try it again," another said. "There are no guns on our deck."

"There are things we're never told. We'll round Holyhead in the Irish Sea, and then we'll know. It'll come quick: take us at midship and the boilers will blow."

There was a lot of talk, fearful speculation, and the children listened well, followed every word with their open mouths and rampant imaginations. They merely picked at their food. The world they lived in seemed a calamitous affair, uncertain and precarious, and it was no wonder they couldn't eat, no matter how empty their bellies. And the ladies at last saw how they frightened the children with their chronicles and prophecy, and then spoke of the voyage ahead and the great cliffs of blue ice floating on the North Atlantic Ocean. That seemed to distract the orphans enough to rouse their appetites. And I was thankful they thought better than to retell the tragedy of the *RMS Titanic* and its collision with an iceberg just five years earlier.

And at the far end of the table the unattached men were intent with their supper, but I noticed now and then that their attention seemed to settle upon two Polish girls in particular, perhaps Lizzy's age. They were travelling with an older woman, a grandmother or an aunt. No one seemed to give notice to the men, their wandering and plotting eyes, sitting shadows. But the girls seemed afraid. Perhaps their journey had been difficult.

I was wary of men, suspicious of what dark thoughts lurked in their singular minds. I suppose it was the company I had kept, the desperate work of privation. I had seen the worst of men, but still I kept hope that they all couldn't be bad in their ways. Was Allan Rose some aberration of nature? There was just no telling night to night. In time I had gained a certain intuitive sensibility. They seemed to guard their ponderings and musings at times, and hid behind a wall of silence, as if they served no cause other than their primal functions. I needed to speak to Isla. She would know the furtive perils of steerage.

Agnes had taken the children to their berths to prepare them for much-needed sleep. Most of the others had left. I asked Isla to stay behind at the table. I had asked for tea, and she seemed to appreciate the gesture. I poured her tea from a kettle.

"I know you have something to say to me," she said, "so please just come out with it. I suppose you have some new insight into the lives of orphans."

"No, not that," I said, "but I do have a dilemma with Gulliver that can wait."

"Well, shall I thank God for that?" She took her cup and held it under her nose briefly, then sipped it sparingly.

"It is the men who sat at the end of the table. They keep to themselves."

"I know the ones." Isla looked up, then back over her shoulder. They were nowhere to be found now.

"I have a bad feeling, that's all. The way they looked at some of the girls."

"They're a tough lot, for sure. Miners, most of them. Some going to the coal mines in Cape Breton, others to mines across the American west. Conditions at home broke many of them. They'll take anything for work. They're from all over Europe and Great Britain, every nationality, looking for a new start. They're not all bad, but there's been trouble in the past. It takes just one of them to goad the others."

"It's the Polish girls. They've been watching them."

"Yes, the youngest and weakest. That's where they start."

"Surely we can intervene before anything happens. We can talk to the grandmother. Perhaps she can speak English. She will need to be vigilant."

"Ah, she is the mother of the girls. Life has been hard for her."

"It need not get harder, surely you agree."

"Perhaps you have misjudged them. Is that a possibility? Not every voyage has its problems."

"No, I've seen them, how they look, and then their under-breath talk. They are like wolves that have come upon a yearling. You said so yourself. Now they wait."

"I must say that you have worked yourself up into quite a lather, Miss Stewart. I'm not so sure that your concerns are merited without proof. However, I know that assaults do happen to immigrant travellers, girls and women. I will speak to the mother. There are certain precautions the family needs to make. She will recognize the uniform as a source of support and encouragement. Don't *you* agree?"

"Why, of course, Isla," I said to appease her.

"It seems you have changed your tune, Miss Stewart. I am most certain that you had admonished the very institution from which you now seek assistance."

"I had only reacted to what I saw on the train. I will admit that I didn't fully understand the work you do."

"Well, it seems we have reached a mutual understanding," Isla said, quite pleased now. "A young woman can hardly know the perplexing nature of life, but you seem eager to learn. I'm happy to see your deference."

I bristled at her condescension and smiled in spite of it. But of course it couldn't last. "I must point out," I said, "that you made reference to my age on the train as well. I may be young, Isla, but I know that scalding a boy's ears will not make him a better boy, merely a convenient boy."

Isla sat shaking her head. Her grey eyes darkened, retreated. "Did your mother not teach you to respect your elders, Miss Stewart? You have a way that is most offensive. I cannot abide it." She got up from the table.

"I mean no disrespect, but my mother taught me to speak up, lest I do without."

"Do without what, dear child?"

"Honesty."

Isla didn't leave at once. She stood looking down at me, puzzling, struggling to comprehend what I had said to her. Her eyes were wide with confusion, and perhaps questions, as if something had been stirred, roused from some unknown place. It seemed, perhaps, I had touched her own past.

"You are an interesting young woman," she said before leaving the dining room. "In your life, you will be despised or admired, but it will be up to you which one you favour."

I sat with her words after she left me, a riddle to consider. And then I became aware of sounds and a blend of smells. Always the soft murmur of voices, but now I could hear the engine of the ship and felt its driving shiver beneath my feet. The faint smell of grease, lubricants for so many moving parts. Then I realized, I was under the ocean. And how strange that the forces of power and order had been established so easily, as if the world had been reinvented on the Irish Sea.

CHAPTER

ELEVEN

THE ATLANTIC OCEAN GREETED US WITH FAIR-WEATHER seas and invited the third-class passengers out onto the foredeck. There was scarcely room to move on the deck as, after a week at sea, below-decks was becoming insufferable with its tomb of odours. The early days of sea sickness had taken a miserable toll.

The gulls had left us, the wind was cool, and everyone was bundled up in their coats. It was the sun and the freshness of the salty air. It was the complete emptiness of the world. And of course, the orphan boys seemed less interested in the vastness of the sea and spat from the rails into the passing white foam below. They were engaged in an activity nevertheless and the Salvation Army mothers seemed strangely indifferent. I suppose they had witnessed such behaviour more than they would care to admit, and now it must have seemed more like a rite of passage than mischief.

We had escaped the Irish Sea intact, thankful for those in uniform manning the upper decks who scanned the horizons with binoculars for signs of U-boat torpedoes coming our way. But the farther away we got from Britain, it seemed, the more we were leaving the war behind as well. I moved with Gulliver along the deck, a good stretch of his legs. Mother Isla walked behind us with a few of the girls while Mother Agnes supervised the hawk and heave of sputum. People talked in groups and there were several languages I didn't understand. I wondered what they were all leaving behind, what had driven them so far from their homes, their countries. I supposed there were many reasons, mostly poverty. And it seemed that the new world had something, some lure that was irresistible. It was the promise of land and opportunity,

I overheard a man from Perth tell another. A vernacular I knew so well. It was the riches from the earth, gold and towering forests, said another, and unlimited fishes from the sea, said still another. Territories still undiscovered. It seemed they all had their good reasons to leave, and good accounts of what lay in wait for them. I was no different, though I had left Edinburgh in rather mitigating circumstances. The promise of Anyox was not my own, but Uncle Calvin's, who painted a rather marvellous picture of a city with its boundless *opportunity* — that encouraging word.

And still I listened as we walked among the passengers. There were conversations that at times seemed guarded, not meant for the ears of others, but still I picked up a word or two, mostly worry and gossip. My listening was the kind that was tuned to a certain quality, one of provocation. I had to filter what entered my awareness, my eyes discretely connecting the words with the speaker. And then something broke through, rough and crude. It came from behind us. I turned and there were several men leaning against the bulwark of the ship, the sun revealing them now, though the shadow of their caps hid their eyes, perhaps giving them a sense of protection, anonymity. It was the Polish girls. They followed behind Isla with their mother. The men had been harassing them for days and now called them out like livestock. One with the common dialect of the rural Scot.

"Hello, sweetheart," he said, "I've got something for you."

"Don't be shy," said another.

I wasn't sure if the girls understood English, but it seemed they had a good idea what the men were after. Their lovely faces crumpled, their hands to their mouths as if sickened. Isla stopped and took them by the arms and pushed them ahead. The mother scowled at the men, who jeered at her and made strange animal sounds. Then Isla moved her ahead as well. The orphan children gathered around Isla and seemed frightened by the commotion, the taunts of the men. The other passengers merely looked on, paid little attention as if they didn't want to trouble themselves. There were none of the ship's crew on the deck, only the assembly of immigrants. But Isla stood her ground, faced the men, who seemed uncertain now what to do with the intimidating salvationist with her royal blue authority. Her eyes as sharp as knives. One seemed braver than the others and stepped away from the bulwark.

"I suggest you keep moving, old woman," he warned, "if you know what's good for you."

Some of the children began to cry and pulled at her frock. No one seemed to want to help her, and I could see that she measured the situation with a certain maternal intelligence. And then she looked about for an answer for the men, for assistance of some kind, but found none. She seemed resigned to her duty and slowly turned away. But something in me could not let such mean and indecent behaviour go without consequence. That something was contrary to the expected representation of my gender, a subordinate role to play. I had no responsibility other than for myself. I was free, unknown, cauterized from my past. And Isla seemed to understand what I was about to do and pulled Gulliver away from my skirt.

I walked up to them with my gall and temper. They all had the same sly and devilish smirk as if I were some greater prize. I had no plan of what I would do or say. I wanted only to look into their eyes, to see who they were, to show them that I knew what they were up to, that such conduct in plain view of children, or any civilized living soul, was unacceptable.

"Now that doesn't set a good example for the children," I said as loud as I dared to the one I believed to be the ringleader. I wanted the other passengers to hear. "You have frightened them, and you have upset the older girls. There is nothing manly about that at all. I would appreciate it very much if you would keep your comments to yourself. Better still, don't dare look their way if you know what's good for you." How strange and unexpected that I used his own threat. I quickly regretted it. He reared back, and his lifted chin revealed his eyes now, a feral malignancy that prickled the skin of my neck.

And then all at once one of them surged toward me, his hand raised as if to strike me down, but the ringleader took hold of it, snatched it out of the air. Then he spoke in a low guttural voice meant only for me.

"You are a Scots whore, and this I know," he said, his breath hot with liquor, "and you belong to me. You shouldn't be running away, Mary."

His words stunned me and I was suddenly breathless as death. No words, no denial, no dissent. I searched his face, the rough sallow skin and the small pitiless eyes. In the light of the day, I knew him, his voice, his smell, and the patched filthy clothes. I felt faint, immovable, and then an arm around my shoulder pulled me back. It was Isla, and with her, a Junior Second Officer, a young man scarcely out of his teens.

"Now move along," he said to the men. "No trouble now. Move along."

Oh, he was as sparing as can be, not an accusing bone in him, but a gentle nudge with a hand was all that was needed. I was grateful for whatever he possessed that moved the men away. I suppose it was his uniform and the hierarchy of rank and command above him. And many thanked him for it, and he was clearly pleased as he nodded to them in return. But I wanted to see where the men would go, to keep an eye on their whereabouts. I looked down through the crowd of immigrants, to the backs of the men moving away. I was startled to see that one of them had stopped. It was the ringleader and he was looking right back at me, through the same crowd and with the same scrutiny as if there was unfinished business between us. And then I began to shake for I knew what he wanted. I stood undone, seized by the memory of his violence for a long and unsettling minute before he continued on.

Later on, after our supper, we took the children to the playroom. There had been looks between Isla and Agnes, the silent language of salvationists. I was left out, of course, being the interloper and all. But I had a feeling that I would know what it was soon enough. It came when Agnes was reading to the children from *The Jolly Miller*. They sat in a circle playing at a game of verse. They were occupied so when Isla sat down with me.

"You know, Mary," she began in a kindly way, "what you did up on the foredeck with those louts took a bit of courage. I'll say that. And God knows they surely needed a bit of dressing down. No one else stepped forward, but you did."

It seemed that perhaps she was an *admirer* now. But her face turned sour all at once, and the air between us oddly thickened.

"I heard the man speak to you," she said, "and I do believe I heard him correctly. You seem quite capable of holding your own with men. However, I do not believe that such an unabashed attribute should be exposed to the children. Now, it is none of my business what it all means. The man used filthy language. I have no interest in hearing your explanation. So please listen."

"Do I have a choice?"

"I'm sure you know what I'm about to say. Please take no offence. This will be your last visit with the children. I must uphold certain standards. I am a servicewoman in the Salvation Army. I can spare you no quarter. I'm sure that you understand. I thank you for your brief service."

I was trying to understand, but it deeply troubled me. "What it is that you think I have done, Isla? I was simply standing up for what was right."

"Please, that's enough."

"You cannot dismiss me so easily. I am not in your charge. I thought perhaps you admired me, but only to realize that you despise me. I can only say that it's a shame that narrow-mindedness has become a virtue."

"I don't despise you. I just don't think the world is ready for you, Mary."

Her stone face. She was clearly adamant. "I would like to know Gulliver's full name," I said curtly, "and his village."

"And why is that?"

"So I won't forget him."

"I suppose, if you must. It is Gulliver Fraser. He comes from the lands about Inverness. Many of the children are Highland stock."

"Thank you."

"You thank me now?"

"I don't mind you, Isla. You're a strong woman, and I do admire that. But I have a different notion of things."

"I've noticed."

"Very well, we understand one another, then."

"Yes, it seems so. And there is one more important thing you should know. Perhaps you already do. The man in question was not distracted by the young Polish girls at our supper tonight. It was you, Mary. So take heed in all that you do until we reach Canada. Stay away from the dark corridors, and if you must, never go about on your own."

"I thank you for your concern, Isla. I know where he is. He's in the smoking salon with the others."

"Yes, well, I can only say that I wish you well with your endeavours. They will be interesting, I'm quite sure. You seem to choose the toughest row to hoe, as they say. Your future will be long and hard. You might want to be more agreeable with your elders at times. There's no shame in capitulation, you know."

There was a vain part of me that wanted to convince her that she had misjudged me, but people, I was learning, tended to get stuck in their ways like wagon ruts in the moors. I suppose I was no different, eager to challenge, eager to make her wrong as well. But before I could say another word, she abruptly got up and returned to the children.

The dark steerage was steeped in shadows and sheltered the eyes of the watchers. I thought that I would go up on the deck to watch the sun set. Many did, leaning against the railing, a last bit of sunlight and fresh air before retiring to the stuffy bunks.

I felt safe enough. And there were others from first class. I recognized their stylish ensembles, the way they laughed, hearty, heads thrown back pretentiously. Why did I resent them? I was wistful now, thinking how attached I had become to Gulliver, a boy who scarcely said a word to me. I suppose it was his vulnerability that stirred something in me. I knew what that felt like, the uncertainty of life — the fear of one's annihilation — the misery of the dirt-poor. And yet I mitigated such insecurity with the only thing at my disposal, my wayward mouth. And, of course, Gulliver had no such thing. He had his silence, his contrariness.

I had my coat fastened and my shawl wrapped about my shoulders, my tam pulled down tight. The cold rushed in from Greenland, but I faced its aliveness with the sun sinking low. A merchant ship moved through the gold shimmer of it, a welcome accompaniment. Danger seemed impossible on a bronze sea, but soon I began to see massifs of ice that appeared blue-gold, capped with a brilliant white. Icebergs that were far away, that had a certain cold loneliness. But it wasn't long before I felt a presence beside me. I turned, and it was him.

"What do you want?" I snapped.

"Oh, aren't you the one," he said. "You fancy being in control now, but that's not always the way. You remember how it was between us. Yes, I am certain you will never forget."

"I don't know what you're talking about, sir," I said, trying to keep my distance. I wouldn't acknowledge him in the presence of others. "And I am certain I do not know you. Please leave me be as I am expecting someone."

"Are you, now? I've been watching you and wager that to be a lie. Isn't that so?"

"He'll be here any minute. He won't like the looks of you one bit. So off you go."

"That's a fine story," he said. "It could be the old ladies with their brats, but you are expecting no man." And then he looked around the deck warily, a quick inventory. "I have a few shillings and a nice bunk," he went on. "That's what I want, something for my loneliness. And I know you can give it. Why pretend to be something you're not? You surely didn't fool me."

"Why can't you leave me alone?" I said in a hushed growl. "You beat me badly and you'll never touch me again. I'm done with that life. Can't you see? I'm done with that life!"

"I'm a different man, Mary. You see, when a woman parts her legs for a man, it's like a marriage. So I want to show you that I might be made a proper man. A husband for you."

"That will never be. Never. You're drunk and you're sick!"

"How can you say that? Come with me. A nice warm bunk."

"No, that's all behind me now. Please, I beg of you!"

"How strange that Jimmy dies and then you leave. You didn't tell me. Just slipped away. But I found you, Mary."

The longer it went on, the more frightened I became. He wasn't a man to be refused. But it would be dark soon and I needed to leave. I tried to move past him but he seized my arm and pulled me up against him.

"You're all alone, Mary. You see, I know you and your eager sex. There's no one here to help you now. These people don't care. A family squabble, that's all it is."

"Leave me be!" I shouted now. Some of the passengers turned, and others moved away.

"See how it is? Now come along."

I fought him, but I was no match for him. It was like Jimmy. The power of the heartless and remorseless, the power over one, the credo of the shameless. I had nothing to defend myself. No knife, only my impotent cleverness.

But from across the deck someone moved toward us. It was a man in the dying light. His hand was raised as if to hail a carriage, as if to address a friend. As he got closer I recognized him. It was the businessman I had spurned on the train, a man I had threatened with a cold and watery grave if he ever laid a hand on me or looked my way. My regret was bitter in my mouth. I wanted to take it back before he recognized me, before he gladly kept his part of the bargain and left me in the clutches of a most brutal man.

"Now what is this?" he said, ignoring me. I thought he surely would have remembered me, though the light was dim, lending a fuzziness to shapes and things.

"None of your business. A family matter. Mind yourself, sir."

"Well, that is very interesting indeed, my dear fellow. You see, Miss Stewart is an acquaintance of mine, and it seems that you are unwanted. The First Officer is a good friend, one I trust to exercise a certain justice at sea. Now if you would, please release my friend before I call for his assistance. He has been known to have offenders summarily arrested upon arrival at the next port. So, what will it be?"

His eyes retreated back into their infernal wells as he regarded the businessman. He muttered some obscenity in his direction and then wandered off like the drunk I knew he was. The businessman stood before me. He lifted the palms of his hand and slightly tilted his head as if in appeal.

"So, it seems, Miss Stewart," he said, "that I have violated one of your conditions. I do believe the suffragettes, at your beckoning, will now bundle me up and toss me overboard. Am I correct?"

"You have me at a loss for words," I said, still quaking with fear, but relieved. "It doesn't happen often, I assure you, but your arrival and intervention are much appreciated."

"How interesting it was to hear that man's solicitation. It seemed he was in no bargaining mood. His insistence was about to place you in harm. He was a scoundrel of the worst kind. I must say that many paid little notice. You both are clearly from steerage. But of course I saw through the failing light the tartan shawl and the scarlet glow of the rose on your cap. I knew it was you."

"I was rather firm with you on the train, sir. I'm surprised you came to my rescue."

"Well, I like to think that I am a noble fellow. The rescue of a damsel in distress and all that. But you see, I saw something in the man. I saw a bit of myself, the same insistence, the same goal. An appalling realization, truth be told. I have no excuse other than loneliness. It's a disease of the mind. Only a woman can relieve it."

"Get yourself a wife, sir. Take her with you on your travels."

"Ah, but I do have a wife," he said solemnly.

"You seem an intelligent man, sir, but I fail to see your predicament."

"I cannot form an argument to refute what you have said, Miss Stewart. I clearly cannot. You have made me quite reflective. You are an unusual young woman. What city awaits you? I am curious what would attract your temperament."

"The wild British Columbia coast, of course. I am due in the city of Anyox in early summer."

"Well, that's surely a feral land, and suited to your proclivities, no doubt. Now it is getting late. I will have a steward escort you to your quarters."

"Can you tell me your name now, sir?" The dying light favoured him, made him look much younger. I didn't want to return to my quarters, to the threat that surely lingered there.

"I must decline," he said. "I wish to remain anonymous with you. You see, I do not wish to shame myself any further."

The horrible businessman who had petitioned me with his arrogance and presumption. And now his shame, and my own that I dismissed to consider his warm bed, encouraged me take his arm. Oh, he was startled by my changeable mood, but offered no resistance. Above us, the heavens swam in a black sea of stars, its thrilling and dizzying infinity. And below us in the human pool of the ship, the delirium of the black-hearted.

CHAPTER

TWELVE

A GREAT CROWD HAD GATHERED ON THE FOREDECK WHEN it was announced that we had arrived in Canada. At first a distant bit of land, then fishing boats and gulls, and finally a harbour opening to greet us. It wasn't much different than Liverpool on the River Mersey, and now the Saint John River, and Saint John itself gushing the smoke of industry beyond the peripheral docks. I got caught up in the crush of passengers disembarking the ship. All five hundred from steerage so eager to be on land, to feel the unmoving ground beneath their feet. I was the same. My insides, it seemed, had been gently heaving this way and that, a kind of rhythm one develops on ocean voyages — sea legs, some call it. Well, I was happy to return to *terra firma* and feel the solidity of it, motionless and rigid, and of course, the solace of having survived the crossing. And a long line of soldiers still bearing their injuries were helped down the gangway to the dock, slowly and forever changed. I suppose they were more than happy to be home and alive.

There was a look of relief among the immigrants, but it was soon replaced with the anxiety of what would come next, holding their immigration cards as the immigration officers pushed us along with whistles and commands. I looked back at the ship, the *SS Missanabie*, one last time. There was no sign of *him*. I breathed a little easier now. It seemed he had moved on, perhaps destined for Boston, or some outpost a thousand miles away. And the businessman, I would never see again. We seemed to have reconciled matters between us, two souls at opposite ends of our social hierarchy. There was the meeting of accommodation, and the acceptance and acknowledgement of human longing. The details of such an arrangement were less important than the principles of kind regard. What prompted his redemption? What motivated my consent? I suppose it was a matter of choice and convenience, without control and domination, or perhaps I had simply retained a certain familiarity with men his age. It was not so hard, really, when the fruit was personal security and not companionship. And my shame was voiceless, muted. It seemed to be a fault in my character, to justify so easily what I wanted. But fear has always been the great persuader.

Somewhere ahead of me were the matrons of the Salvation Army with the children. There was a building, the *immigration shed*, they called it, where the medical examinations were held, and perhaps quarantine for the hapless. I couldn't see them. I couldn't see Gulliver. But he had the gift that I had given him, a piece of paper, one that he could never lose, words that he could never forget, words that I prayed would help reunite them one day.

Dougie Fraser, born in 1907, Inverness, Scotland

The long lineups, the questions, the nervous answers, and finally the Medical Examination stamp and Civil Examination stamp on my immigration card — *vaccination protected*, it read, certified by the flourish of a surgeon's pen. And the crowds moved on, together, making their way to temporary accommodation and then the train. I just followed with my suitcase, the stale smell of my clothes now mingling with a collective mustiness. During the progression I was unceremoniously shoved and fell to the ground, perhaps by a sudden surge of panic when a child had been separated from a mother. I was helped to my feet. Order was restored. We moved, we crept, strangely anonymous, shoulder to shoulder and heel to toe like refugees on a long march to freedom. We were refugees, really, seeking refuge from poverty, from scarcity and exhaustion. There was such a will to endure, whole families placing their trust in a new country that didn't look so strange. Most were familiar with ports by the sea, the drift of filthy smog from coal fires and foundries. A transplanted world. Some would stay and begin again, and others like myself would come to know the breadth of Canada.

The press of cots and bodies in our lodging, much like steerage, but more so, like the packed herring of my mother's *silver darlings*. I overheard an immigration officer tell a family that it was more than three thousand miles to Vancouver. Now, I knew that Canada was vast but still I gasped loud enough for him to notice.

"If that's where you're going, Miss," he said turning to me, "you'll get a feel for this country soon enough. Hills and mountains and a bit of prairie in between. You'll be there in a week."

I smiled out of courtesy, mulling over such distance in comparison to Scotland's two-hundred-mile width. It seemed a bit too daunting to consider just then, the where and the how. I realized that I would need help along the way, a guiding hand, a pointing finger. Uncle Calvin had said as much in his letter.

We retired early, a warehouse of immigrants, and soon the shuffle of bodies subsided, and then only a soft murmur of voices remained, and then a cry, a cough, and finally the mercy of sleep. But of course, I was like most others, looking up into the dark rafters for some measure of peace, something to ease the grief of things left behind, a home, a family perhaps, and every echo of our lives. It took great courage, I was beginning to understand, to leave everything that one held dear for a chance at a better life.

In the morning a kind woman at a bank helped me exchange my Bank of Scotland notes for Canadian dollars. There was train fare to purchase at Union Station, and I moved through the street now with the others, watchful of the city. There were horses and carriages and motor cars, electric street cars on a street without cobbles, a street lined with telegraph poles, and buildings cramped and new, more wood than stone. There were squat buildings, no rising tenements that I could see. There seemed to be a hurriedness to it all, a certain haste to grow, to become, in the streets of Saint John.

At last the enterprise of arrival had been satisfied, tickets purchased, luggage stowed, and we boarded the train. I had removed a handbag with pen and paper from my suitcase. Lizzy would be worried. I would write to her once I was settled. I found my seat and after what seemed like a long time, the train began to move, unannounced and rather unceremoniously, suddenly lurching forward like a beast with a hunger for distance. There was something satisfied in me now, a sense of relief to be on my way. I was in Canada and, like the immigrant passengers around me, sat in repose with my face pressed to the windows, curious and hopeful, watching Saint John unfold before us, then soon receding into the wake of steel, a city that received us and then released us to our futures. I felt part of a collective, a community of like-minded souls with the same dreams. But how strange that most kept to themselves, no open communion, no fellowship other than the shared space of that accord.

As the land rushed by, I wasn't so keen to see it all, the broken earth with its smouldering brush piles, and then a green wilderness that seemed unending. The click and sway of the train made me feel sleepy, uninterested, and a bit melancholy. I was travelling to the far ends of the country. There was too much time to think now, to reflect on the distressing things of the voyage, of my life. And I couldn't look ahead, so uncertain and unclear Anyox was in my head. What was it? Perhaps like Saint John, or Liverpool, or ... Oh, Edinburgh.

I went to the immigrant dining car and sat at a table. A steward brought me a pot of tea and a lovely scone and a pad of butter. I was so hungry that I doubted my competence with pen and ink. So I rested a moment while I ate and sipped my tea. Lizzy would be anxious to hear from me, I knew, that I had made it safely to my new country. But how to be encouraging, optimistic, in a demoralizing world? What did she need from me? I supposed that truth could be obscured by eagerness — misleading, I was sure, but it seemed to me that it would serve Lizzy's mental health. Perhaps encouraging her dreams when she was low with despair, something to carry her through.

June 17th, 1917

Dearest Lizzy;

I have arrived in Canada at last, in Saint John, New Brunswick. I hope this finds you and Da well. I do thank you for the selfless work you do, and I rest assured that Uncle Calvin will support you both until such time as you join me. It was very exciting indeed on the train to Liverpool with so many sights that had been unknown to my eyes. I had imagined them, but I could never had been prepared for the glorious valleys of Scotland, the heath, the rivers and lochs, and the mist that settles in the moors. And Liverpool with its colour and bustle at the Landing Stage docks on the River Mersey. A million people coming and going, it seemed to me, travellers and emigrants, and orphans too. It all seemed so important, so momentous. So many people leaving their homelands for a fresh start. The SS Missanabie was a magnificent ship, room for 1800 passengers. You should have seen the looks on the children when they gazed up at its bow. They must have felt they were in a dream.

And the ocean was astonishing, I must say, to look out from the deck in every direction and see nothing but rolling water the colour of a deep-green bottle. Icebergs in the distance were the size of Arthur's Seat and as blue as a thrush's egg. I suppose I exaggerate, just a little. I will never forget that morning we shared on Arthur's Seat when Edinburgh was bathed in the morning dew. That's a precious memory to return to, Lizzy, when you feel alone.

I am now travelling on the Canadian Pacific Railroad, westbound for Vancouver, British Columbia. I will post this letter at the next stop. There will be more to follow with news of my adventures. That's what it is, Lizzy, an adventure. Now, time will go by soon enough, and you'll be coming to join me. Please don't worry about Da. He wants it that way. It's a chance for his daughters. You see, it will bring him peace to know we are all right, that we have prospered in Anyox. I should be there in early July. It's a bit of a mystery to me, I must say, that strange-sounding city. I'll make a few queries as I get nearer. Perhaps then I will get a sense of where I am going.

Until then,
Your loving sister Mary

That night in my berth, I couldn't sleep once again. I could feel the weight of my leaving, and the responsibilities of a fourteen-year-old girl in my absence, bleak and absolute. Had I a choice, really? I was so far from home just then that I wondered how it all happened. It was something I had done, I knew, my entanglement in a nefarious business, but the reasons seemed so unclear now, my motivations not so excusable. I felt the guilt like a large stone pressed against my chest. I couldn't breathe in the tomb of the berth, in the absence of my own vindication. I fretted until the tears trickled down my temples, and in that space of regret sleep soon overtook me like an act of mercy. But it was not so benevolent. It came with a messenger for the disgraced and culpable, Jimmy McDuff floundering on the floor, gasping at the sight of his own blood, clutching where I had stabbed him without hesitation, without pity. I awoke with a start, a kinder mercy, it would seem, but I was confused, and terrified that he had followed me to Canada.

CHAPTER

THIRTEEN

HILLS AND MOUNTAINS AND A LITTLE BIT OF PRAIRIE IN between, the man had said. I had never seen such space. The sky was like an inverted sea, and the land shimmered beneath it in waves of grass. Up or down, it was all I could take after many unchanging miles. I had to close my eyes, because at times I could have sworn we hadn't moved at all. And, as if to bear my perception wrong, we began to lose some of the passengers, the immigrants with their trunks and suitcases leaving for towns that seemed too insignificant to have names. But there would be a sign that read *Mortlach*, *Emfold*, or *Rush Lake*. It was Saskatchewan, I was told by a steward, and there were farms along the railway, men toiling under the glare of the sun with horses and machinery, plodding along in clouds of dust, and now and then dark-faced children watching us pass. They stood blankly and as stiff as the fence posts that criss-crossed the prairie, perhaps to define a boundary or to keep something out. Not a hedgerow or stone fence in all that space. Everything seemed fashioned from wood. Yet on the prairie, scarcely a tree. It was a curious sweep of geography.

It was the same in every town. The platforms at the train stations were overwhelmed with young men in uniform. They were waiting for the troop trains that would take them east. Perhaps they would board the *SS Missanabie* in Saint John. So many boys giving their lives, so many who would not return. I wondered about the mothers receiving the news. My own mother was spared the news of the deaths of Paul and Robbie. She had died prior, of course, but my father grieved every day for his boys. And I was certain he would never recover. A part of him had given up on life. I was convinced that once Lizzy joined me in Anyox, he would will himself to die.

A woman boarded the train in Swift Current and to my surprise sat beside me. The car had quickly filled to capacity and she had taken the only seat available. I wouldn't begrudge her a seat, but I had enjoyed a certain privacy since Saint John and was somewhat cool with her. She was an older woman, perhaps fifty years old, dressed in a common blue–grey frock and jacket, but strangely dignified. She removed her plain straw hat and placed it on her lap. I smiled pleasantly enough, I thought, as she settled into her seat. But as I turned my attention away from her, I suddenly felt the warmth of her breath on my neck. She gave me what seemed a good measure of scrutiny. Then she leaned even closer.

"I am not an immigrant," she said, with a contradictory strong accent. "I've been in this country twenty years and still I must ride in second class. I wanted a seat of my own. I find it intolerable. And you?"

I turned to her. She had striking blue eyes, slightly almond shaped. Her hair in a long braid was as pale as summer grass. "I am unsure of your question," I said truthfully.

"Ah, yes, a Scot immigrant," she said. "I know the English of the poor. You are young and I would expect a young girl should be with the war effort. But you are going in the opposite direction to be of any help." The chiding lift of her eyebrows.

"And you?" I said, tossing it back at her. She looked at me rather dumbfounded. I was in no mood to be provoked by a stranger.

"And I am unsure of *your* question," she said.

Her manner was a bit too familiar. I felt a surge of resentment, but the others around us were listening the way they do. I wanted no trouble with her. "Are you travelling far?" I asked her.

"Vancouver is my destination, and beyond." She threw up her hand.

"And that is my destination as well."

"Very well, we have established something at last," she said, clearly displeased with me.

I had no idea what vexed the woman. I turned in my seat and faced her squarely. "If you are going to sit in that seat beside me for another minute, madam," I said, "then we should come to an understanding."

"Understanding?"

"Yes. I have travelled far, and I have a long journey ahead of me still. I don't want to argue with you or anyone. I like to keep to myself. And if you wish to speak to me, then please be civil. You are a rude woman, madam. You find it intolerable to be treated like an immigrant, but you were very quick to offend me. You know nothing about me. If you wish to speak to the steward, perhaps he can find you a more suitable seat. It is true that I am an immigrant, and I've seen the discrimination. And I know by your English you were born overseas. So do we not share something in common?"

She sat a moment without saying a word. I wasn't sure if she was fuming or merely stunned. I meant no harm, really. I suppose I had looked approachable, amicable perhaps, but before one admires the bloom on a thistle, be forewarned of its prickle. Then I noticed the woman rubbing her fingers nervously.

"I haven't been myself," she said, her head down.

"Then who have you been?"

She shook her head and fussed with the brim of her straw hat. And then I heard her speak under her breath. "No need for that," she said as quietly as a whisper.

"I beg your pardon, madam?"

"The way you spoke to me. Such words from a young girl like you. But I suppose you were right. I shouldn't have spoken to you the way I did. It comes and goes. I don't understand what is happening to me. Please forgive me, if you can."

I had been quick to defend myself, I knew. I suppose I had good reason to be wary in a strange country. I couldn't let my guard down for a minute. But the sudden change in her demeanour made me reconsider. She was clearly remorseful, and troubled by something that seemed to have nothing to do with our seating arrangements.

"Perhaps we can begin again," I said.

"Yes, that would be nice."

"My name is Mary, and I am bound for Vancouver and beyond."

"And my name is Marta, and I am bound for Vancouver and beyond."

"See, we have one more thing in common, Marta."

"Yes," she said. I detected a weak smile along with her regret.

"I am on my way to the city of Anyox on the north coast of British Columbia. That is my *beyond*."

"And I am on my way to the state of Washington, and that is my *beyond*. Tell me, Mary, what takes you to ...?"

"Anyox."

"That's a strange name. I don't know that city."

"Well," I said, to continue our little game of disclosure, "upon arrival in Anyox, I will begin my new position as a nurse at the city hospital. I have a letter of introduction from the Royal Edinburgh Infirmary." I stole a glance at her to catch her expression, impressing her, and certain to correct her presumptions. But gone was her smile. Instead a sad, grey face.

"You are young and starting a new life," she said.

"I am indeed," I said, perhaps a bit too cavalier.

"I was young like you, Mary. I had your spirit and spleen. It was twenty years ago when we emigrated from Denmark. There was free land to be had. Aksel wanted to be a farmer. Oh, he was strong and good with his hands. And we had our farm. There, much like that one." She pointed out the window.

I looked out to the prairie, to a barn and house atop a rise in the distance. There was something bleak about it, the way the farm's buildings sat, isolated, forlorn, as if it missed its people.

"We raised two sons and a daughter," she went on. "They were born in Canada, but we were always immigrants. It's the language, you know. It takes a while. People make up their minds about you. But we worked hard, growing our wheat, our vegetables, and tending our animals. It was a hard but good life. Then ..."

I turned to her. Her chin trembled like a leaf. "What is it?"

"I am not well, I'm afraid. It's all too much."

"Tell me."

"The war took our sons," she said faintly, her eyes closed and her head bowed as if in prayer. A tear trickled down her cheek. "We were told that they were missing. Were they dead? I had hope, but Aksel said he knew they were gone. Well, the news came in late winter, and it killed him just the same. He dropped like a stone that very day, walking to the barn. I couldn't manage the farm on my own. The bank wanted it back. So now, you see, I am an immigrant once again, with all of you. My sister has left Cape Scott, a Danish settlement on the northern tip of Vancouver Island. It has failed to thrive. She will be waiting for me in Vancouver. She is all I have now. I loaded a trunk and left our home for good. I've always been a strong woman, but the heart can only take so much."

I had been thinking of that very thing, the sad deaths of Paul and Robbie. How strange indeed. I didn't know what to say to her. We had both presumed to know the other. We sat in a kind of sacred space, silent and venerated. "What about your daughter?" I asked curiously. She had made no further mention of her.

"Her name is Lise."

"Where is Lise, Marta?"

"I don't know what happened to her," she said. She seemed surprised by the question, truly uncertain, and then her skin turned frightfully pale. "It was cold, very cold," she went on. "Lise never liked the cold. She fared poorly in winter. She needed to be near the fire. I put a chair there for her. Yes, there was a good fire in the stove. It would burn all night. She never liked the cold. But she was too close to the stove. I told her so with her hair just brushed and long. I had only left her for a minute ..." She stopped and began to rock, her head shaking slowly from side to side, and a Danish prayer, I surmised, fell from her lips like tears.

The other passengers turned and stared at her as if some madness had broken out in their midst. Then they talked among themselves and the steward watched from the aisle. I put up my hand to reassure him and he turned away.

I never knew that life was so full of tragedy and sorrow. I suppose it was simply my naïveté that had restricted calamity and misfortune to Edinburgh, to my humble world. But my journey had taught me one thing, over and over. Despair was everywhere, as if woven into the fabric of humanity, from the trenches of France to the cold of Canadian winters. And I wondered, as Marta rocked through the day, how she could continue. Her whole family gone, vanished from the Earth. What was it that made her go on when all was misery?

As we continued west, I sometimes felt Marta's pain, and the pain of the others. It seemed that everyone had suffered at one time in their lives. It had a way of eliciting certain feelings in me. It made me feel a little more connected than I gave our circumstance credit for. We were not strangers at all. We may have been estranged from our countries of origin, but we all shared the quickening of our lives as our destinations grew near. The fear, the anticipation, and always the uncertainty. Now and then Marta would rest her thin hand on my arm. I allowed it, of course, but I wondered at such times what memory visited her, unannounced and irreconcilable. I wasn't expecting to grow fond of her. When we went to the dining car for our meals, or to our berths for the evening, she would gently place her hand around my arm, perhaps the way a mother takes her daughter's arm. I felt her affection and it pleased me. It seemed to fill a vacancy in me — a gaping hole, really. Before bed she brushed my hair, and then I returned the kindness. It mellowed her moods and mine. She seemed to bless me with a mother's unfulfilled love.

We had entered the shadows of the mountains, deep in the serpentine valleys, and down, down for a day and a night until the sun shone brightly the whole day through and the train left the banks of a wide muddy river, past many houses on hillsides, past burning piles of brush — a common theme of Canadian cities, it seemed. We moved steadily toward the ocean. Vancouver was near and the eagerness on the coach was palpable, save for Marta, who took on a spell of nerves, anxious and silent, a sudden undoing of her disposition that had been calm and endearing. But now I noticed her hand always on my arm, her cheek leaning on my shoulder. Something troubled her, and I could only guess as she held onto me tighter and tighter. She stared out the window, her hand in her mouth like a child when the ocean harbour came into view.

"Marta, what is it?" I asked. "We have arrived in Vancouver at last."

"I haven't been truthful, I'm afraid, Mary. There is no one here for me." And then she covered her mouth with her hand. The fright burned in her eyes.

"I don't understand. Your sister is waiting to take you to Washington, your *beyond*. I heard you clearly, Marta. Surely she will be at the station."

Marta removed a letter from her pocket. She passed it to me. "It's all here."

I removed the letter from the envelope. A language I didn't understand. "I can't read this, Marta. You must read it." She took the letter and stared at the words, her fingers running over the letters. Then she began to read it in English.

Dear Marta,

They are all leaving. One thousand people are leaving Cape Scott. By the time you receive this letter it will be abandoned. The colony has not survived. We all had such great hopes for it. The road the government had promised never materialized. And the winter storms and incessant wind have nearly killed us all. It is no place for the civilized. I leave with both relief and regret. I hope you receive this note before you leave the farm. I cannot wait for you, Marta. I fear that you will come all this way only to find a ruined ideal. We will go to Washington State. Please remain in Swift Current until I can send for you. I am sorry for your losses, the boys and Aksel, and cherished Lise so long ago now. It is more than a mother should have to endure. Keep well, sister.

Your loving Emma
Cape Scott, British Columbia

"Why didn't you tell me, Marta?" I asked, astounded at this sudden revelation.

"You see, I had no choice. I had to leave. I didn't know what I was going to do. I had no plan for myself. How the world is changing so quickly. It makes my head spin. You were a stranger, Mary. I could say anything to you. I would never see you again. What did it matter? Perhaps I thought there would be something in Vancouver. But now that I'm here, there is such fear in me. I have no place to go."

"Perhaps the Salvation Army will help you," I said, trying to be optimistic with such a miserable state of affairs. "I'm sure of it. I will make some inquiries. Yes, that's what we can do."

"I'm so afraid, Mary. Take me with you. You can see how we get along. You can feel it. Tell me that you do."

Marta had both her hands on my arm now, her fingernails digging, clutching. It seemed she would never let go. There was something broken in her that at times remained latent and appeased, but then would appear unexpectedly like a rash on her pale skin, like a nightmare in her dreams, a nightmare that could be roused in a moment's reflection.

PART TWO

HIDDEN WATER

CHAPTER
FOURTEEN

I LOOKED UP BRIEFLY TO THE BLUE-GREEN MOUNTAINS, twin peaks still with snow as we hurried along the harbour dock with crowds of people. Marta held on to me as always, but more so now, like a child fearing separation from her mother. I carried my suitcase toward the Canadian Pacific Steamship landing and felt panicked because I didn't know what to do with her. She was clearly unwell, stricken with so many unthinkable deaths. She had no paid passage, no destination but her sad appeal to me. And her trunk was sitting on the train terminal platform, unclaimed. I had my ticket for the *Princess May*, a steamship that would take me to Anyox. They were expecting me. I felt a new urgency. I thought of breaking free of her. Surely, she would understand. She had to be on her own now. I couldn't care for her.

I held her arms and looked into her trusting blue eyes. "Marta, I have to go on my own. We must part ways now. I have work to do in a new city. I'll find you a policeman to help you. Do you understand what I'm saying?"

"No, Mary, you must take me. Don't you see? We must hurry now."

Something passed in front of her eyes just then, a shadow, perhaps, but the clouds had gathered against the mountains and the sun was absent in the harbour. Her insistence alarmed me. I was truly lost, unable to reassure her. "I'm sorry, Marta, I can't help you."

"Don't you know who I am?"

"Yes, of course I know who you are."

"Then take me with you, Mary." she pleaded. "We must go now. We must hurry."

"You are not making sense, Marta. You confuse me, you surely do, and I am unable to sort it all out for you. You were a wonderful companion on the coach. I do care about you, but now ..."

I felt her give way slightly, as if her legs had weakened, but then strangely I heard her name called out from some distance behind us. It wasn't a common name. Then it came again, but closer, a woman's voice. I turned and could see a woman hurrying through the crowd, her hand raised, calling out rather frantically. There was nothing to do but wait for her. I thought perhaps the woman would continue on past us. But I had a feeling she wouldn't as I saw something in Marta's face, recognition of the voice and of the woman who stopped breathless before us.

"Where do you think you are taking my sister?" she said, scalding me with her anger.

"I'm not taking your sister anywhere, madam," I answered, trying to remain calm and loosening Marta's grip on my arm.

"I will call the police. Kidnapping is an offence that will see you in prison. Let her go!"

"Marta insisted on coming with me, but I do not wish to oblige her as I am expected in another city. There is no reason to be angry, madam. I have done nothing untoward. Your sister needs to be truthful. Then perhaps you will withdraw your caution."

"Marta?"

"I changed my mind," Marta said. "That is true. This lovely girl is the same age as ..."

"No, Marta. You must come with me. I explained it all in the letter."

"Marta read me the letter," I said.

"This is no longer your business," the woman said bluntly.

"Hear me out, madam. The letter said that you were leaving Cape Scott for Washington. You told her not to come. You said that you would send for her."

"Marta, what have you done? I told you to come here. I would meet you at the Vancouver Terminal and take you to Washington. Why did you lie to this woman?"

"I had a change of mind, that is all. A mother and daughter, Emma. You can see for yourself."

"No, sweet sister, your Lise is dead. We must leave this woman now. Come along, Marta. I have it all arranged. They are waiting for you."

"Who is waiting for me, Em? Who?"

I stood slackly as Marta's sister pulled her away. She said nothing further to me. It was abrupt and unsettling, to say the least. And Marta turned back to me, a hand reaching and her mouth open in what seemed a dying prayer. A certain dread seemed to envelop her, that veil I had seen before. Who was waiting for her? Then the crowd swallowed them whole. There was no further sign of them. I walked away and continued toward the steamship dock, but the destroyed look of Marta would not leave me so easily. I stopped and looked back several times; there was nothing but the echo of her name.

At the steamship landing I boarded the *Princess May*, one funnel and half the length and beam of the *SS Missanabie*. I stood on the deck after I had settled into my berth, which was happily above the waterline. I will pray for you, Marta, I said silently to myself. It had been an awful wrenching-apart. I looked to Vancouver as the steamer pulled away from Coal Harbour. I had paid little attention to the city. There was no introduction. There was only the realization that I had come a long way and the water churning oily-green below me was the Pacific Ocean. But I had an impression of what surrounded me, a heaviness that I felt under a steel-grey sky. It was the mountains and the forests, their rising from the sea that was dark and unknowable. The smell of wood smoke and the sting of salted air, an unfamiliar blend. Ships and tugboats signalling their existence, and all about the harbour the shrill of ubiquitous gulls. I couldn't stay on the deck another minute as the mood of the city made me homesick for Edinburgh, for the purple-misted heath of the highlands and Arthur's Seat, for Lizzy and "The Fish Gutter's Song."

Haud the fishie by the gills,
Rug the knife along its belly ...

But before I turned away I removed my handkerchief from my coat pocket. I had tears of sorrow, and such loneliness. But something fell out of my pocket. It was a folded note, hardly noticeable. I picked it up before it blew away into the harbour. A difficult scrawl.

The good businessman told me after a good coaxing
where you're off to. He'll recover soon enough. I'm not
evil like you think. I'll be satisfied with your change of
heart.

Quinn

Quinn. I hadn't been willing to say his name aloud or even in my thoughts. And yet there it was. What did the businessman tell him, the poor fellow? Perhaps he put him off to another port, another city, or he was bound for the mines of America as Isla had said. But it was Quinn who surely pushed me to the ground in Saint John to slip the note into my coat pocket. I hadn't wanted to remember his name, but now it filled my head with its torments. I let the note fall from my hand and a breeze tossed it out into the water, where it was lost in the wake of the ship. I was exhausted and had to return to my berth. It seemed that I would need to sleep away the rest of my life to forget him. I had lost track of how many days I'd been away, but it felt like a year had gone by and still there seemed no end to troubles.

I stared up into the ceiling. The hum of the engines like a mariner's lullaby. The scale of Canada was most difficult to comprehend. I had travelled the breadth of it, but in the narrow confines of a railway. It could not accommodate anything beyond its limitations. There was so much more, and at times I forgot why I was there at all, what purpose was served by such an arduous journey. A moment of kindness to Gulliver? And the suffering Marta a perplexing affinity. Perhaps she appeared to remind me of the frailty of life, though I was certain I knew that fact well enough. And as thoughts came and went like coaches on a passing train, it was clear that I could not reconcile the horrid Quinn, or the world, and finally, like charity, fell fast asleep.

We steamed up the coast for two days. I kept to myself and was indifferent to the passengers, aloof you might say. I regarded them with a certain scrutiny. Most were well dressed, or modestly dressed. There were no rough men on that ship that I could see. There was a certain purpose in my demeanour, a throttling back of my vexations. I didn't need or require others' attention. I would agree with Uncle Calvin, for the time being, to censure myself. And so I watched the narrow passages of Queen Charlotte Strait from the deck and from the dining salon, the steep rising mountains and the endless coastline with its flood of mist and low-slung clouds that obliterated the peaks of the mountains. The sun would break through now and then, but rarely it seemed, and all the world was transformed. Colour seemed to burst from the gloom, brilliant and gilded gold, and the ocean emerald and not so black, not so terrifying. But sadly the sun wouldn't last for long. And how the captain of the steamer found his way between the rocks and tides and the countless islands was a mystery, and then a narrow inlet that seemed to go on and on, but a town at the end of it, Ocean Falls with its wood mills spouting smoke and steam.

There were many ports of call along the coast. Goods and mail were delivered and passengers disembarked, embarked, and we would be off again. It seemed that it would take forever to reach Anyox. And then the next morning as I sat in the dining salon enjoying a rare breakfast of eggs and sausages, I overheard two middle-aged gentlemen at a table next to me speak of it, Anyox, the mysterious, the unreachable. They seemed to be businessmen. At least they had that certain look of affluence.

"Excuse me, gentlemen," I said. They both turned to me and seemed to be in good temper. "I did not intend to listen to your conversation, but I did overhear you refer to the city of Anyox."

"The city of Anyox, you say?" one said rather curiously.

"Yes, I would like to know how far until we reach that city."

"You call it a city, Miss?" the other said. They both seemed surprised by my query.

"Yes, I understand that Anyox has all the modern amenities of a grand city. I've been travelling for weeks and I am anxious to arrive at my destination. Surely you know of it."

Oddly, they both laughed. I didn't understand. "Did I say something amusing, gentlemen?" I could feel the unloosening of my tongue, but as providence would have it, they each turned to the other and seemed to decide that they would assist me.

"Prince Rupert is our destination, Miss," one said, "and it happens to be the next port of call for this good ship. We are in the cannery business. Salmon, Miss, the likes you've never seen. But we know Anyox. Don't we, George?"

"You will be there in five hours," George said. "And yes, it's a grand city. I would say one of the most beautiful cities in the world with its forested mountains and snow-capped peaks, and above it all, the splendid blue sky. It is set in a magnificent harbour. There are wooded islands scattered all about the channel. A pristine paradise. You will want for nothing in Anyox. I know there are many who live like kings. The smelter has made many a rich man. Copper is a softer gold. Isn't that so, Gordon?"

"The ships are taking people there all the time just to see its beauty. The finished copper slabs ablaze in the sun awaiting shipment. Now that's a sight. You'll see for yourself. Whatever you've heard, it'll be that and then some."

I watched their faces. Stone sober. "Well, I thank you very much, gentlemen," I said. "I'm sure it will be just as you say."

When the *Princess May* began to pull away from Prince Rupert, I felt much better. I had a sense of relief that my journey would soon be over, that my new life was just over the horizon. I felt invigorated. I looked back at that coastal town, like so many with its docks and ships and upland houses hewn out of the forests. Wood smoke from chimneys plumed like thin cotton. And the fishing fleet was tied fast to the canneries where the two gentlemen waved their hats madly and seemed to cheer for no reason at all.

It wasn't long before we entered Portland Inlet, an arm of ocean, a firth penetrating the mountains as far as I could see. The afternoon was overcast with high clouds, but warm. I joined passengers on the deck as there were killer whales about, black and white, swift, magnificent creatures with their tall black fins that drew gasps from the onlookers. It was thrilling indeed, and then they were gone. But still so much to see. There were constant gulls abreast the ship, never gaining and never falling behind, and great birds lifting from their forest perches with their white noble crowns like aristocrats, surely eagles of that wild colony. I wondered if I could come to like the British Columbia coast with its immeasurable bays and arms, and massive forested upheavals, all unending, incomprehensible. It truly seemed that Portland Inlet would never end, never cease to be. Somewhere a city. Then the inlet gave way at last, but to yet another sea, Observatory Inlet.

The ship plodded on into the late afternoon. Then the air began to cool. I snugged my tartan shawl under my chin. The gulls disappeared. I felt a drop of rain on my cheek, and then several on my fingers that held fast to the railing. A sharp gust of wind and the sky darkened. The sea churned and the green-black crowns of waves collapsed and foamed. The other passengers returned to the sanctuary of the ship as a black cloud settled low over the inlet and it began to rain in earnest. I stayed a minute longer. I didn't know why I hesitated, but I thought I saw something. I looked off to the port side of the ship, a vague impression, a break in the landscape, a smudge of smoke, perhaps Anyox at last.

It was all so vague. As we got nearer, the amorphous haze began to reveal its secrets, dark brooding buildings of all sizes but without form or definition. It seemed a muddy conglomeration in the rain. I tried to find the city in such obscurity, the city I had travelled so far to see. The ship signalled as we approached a sheltered harbour, and then the pull and shudder of its engines. I could see other ships tied against a wide sweeping wharf. And then there it was, against the rising grey mountains, what had to be the machinery of production, the copper works, the smelter itself, an enormous warehouse-like structure with a towering chimney spewing great clouds that drifted up and over what was surely a town, and not a city at all. It appeared funereal and black under a low ceiling of gauzy clouds, and the air so fouled with the smell of sulphur, of rotten eggs. It seemed a colourless wasteland of stumps and industry, and squat houses row on row like inky toadstools. My legs duly sagged beneath me — the cannery men be damned. The storm was upon us now. I felt a sudden disenchantment, and such discouragement and distress that I thought I would become physically ill. And then as I stood slackly and soaked to my skin, I spoke aloud, but the words shattered in my mouth like glass.

"Oh, where is my forbearance and willingness now, good uncle?"

CHAPTER

FIFTEEN

I WILL ADMIT THAT I DID NOT WISH TO DISEMBARK FROM that ship into the driving rain. I would not have been a fool to have left with the tide, but reluctant or not, I stepped onto the greasy wharf with my suitcase and pride. I suppose the lifted chin kept me from bawling, gave me a certain confidence, if not haughtiness. The girl with the umbrella, my welcome party as it turned out, knew very well what had come over me. It seemed that shock of arrival at that black harbour was not mine alone. She rushed up to me and offered me shelter from the rain.

"Miss Stewart," she said excitedly, nearly shouting. "Happy Dominion Day!"

"Thank you, I suppose."

"I knew it had to be you. I had no doubt as I am a good judge of people. I had you for the nursing type. My name is Violet Daly. I am a nurse at the hospital and will help you get settled. You will get used to it. They all do. It's not so welcoming in the rain, but welcome to Anyox anyway."

"The smell," I said. It was all I could think of saying. It seemed important not to vomit on her. It would have been a shame. She was a pretty girl with a shock of red hair and petite upturned nose. And a soft British accent.

"The sulphur," she said. "It's not so bad in the rain." She picked up my suitcase and started up the wharf. We joined other new arrivals who hurried off to their destinations. It was all a bit of a mad dash to get out of the squall and gloom.

"And will I get used to that?" I wanted to know.

"It's the price you pay," she said. "You will live in a fine apartment, Miss Stewart. Think of that. All the amenities. Everything a girl needs."

"Please, call me Mary. You make me feel rather doddering. Likely we're the same age."

"All right, Mary. It's always best to be a bit formal at the beginning of a friendship, at least until you know what kind of girl you're dealing with."

"And you know that already?"

"Oh, you're funny, Mary. We're going to get along grand."

I felt sorry for her. She may have had me for the nursing type, whatever that was, but certainly she couldn't have possibly detected my more irreverent traits. I felt a shift inside me. I had survived the long journey intact. There would be the return to my old self, but still I would have to be measured, prudent, and accommodating, for a while at least. I felt the tension of bottling up every little thing. I wanted to shout, but it was certain that there would be many tears before then.

We started up a grade, a wooden sidewalk along a wooden road. How strange, I thought. And then I turned to look back at the bustle of the wharf, the scattering of people in the rain. I wanted to get a sense of place, where I had landed for future reference. There was all manner of buildings built along the docks, freight sheds and floats, a general store, and derricks and cranes. A crew carried supplies from the steamship and loaded a tiny locomotive. And the roar of the smelter's breath beyond, the changeless and requisite backdrop to it all.

As we continued on with the wind tugging at the umbrella and the rain slapping the back of our legs, I wondered what Violet Daly possessed to have greeted me with such felicity. I did appreciate it, not quite forgetting the gruff reception I had received from the thick-bodied Nurse Hare at Edinburgh Royal Infirmary. Well, she was fat. I could say that now. Heft seemed to give a woman a measure of power, perhaps licence to intimidate. Well, Violet was slim and couldn't terrorize a mouse, I was sure. Then she pointed to an apartment higher up on the hill.

"There it is," she said. Even that drew a smile.

The apartment was two storeys and all around it stumps from the fallen forest. We marched up the slick wooden road, past small houses, each similar in design and colour, russet-brown with white trim, neat among the remnants of the forest. There were no motor cars, not a horse and carriage, and not a tram that I could see. It seemed to be a pedestrian town, and yes, it was a town. It had not been my invention that Anyox be a city. I could thank my overzealous uncle for that; nevertheless, my imagination was duly crushed. And then we reached the apartment and Violet led me up a flight of stairs to the second floor and then along the balcony. She stopped at room twenty-two and shook the rain from her umbrella.

"Are you excited?" she asked me.

It seemed an optimistic question. I was exhausted, wet, and dirty. Excitement was not part of my vocabulary just then, but I smiled. Violet deserved that. She went in and I followed behind her. She put my suitcase down and then turned on the light switch. The dark room brightened. It was a fully furnished flat. How lovely, I thought. I dripped onto the floor and shivered and watched her. She went to the windows and opened the curtains, but there was only a grey light beyond the window glass.

"There is your bedroom," she said opening a door. "All to yourself. And a bathroom with a bathtub. Hot and cold running water, and a kitchen with stove and icebox. Coal for the heater for those chilly nights. Everything a girl needs." Her outstretched hand like a parody.

Violet was a rather whimsical girl and gave quite the sales pitch, but rather unnecessarily. She hadn't known the tenements of Edinburgh, the stacked and rancid poverty that had been my home. But I did have a concern, something she didn't mention. "So, Violet, how is all this to be paid for? I haven't yet earned a shilling."

"A shilling, a penny, it doesn't matter. The Company pays for it all. There will be some minimal rent, but don't you worry, Mary, the Company owns everything in Anyox. In fact, it *is* Anyox. Now, you're likely tired from your journey. I will leave you as I must return to duty. Help yourself to the kitchen. Perhaps make some tea. Tomorrow, the hospital."

"You have been a most gracious host. It seems you have gone out of your way to make me feel welcome. That is not so common."

"That's very kind of you, Mary," Violet said, "but I believe that one should extend every courtesy to a new roommate."

"Oh, roommate," I said, feeling all at once foolish that I hadn't understood the arrangement. But she hadn't said a thing about it.

"I may not have mentioned it. Silly me. But I wanted to make sure."

"In case you discovered I was a murderer?"

"Something like that."

"Likely you wouldn't know, would you?" I laughed not because it was absurdly funny, but out of nervousness. My own private irony.

"See, Mary, I was right about you. I have a feeling we're to be fast friends."

I was rather relieved when Violet left me alone. It seemed to me that the girl could be exhausting. Now there was only one thing I wanted to do. I went to the bathroom and began to fill the tub. I felt unclean — unswept and begrimed, as it were. And I was certainly trail-weary. I couldn't think about where I was now, what it took to get to that remote wilderness. There would be time for that, time to reflect and get acquainted with Anyox. And soon the tub was filled and it steamed and I removed my shabby clothes and settled down into the soothing water. At once I noticed my flimsy, bone-thin legs, my emaciated thighs as white as porcelain. I had lost weight. I had no strength in my limbs. It seemed that

I had aged. Perhaps that was what Violet had seen, an older girl in my body.

And I sank low into the tub and for the first time in a long while the strain in my body, the taut and rigid sinew and muscle, began to loosen. I felt sleepy. My mind drifted. I followed the memories of my journey, of people I hardly knew, orphans and salvationists, a businessman and a madwoman who was not mad at all. They seemed to me like characters in a play: my play. And Violet was a funny duck, to be sure.

Sleep came like a kindness after my bath. There were linens in a closet and I had hastily made my bed and climbed in. I slept deeply, so deeply that it took the tugging on my shoulder to rouse me in the morning. Who was that red-haired girl who shrieked into my face like a banshee, a nightmare loosed in my room, wailing warnings of impending death?

"Mary, Mary, come on now," she implored robustly, "up you get. The Matron Nurse is waiting. You can't keep her waiting. It's not the way to begin. No, not at all. Mary, get up or I'll be in for it!"

It took a moment to comprehend that I was no longer dreaming, that I had awoken in Anyox and that girl was Violet Daly, my flatmate. "Violet, I hear you. I'm awake. I must have overslept. You can cease with your convulsions."

"That's fine for you to say, Mary. The Matron Nurse will need to see your schooling credentials. Everyone calls her Nurse Stricker. Get dressed. There's no uniform for you. You will see her first. She doesn't like to be kept waiting. Up you go."

I climbed out of bed. "Why are you so agitated, Violet?"

"Because I was given the responsibility to get you, and to get you to the hospital at nine o'clock sharp."

"And if I'm late, what, you'll be shot at noon?"

"Oh, Mary, not now. Hurry!"

I managed to get dressed in a rumpled, mothballed outfit. A faded blue, but it had to suffice. I wasn't worried about the off smell as the sulphur seemed to me far more repelling. And I didn't have time for a bite to eat with Violet's dire consequences of tardiness, only to retrieve my letter of introduction. She pulled my arm as we followed the wooden road once again toward the base of a hill above the harbour. Townsfolk were leaving their selfsame houses for work and business, all at once as if answering to the gods of time. The thump of footfall on wood, and carpenters at work on more rows of company houses, sawing boards and pounding nails like a thousand discordant drums no Highlander would tolerate. The day was different: urgent yes, but the sun was shining. I had doubts that it ever shone in Anyox. And there it was coming over the mountains like good news. But Violet did not cease with her encouragement of promptness and found it necessary to caution me for one of my most endearing affections.

"Now, you are a funny girl, Mary," she said, "and you make me laugh. You have a way about you. I don't know what it is, but you can't let it loose with the matron. She will not be amused. Not for a minute."

"Violet, I must point out that I did not just fall out of a tree. I know when to be serious, professional, and accommodating. No need to worry. I won't blame you much."

"I may die on this day," she lamented.

"Then, Violet, be thankful we're going to the hospital."

She was beyond appeasing. I suppose it was my own nerves that prompted my teasing. It seemed to offer a measure of relief, the more benign usage of satire, at least. And as we neared the hospital I just had to look over my shoulder now and then to understand Anyox. It was strange, a town hacked out of the British Columbia wilderness. And I began to notice that the few trees that remained were grey in appearance. There was no greenery, which was a clue that they were not alive. The whole hillside above the hospital seemed to be dying or dead. The dead trees that had been cut down littered the hill. And the hill grew into a mountain. The whole town, it seemed to me, was suffering the same fate. There were no gardens, no flowers, and not a bird about. And I spun around, walking backwards, and the smelter plume drifted over the town, clung to the mountain slopes and seemed to fuse with the snowy peaks.

"If you survive the matron, Mary," Violet said, "you'll get used to it."

"Get used to what?"

"The way the smelter works. Today the wind is blowing the plume away. You can put your clothes out on the line. Now come on."

It looked like a house to me, stairs and a veranda, and not a hospital at all. I followed Violet up the steep staircase and inside. All was very clean, at least, whitewashed and bright. A nurse turned as we marched down a hallway toward an office. She stopped what she was doing as if my arrival were something notable. Violet stopped outside the door.

"Go, in," she said.

"Thank you, Violet," a voice said, which I took to be *the matron*.

I walked in. She was standing, silver haired and unsmiling. Why do women of authority address the underlings with a dreadful lifted chin? It was her intention, I suppose, to remind me of my place before I could utter a single word. I found it absurd and unpleasant to look up her nose.

"Have a seat," she said. I sat as she continued, but she remained standing. "I am the matron of the hospital. I have several responsibilities, nursing being one of them. The nurses here call me Nurse Stricker. I hope you had a pleasant voyage. Miss Stewart, isn't it?"

"Mary Stewart, madam. And yes, the voyage was long but tolerable. And were you not expecting me?"

"I was expecting a nurse. Now, if you could be so kind and show me your nursing credentials."

"Credentials?"

"You had your training from the Edinburgh Royal Infirmary, did you not?"

"I had my training," I said ambiguously. I started to worry. I handed her the letter from Nurse Monck. She sat down at her desk and regarded it carefully. She had a cup of tea and her hand reached for it without looking. She took a thoughtful sip — the smell of lavender. I watched her eyes consider the words, her eyebrows reacting, twitching skeptically.

"The Edinburgh Royal Infirmary," she said, "most prestigious." A quick smile before she read on. She seemed pleased, and I was most relieved. Then a man in a white smock poked his head into the office and interrupted her. The doctor, no doubt.

"Oh, Dr. Trig," she said. "This young lady is a candidate for one of our nursing positions."

"Well, good luck to you," he said.

"Good luck?" Something was truly amiss.

"I'm sure you have nothing to worry about."

"Thank you," I said politely. That smile on his face seemed to be for me as he hadn't a question for Nurse Stricker, or anything else to say. He stood there rather foolishly, a bit too long, it would seem, judging by the subtle rolling of the matron's eyes. He must have noticed and abruptly left.

I felt slightly uncomfortable by that odd interaction with the doctor. I seemed to lose my concentration. He was quite young for a doctor, perhaps thirty-five years old, and tall and handsome, I will admit. And I noticed Nurse Stricker watching me, perhaps taking note of my reaction.

"Dr. Trig is a good doctor," she said. "Some think he's too young, but he was instrumental in acquiring the X-ray equipment and making this hospital a modern, fully functioning eighteen-bed hospital. And he's married and has a young child. Can I read this now?"

That was rather strange, I thought, his manner, and her reaction like a forewarning. "Yes, please continue," I said. She read it aloud.

Anyox Hospital
British Columbia, Canada

Dear Hospital Matron,

It is my pleasure to introduce you to Nurse Mary Stewart.
She was under my charge during her stay at the infirmary.
I found her keen in mind and exemplary in her work. She
exercised sound judgement and care at all times, and of
course, with the required nursing acumen. She possesses a
rare empathy needed in this profession, and perhaps has a
gift in that regard. Mary has all the qualities necessary for a
long nursing career. I am most certain that you will concur
with my observations. I highly recommend her for service in
your city.

Sincerely,
Fiona Monck
Senior Nurse
Edinburgh Royal Infirmary

She put the letter down on her desk. "This is the *Granby*
Hospital in Anyox," she corrected.
"Yes, Nurse Stricker."
"And these are your nursing credentials?"
"I suppose they are."
"Suppose?"
"Yes."
"You did not complete your nurse's training?"
"No, I suppose I didn't."
"Well then, do you *suppose* you could tell me how long you did
train at the Royal Infirmary?"
"It wasn't long."

"Young lady, you cannot tell me how long you worked under Nurse Monck? You suppose nothing." The tone of her voice climbed the stairs of irritation.

I looked down at my fingers, laced nicely on my lap. How could it be that I travelled so far only to be questioned in such a way? It had all been arranged by Uncle Calvin. I couldn't answer her. I couldn't look up at her puckered mouth that doubted me. And she wasn't fat, only a tight, narrow face. No heft at all.

"Speak up," she said.

I couldn't. I was feeling quite anxious now. My clever mouth abandoned me.

"Speak up!"

She hurt my ears that time. I didn't know why, but I thought of my mother just then. *Speak up, Mary.* There was a time when I couldn't speak up, when the words lodged in my throat, as hard as stones. Like a spell, I couldn't find the will to free them. What was I to say to this woman now, who, it seemed, held my future in her hands? I felt the inadequacies of my offering, my proposition unconvincing and inconsequential. *Speak up, Mary.*

CHAPTER

SIXTEEN

WE HAD ONCE LIVED NEAR THE BEACH ON HIGH STREET IN Portobello, a place for tourists and city folk to sink their alabaster feet into the golden sands. Perhaps make daring dashes into the frigid waters of the Firth of Forth. There were donkey rides for tourists, and the Portobello pier for long strolls. My mother was home from the fishery at the end of summer. It was a sunny day with a good heat in the afternoon. I went with Paul and Robbie. They were supposed to look after me, a bothersome responsibility for older brothers, but I was sufficiently independent at nine years old to let them off the hook to chase a loose pair of donkeys down the beach. Great fun for spirited boys. A thousand people faced the water, gaining their nerve or simply enjoying the day. I was on my own, lost in the sunbathing congregation. Now, that wasn't so unusual. I was an inquisitive girl and could entertain myself well enough.

But I withdrew from the crowd, moving away to explore the things brought in by tides and storms. And when I heard a man call from a tent, I was curious because I had seen two puppies outside the flap of that very tent earlier on. I worked my way toward the tent. There was a little opening in the flap. I stood before it and could hear the puppies' tiny voices like mewling kittens.

"Come in, come in," a kind voice said. It was the man once again. He must have seen me from the opening.

I hesitated. I knew that I shouldn't, but the little beggars could see my shadow against the canvass wall of the tent and began to squeal excitedly. I poked my head in.

"Don't be afraid," the man said.

I went all the way in. The puppies were very cute, adorable in their black and white fluff. Border collies. I knew the breed well enough. I knelt down to pet them.

"Would you like one?" the man asked.

I hadn't been interested in him, only the puppies, and didn't notice much about him other than his voice, but as I turned to his question, he was standing completely naked. An awful sight for a girl. A hairy bulging man, pink as a baby with his little thing in his hand. I backed up to the door. I wanted to scream for my brothers, but I couldn't find my voice. And then the man stepped toward me, seeing my fright. He quickly covered himself with a towel.

"I'll give you one if you don't say a word," he said. "It'll be yours. A puppy all to yourself. It's a secret, that's all it is."

There was something about the offer that made sense to me. I could say nothing, and certainly no one would listen to a girl, and take one of them home. Perhaps it was only a mistake. I wanted the one with the white patch over his eye. I would train him well. He would sit and roll over and fetch a ball for me. He would run through the tall grass under the Salisbury Crags. I would call him and he would come.

I took the puppy home, but I should have known that our flat had no place for a herding dog. I hadn't thought it through, of course. I suppose I didn't much care. I only wanted a puppy to love, and for it to love me.

My mother stood over me with her folded arms as I held the puppy. She wasn't happy at all.

"Do your brothers know about this, Mary?"

"No, they don't," I said. "They're chasing donkeys down the beach. I suppose they are still."

"So, this is all your scheming?"

"I suppose it is."

Then she knelt down to me. She often did that with us children when there were important matters to discuss. Her broad face was mostly without displeasure or ire. But she had a way. "Now, how did you come to have a puppy, Mary?" she said reasonably.

"He was just there." My unreasonable answer.

"And where was that?"

"At the beach."

"Don't you think, Mary, that someone, perhaps a tourist, has lost their little dog?"

"No, that's not how it was."

"Then how was it?"

"I cannot say."

"You cannot say?"

"No, Mother, I cannot."

"There's something you're not telling me, Mary. A mother knows when her child holds back the truth. And I suggest you come out with it."

I stood holding the little dog. It licked my face affectionately, wiggled in my arms. I wanted him so much. So I said nothing.

"Speak up, Mary."

I shook my head, immovable.

"Speak up, Mary," she said, a change in her tone now. "It's a thing you will face all of your life. The truth will not harm you, though there may be sanctuary in keeping your mouth shut. It might serve a purpose if some greater good will come of it. You need to face what you've done. Now speak up!"

My face was burning with worry now. The little dog wasn't mine at all. "A man in a tent," I said with a burst. "He said I could have it."

"A man in a tent with a puppy?"

"At the beach."

"And what else?"

"He wasn't wearing a stitch of clothes. A hairy man. He said I could have a puppy if I didn't say a word." I was crying now, inconsolable, and then my mother's fingers wiped the tears from my cheeks and she pulled my anguished little face against her shoulder.

So it was that I told the truth. I spoke up. And then my father came home from the docks, but not for long before he went back out the door. I could hear his feet drumming down the stairs. I watched him from the window, how he hurried down the narrow street, long urgent strides. He had arrived at the beach just in time to see the Edinburgh police taking the man away. It turned out that he had begun the day with six puppies in his tent.

Nurse Stricker was far more patient than I had given her credit for. She didn't dismiss me outright during my deliberation. She must have thought my answer worth waiting for. I drew a deep breath, preparing myself for the worst.

"I did train all of one day at the Edinburgh Royal Infirmary," I said. "Now, I will admit that Nurse Monck was most generous with her words. And I will further admit my embarrassment, Nurse Stricker, for I truly believed all was in order. My uncle made the necessary arrangements." How desperate he was to be rid of me. What other deceit had he hidden? I would write to Lizzy at once, no matter the outcome of that day.

"This is most unusual, Miss Stewart. I do have your uncle's letter. He assured the Granby Hospital that you had all the required nursing skills. Yes, he convinced our doctors, impressed them, I would say. And the Company has provided you with accommodation at my request, but I cannot see how you can be of service to Anyox with such limited experience. Nurse Daly, whom you have met, has completed her two-year training at the Vancouver City Hospital. What am I to do with you? How could you have possibly attained the knowledge to become a nurse in one day? I find the very presumption to be outrageous, to be quite frank. And why would Nurse Monck refer to you as Nurse Stewart? It is highly unusual, if not troubling."

I had to be quick, and careful now. "It was a day of intense instruction, Nurse Stricker," I began. "There was a man at the end of his life. His name was Mr. Graham and he had a long life. But at the end he was sick and he vomited and made a mess of himself.

Sadly, he soon passed away. I took the gentleman into a quiet room and cleaned him up the best I could. I made him proper for the morgue. You see, I spoke to him, told him that everything was all right, that he was safe in the hands of God. But it was only a body, you see. His spirit was about, and that was what I spoke to.

"Many soldiers were coming into the infirmary with dreadful wounds. There were dressings to be changed, stumps and holes, and broken boys to comfort. And one, not a soldier, but a local lad. He had a wound in his belly, a belly black and distended. He was bleeding inside. It was a knife wound and it fouled and he died. There were a hundred beds or so, all manner of disease and afflictions. I was duly run off my feet to keep up, to offer assistance to the nurses, to Nurse Monck who saw that I was of use, some value to the ward. She said I had a quality of caring that couldn't be taught. A compliment, I dearly hoped. She called me Nurse Stewart after that, perhaps to inspire me, and she surely did. And at the end of that day she saw how I admired a photograph of Dr. Elsie Inglis on a wall. I learned that Dr. Inglis was a compassionate woman, headstrong, and a campaigner in the Scottish suffragette movement. Now she leads her medical teams in France. I am by no means comparing myself to her, but a nurse, you see, tends to the sick, injured, or aged and assists the surgeon in his work."

She just looked at me, her mouth opened slightly, disbelieving, it seemed. Quite a day at the infirmary. "Well, something to consider, Miss Stewart," she said, composed now. "I was trained in London under Dr. Inglis, who as I recall was not pleased with the care of female patients and returned to Edinburgh to establish a maternity hospital for the poor. And here at the Granby Hospital, servicemen who left for the war a year ago are returning home now, many without parts of themselves. There's a young man with a hole in his back that won't heal properly. It's a foul wound. He needs special care. Is that something you could tolerate?"

"If he can tolerate a hole in his back, then surely I can tolerate tending him."

She made a noise through her nose. "You make a compelling argument," she said, "but I do not know why I listen to it. Now, before I make my final decision," she said, "I want to warn you."

"Yes, Nurse Stricker."

"There has been great debate over a women's right to vote in British Columbia. There was a referendum on the matter last September. And women were granted the right to vote in April of this year. Although I can sympathize with women, I must insist that you refrain from overstating the matter in the presence of the doctors on the ward. Do you understand?"

"I want to understand."

"Miss Stewart," she said leaning forward for great emphasis, "you have found yourself in a company town. It is solely the enterprise of men. It is a town built by men, for men, and with a lot of capital. Six hundred men at work mining the copper. The company provides our lodging, our medical expenses, and our food. We are in the employ of the Granby Consolidated Mining, Smelting and Power Company. Nothing in Anyox exists without men. It is the domain of men. The men provide for their families. Yes, women and children. There can be no disruption to the smelter. It is the world you have arrived in. Now, do you understand?"

"I think so, Nurse Stricker."

"You're not so sure."

"I'm not sure of many things, truth be told, but a true understanding of anything requires a certain curiosity. Scottish Enlightenment."

She stared at me now. I spoke plain as I felt she had made up her mind in my favour. But perhaps the *Enlightenment* reference was a bit too cheeky. I wanted to take it back.

"You will not be filling Nurse Daly's head with your opinions. She is young, impressionable. Do you hear me?"

"I form my opinions from my own *impressions*, Nurse Stricker. I am certain Violet is no different."

More nasal mulling. It must have helped her think. "I will take a chance on you," she said, perhaps intrigued more than impressed. "I will expect you tomorrow. I will place you on probation. All you need to do is prove your worth."

"With God's help."

"You seem to be a reverent girl," she said with a thin smile. "There are several churches in Anyox: Presbyterian, Anglican, and Catholic. I am sure one of them will suit your needs. I am pleased to know that you are a godly young woman. The town needs more devout ladies."

"And what of the ungodly women?"

"You may see them soon enough. They come from the shanties beyond the slagheap. But don't concern yourself with those lot. You will have all you can manage keeping the *good* citizens of Anyox in good health."

Shanties beyond the slagheap? That certainly didn't sound encouraging. But, of course, I was a *curious* girl, although I never had ambitions to be a nurse — or a prostitute, for that matter. I didn't recall wanting to be anything living in Dumbiedykes. I suppose I wanted out, wanted food on the table, wanted things for my father and Lizzy. But now I was certain that I would learn all I could about the *ungodly* women of Anyox. I felt the tug of injustice, of course.

"Nurse Stricker," I said, "a nurse, after all, is duty bound to nourish and foster good health and to care for the sick. But who in Anyox declares one a good citizen, or heaven forbid, ungodly?"

"Never you mind, Miss Stewart," she said curtly. "Don't you make me regret this!"

"No need for concern, Nurse Stricker. I will not leave anything undone. I can assure you."

As I got up to leave, Nurse Stricker sat staring into space, a knitted frown of consternation. I wondered what she was regretting. And as I got to the door she seemed to have gathered herself.

"I must admit that I find you rather brash," she said. She reared her head back in an incredulous way.

"And that may be considered a brash statement as well, Nurse Stricker. We all can be brash. It is not my intention. I wanted only to provide you with the evidence of my competence. That is not brash. I advocate for myself. If you consider that a virtue, then we shall get along just fine."

"Some would call such veracity arrogance."

"I have been bullied in my life, Nurse Stricker, by those who wished to control me, who wanted me to be what *they* wanted me to be. I won't be bullied."

"I'm tiring now," she said. "Go to the library. Study the reference material. The hospital keeps several manuals and texts." She held her hand up like one who wishes to volunteer, or perhaps surrender.

"Yes, Nurse Stricker."

As I made my way out, down the hall, I looked into the rooms, to the patients in their beds, the white-washed interiors — an unexpected orderliness. And then out the window to the hill behind the hospital, its shattered trees and stumps. A primitive upheaval. The contrast was implausible.

CHAPTER
SEVENTEEN

I HAD THE AFTERNOON TO WRITE TO LIZZY, BUT YET AGAIN, I had the same unsettling thought. What would I say to her? Oh, Anyox was not the *Eden* of Uncle's imagination, or contrivance, for that matter. I could tell her that it was breathtaking — as long as you didn't breathe. I could write of the verdant forests — as long as I didn't tell her that it was meant in the past tense and that the return of birds had been permanently delayed. I could have mentioned that the gloom on dull, sunless days was only temporary due to the latitude of being that far north. The sun was duly extinguished. Of course, I wouldn't tell her that Anyox is located at fifty-five degrees latitude, one degree less than Edinburgh, and that the light remained in the wooden streets of Anyox far into the evening. Possibly, I could tell her that the Anyox hospital where I was now employed, though I would skip the part about my probation, was referred to as the Granby Hospital, as the town is all things *Granby*, as it turned out. Granby was *the Company*, owners of Anyox, of course, and then there was Granby Bay, the newly built Granby Hotel, Granby Bay School, and the Granby General Store. I suppose the owners wanted to leave little doubt who to thank.

I may have seemed ungrateful if I had written what I felt, what I really saw, what the business of mining was all about. And part of me didn't want her to come, didn't want to see the look on her face when she stepped off the steamship in the cold and miserable rain. I wouldn't do a thing to break Lizzy's heart. So I would be the illusionist once again, painting a tolerable portrait of a town, not a city, something for her to imagine in her darkest hours. I knew there would be many. If it was a cruel trick that I played, it was only because I couldn't leave her in Dumbiedykes to wither away. And I knew what a shock it was for me; therefore, I would sprinkle my narrative with bits of truth, insights, things I knew she could manage.

July 2nd, 1917

Dearest Lizzy,

You will be pleased to know that I have arrived in Anyox at last after a long journey across Canada. To say that my new country is immense would be an understatement. Nevertheless, I am here and in good health, apart from some of my weight which I lost along the way. Don't dismay, it will surely return. There is a general store with ample food and supplies. There is such wilderness here, Lizzy, such astonishing sights on the steamship as we travelled up Observatory Inlet. Killer whales and eagles and trees of unimaginable proportions. The Pacific Ocean here is deep and as green as the forest and seems to be the predominant colour of the west coast of British Columbia.

Well, back to Anyox. It is a town of wooden roads. You can hear the footfall of the men as they hurry off to work in the mine or the smelter. It is truly a mining town. I won't try to fool you, Lizzy. The smelter stacks smoke all day and night, like giant chimneys. It's a copper-mining town. And they say everyone earns good wages and benefits from a good standard of living. No poverty here. You must practise your writing and your sums for you will soon be here with me. There'll be school for you here, so keep up your schooling if you can. I know it'll be hard to find the time. But I hope things are easier for you and Da now that Uncle Calvin is providing assistance. You will tell me if things are contrary,

Lizzy. Write to me as soon as you receive this letter. Tell me about Edinburgh. Spare no details. I want to hear it all.

There is something that happens to one's feelings about a place once we leave it. You remember the loveliness, and not so much what you could no longer live with. It's a melancholy dilemma, homesick for the familiar, but not for the insufferable conditions of Old Town. You long for the country, the romantic notion of our history, our society of lands and battles, and pride and honour, of course. I suppose those are the things that remain in the hearts of Scots who left. It follows them around the world. There's no going back. There seems to be limitless opportunity here, Lizzy. The scale of Canada would suggest that. But at times I miss Scotland dearly. So tell me about your days. I will look forward to your letter with anticipation and excitement.

Your loving and devoted sister,
Mary
Anyox, British Columbia

I tramped down the hill to the harbour, down the wooden road and down the wooden sidewalk, past men in white sweaters playing a game of tennis on a wooden tennis court. One couldn't casually amble down rough-hewed planks. And it seemed that I would never touch the ground again, as if it were forbidden, or perhaps something lurked there under the wood like trolls. The wharf and harbour were the centre of commerce and where the Granby administration kept their offices. I had taken notice as Violet led me up through the rain. And now there were times in the sunshine when the world felt quite normal, when the wind kindly pushed the smell and plume away, when townsfolk carried out their business and ships arrived and departed with great fanfare. I quickly learned that the steamships were the link with the outside world, and there always seemed to be a gathering waiting for arrivals — or waiting to depart. I smiled at every passerby and paused to watch young boys with their fishing poles sitting on the edge of the wharf. I suppose it was the hill that blocked the smelter from my view that lifted my mood, a hill with several large homes among the remnants of the forest. There was definitely a raw feel to the town, something built in haste, but still it seemed to contain all the amenities one would need. That part, at least, Uncle Calvin had right.

And beyond the boys, I noticed a strange figure in a long boat. He was just sitting there watching, it seemed, not doing anything really. He was dark skinned like the young boys I had seen on the prairies. I didn't know what to think. As children in Scotland, we were taught about life in Canada and the people who lived there before colonization. They called them savages. I turned away finally, unable to account for his presence in Granby Bay, in Anyox.

I went into the post office and removed the envelope from my handbag. There was a gentleman behind a wicket, a balding little man in a waistcoat. He looked up as I approached him. He noticed the envelope in my hand.

"You'll need a post office box, Miss," he said, "if you wish a reply."

"Yes, and I suppose you know every number for every household and business by heart." I surprised myself with the speculative nature of my comment, but I suppose I wanted to get a sense of things, the town, how it operated. And perhaps the *shanties*.

"I surely do." He removed a blank card from a stack and pushed it to me. "Kindly fill in your information."

There was pen and ink for my convenience and I made the appropriate notations and pushed it back to him. He gave it a quick inspection.

"Very well, Miss Stewart," he said. He entered my post office box number on the card, then copied it all into a ledger, all very formal. He handed me the card. "Keep this in a safe place."

"Yes, of course."

"I was expecting you," he went on. "Violet Daly tells me that you will be working at the hospital."

"That's right," I said. He seemed quite affable. "And what is your name, sir?" I thought that I should get acquainted with Anyox in a more personal way.

"Postmaster Curly," he said.

"Well, Mr. Curly," I said, taking the envelope and adding my new address to it, "can you tell me where I can find the Anyox Library? I would like to review some reference material. Medical journals and such."

"Yes, up the boardwalk. Not far, past the provincial police office. That will be one cent for the war tax postage and two cents regular postage. Three pennies."

I removed several coins from my handbag and placed them before him. He took three large one-cent pieces.

"So, Mr. Curly, if a friend or relative arrived in town, how would they get in touch with me?"

"Certainly, I could confirm your residency in Anyox, but your dwelling information is with Granby. Their offices are just up the way as well. They are the owners, Miss Stewart, landlords, if you will."

"All dwellings, Mr. Curly?"

"Why, yes."

"And the dwellings beyond the slagheap?" I laughed pretentiously.

He stared at me as if I had just committed the most awful sin. "They don't exist," he said bluntly.

"Indeed, Mr. Curly," I said with a scandalous flare. "Now, you have been very helpful. Thank you."

"Good day, Miss Stewart."

There was little doubt regarding the infamy of the shanties. And as I walked up the slight grade toward the library I turned and tried to look beyond the hill, but the smelter was obscured still, no matter how hard I tried to peer through the few lifeless trees. There was only the drifting plume of the stacks. I wanted a good look at it all, the very reason for the town's existence. It wasn't a regular town with its collection of industry and businesses of the marketplace. No streets jammed with motor cars and trams. No train stations like Waverly or Lime Street. It seemed rather medieval, even feudal. Lord Granby. There had to be one person who could explain it all.

I went into the Anyox Library as a mother and two children left with an armful of books. They appeared happy, content with their selections. I smiled, of course. All seemed so carefree, conventional. The library was tiny by comparison to Edinburgh with its library halls and stone sculpting, elaborate wooden veneers and polished chairs where humped-back intellectuals scoured the texts under green-shaded lamps for no other reason than to resolve an argument or test their declining memories. But I did see a table and a lamp before a wall marked *Anyox Hospital — Reference*. No Granby. Perhaps they were at odds.

There was one other person in the library, which was a one-room affair. A woman, the librarian, I assumed, was sitting at a desk and raised her head now and then and peered over her eyeglasses. She wore a blue–grey suit, a kind of furry suede. She never addressed me or smiled, just a look of distrust. I soon felt rather unsettled. I considered asking her what ailed her, but I thought better of it.

"Excuse me, madam, but I am looking for medical texts, anatomy, diseases, and the like."

"Are you with the hospital?" she asked.

"Yes. My name is Mary Stewart, and I have been hired as a nurse and have been asked by Nurse Stricker to study all that I can. I am a bit behind the other nurses. But I wish to catch up on my studies."

"You're the new one. I thought so. Very well. They're right in front of you. Reference books mustn't leave the library."

"Do I need a library card for the other books?"

"I've made up a card for you, Miss Stewart. Sooner or later the new ones come in and wish to take out a book. Especially in the winter. It tends to be extra long in Anyox."

I noticed a name plate on her desk — *Mrs. Moffatt.* "Well, Mrs. Moffatt, I should begin my studies." But there was one more thing. "Mrs. Moffatt, do you keep a town census?"

"Yes, we do, but it is not for public viewing," she said brusquely. I noticed that she twitched, perhaps a tic. Still, she seemed as nervous as an extricated mole.

"I see. Well, thank you."

I removed several books from the shelf. *The Practical Medicine Series, Textbook of Pathology for Students, The Clinical Anatomy of the Human Body, Contagions and Blood Diseases,* and *Women's Guide to Health.* How did that one make it into the library? I wondered. I would start with anatomy. I was beginning to feel excited. It was rather fun, as if I were playing a game of make-believe. But it was real enough, and there would be a soldier that I needed to attend to the following day, a hole in his back that wouldn't close. There would be nothing make-believe about that. Nevertheless, I couldn't help but feel a sense of accomplishment now that I had arrived in Anyox. I would have shouted out my praises if I hadn't thought Mrs. Moffatt would have fainted.

But the last book I removed from the shelf stopped me cold. *Venereal Diseases: A Manual for Students and Practitioners.* I opened it randomly to a rather graphic illustration. I quickly closed it. It was then when I realized something wanted me to remember, an association, a sisterhood. But I rejected the notion outright. I didn't believe that the *ungodly women* were my kindred spirts, that I owed them something. On the contrary, I felt a wave of paranoia that they would *know* me somehow, that my truth would come out and my new-found career would be in ruins. But how absurd.

I looked up self-consciously, and Mrs. Moffatt quickly closed a drawer in her desk. It thumped. She just sat watching me. It startled me, as if she had read my mind. She had that strange look on her face, a bit crumpled, as if she was about to break out in tears. It seemed she wanted to tell me something. She sipped from a teacup, her eyes nearly boiling over.

"Is there something on your mind, Mrs. Moffatt?" I asked. I all but dreaded her response.

"I'll be gone sometime in the coming autumn," she said tearfully. She got up from her desk and moved closer to me.

"And why is that?"

"They're replacing me with ..." she said but couldn't continue. I felt quite bad for her. And then her stalled speech, like a soap bubble, suddenly burst. "The Company. Yes, it's true. They're replacing me with a niece of someone, a shareholder, no doubt. An American girl from the East Coast. She'll be here in the autumn. Can you imagine that? This was my job. I had come all the way from Victoria to take this position. Left a good life with my sister. But I have to go back. She has children now. There's no room for me. A terrible thing to do. I don't mean to carry on, but you seem like a good person. I just had to get it out. Most ladies are well connected with the Company. I dare not confide in anyone. But you're new. It's not fair. It's just not."

"It doesn't seem right at all. Is there anything you can do?" Luckily for me she wasn't a mind reader, only a disgruntled employee.

"What can I do, Miss Stewart? They've made up their minds."

"I do believe in fairness in business and to be fair in one's dealings with people. But there is one thing you can do. *Forgive your enemy but remember the bastard's name.* A Scottish proverb."

"That's quite amusing." She laughed tentatively.

"Keep it in your pocket. You'll never know when you may need to pull it out and put it to good use."

"You seem to be a clever girl. You'll do well here, if you keep your counsel. Don't be overly curious, Miss Stewart. There are things to hide in Anyox, and they don't want to be found." She turned guardedly to the door, the perfume of alcohol faint on her lingering breath.

"There are a few things I'm curious about, Mrs. Moffatt. The lay of the land being one. There must be an official who acts in the capacity of a mayor or reeve in Anyox, who does not belong to the Company in some capacity. Someone to show me what is what."

"One of the churches, perhaps. I won't assume your particular denomination, Miss Stewart, but the Anglican church has someone who may be able to assist you. Pastor Burke is a knowledgeable and caring man, though I cannot bring myself to divulge my dilemma to him. It may be *his* niece for all I know. You can follow the road down the hill. You will see it just before the smelter comes into view."

"Are you feeling better, Mrs. Moffatt?"

"I am, actually. I don't know why. Perhaps what I needed was a sympathetic ear. I have spells of nerves when I meet someone new. I'm afraid to say the wrong thing to the wrong person."

"It is my understanding, even after my short time here, that Anyox is a man's town."

"Stifle, that's what they do. And if you're braver than most and march into the Granby offices with a grievance, they will gladly give you a one-way steamship ticket for your trouble."

"A wee fiefdom, wouldn't you say?"

Although the day was long, I had accomplished a great deal, to my mind at least. The visit to the Anglican church would have to wait. I returned to my flat. Violet was still at the hospital. I wasn't sure when her shift would end, but it was near dark when I heard voices on the wooden street below the apartment. I looked out the window. It was Violet standing under the streetlight. A man was with her but remained in the shadow. I couldn't tell who it was, and of course, why would I, having just arrived in Anyox? Violet hadn't said anything about a boyfriend, or any male acquaintance, for that matter. But the tall figure leaned toward her all at once and kissed her cheek. I saw him as he came into the light, the profile, the boyish shape of his head. It was Dr. Trig.

CHAPTER

EIGHTEEN

I WAS GIVEN A UNIFORM TO WEAR, A NURSE'S STARCHED frock and bib, as white as the snowy ridges. Of course, the mountain tops could be seen only when the plume from the smelter was pushed up Hidden Creek by a stiff sea breeze, and there it smothered the trees in sulphur gases. And as I was led down the hallway by Nurse Stricker, I found it rather remarkable in an unremarkable way that out every window in the hospital the plume was the first thing to be seen. The coughing stack and the solemn grey of the smelter. It was an anchor, a reminder why we were there at all. I found it distracting at first, as if something were about to happen, that the plume would cease and a fresh new world would be revealed. But it was a town without an unfading history, without generations of building and rebuilding, without functional self-sufficiency, and perhaps a vision for its future.

I quickly realized that I had to abandon my opinions, some at least, as suggested plainly by the matron. There was a certain acceptance that one had to adopt — gratitude to the smelter god. I found myself in the wilds of a new country. It was vastly raw and isolated, but it was surely a better life than the one I had left behind, was it not? And I was sure, too, that the young soldier lying before me with the weeping bandage cared less about the spoiled vistas than a chance to be well again. He was in a room with four other beds, some with drawn-curtained partitions.

"See for yourself," Nurse Stricker said, holding a clipboard as if I was going to be marked. "You may remove the bandage." There was a trolley with medical supplies at the ready.

The soldier was facing away from us as if he had been arranged for my viewing. He was staring at the wall. I didn't regard the bandage or its placement on his back in any detail straight away. "I would like to see him first," I said.

"Nurse Stewart," she said in a tone to inform me of my error, and then with noticeable pauses and emphasis, "please listen. You must place your attention on the patient's wound. You must familiarize yourself sufficiently in order to administer proper care."

"Yes, Nurse Stricker," I said. "I certainly concur. However, if I am to familiarize myself with the patient's injury, shouldn't the first order of business be with him, the person with the injury?"

She turned to me with such alertness, a sudden squint about her as if she hadn't heard me correctly. Then her hard face softened. "Very well," she said. There was a certain ambiguity in her manner as she gently took hold of the patient's shoulder and rolled him so that I could see him.

He was frightened, eyes looking aslant, uncertain. "What is your name, soldier?" I asked. He was young like most of them, his black hair swept to one side, though a few strands hung down over an eye.

"Tom Haney," he said. He lifted his eyes to me.

"Do you have family in Anyox, Tom?"

"No, they're all back east. The Company said they'd have a job for me when I returned. I'm hoping to get back to the smelter. I just want to be useful, Nurse."

"Yes, well, it's our job to make sure of that."

"Do you have a name?" he asked me.

"Mary," I said, "but Nurse Stewart if you're in need of me." As I looked down at him, I noticed how gaunt his cheeks were, his thinness of limb. His eyes stared out from their dark wells, and behind them, I was sure, terrible things that I would never know. And then I felt a jab to my arm. Nurse Stricker motioned me outside the room. I smiled at Tom and then followed behind her.

He had a name now, and a face. And it seemed to me that Tom Haney had a lot more to say.

Out in the hallway I knew that I was going to get a lecture. It wasn't just her free hand resting on her hip. And she wasn't a tall woman, but still it seemed that she looked down at me. Perhaps it was only her position that I felt, pushing me downward.

"Nurse Stewart," she said, "this is not the Royal Infirmary, and I do not care that Nurse Monck thinks it a gift you have. You cannot have too much of *you* in your dealings with a patient. Emotional attachment will sully your chances of a career. You simply must distance yourself from the patient — *Tom*, as you so casually called him — if you are to provide him with the best of care. His injury is not resolving and he is wasting away. And I warned you about expressing your opinions."

"I don't believe I gave an opinion, Nurse Stricker. I had it in my mind that it was good nursing practice." I suppose I was hopeless with my opinions, but my mother once said to settle an argument, *It's not an opinion if it's true.* I tended to believe such self-evident axioms, perhaps to my detriment.

"Can you be taught? I'm beginning to wonder."

"Yes, of course, Nurse Stricker." She had a way that gnawed at my sensibilities. She made me feel rather incompetent. Perhaps that is what she intended, as if it were a lesson, something to learn. I decided not to believe her. I would believe Nurse Monck instead.

"I'm going to bring Nurse Daly into the room. You can watch her. I want you to get a proper start in our hospital. Empty your head of every idea, every notion, that you have brought with you. You will be taught or you will be finished. Now, do you understand?"

There the green flare of her eyes. I could see that she would have been an attractive young woman, and perhaps her mind not so made up about things, the way the world should be, not so absolute. But now she didn't seem to allow for change, and yet she *allowed* me to stay after that first interview. Perhaps, and I hoped, she saw something in me that spoke to some latent truth in her, a truth now obscured by responsibility and protocol. I felt a strong motivation at such times, a desire to express myself in all my *brash* glory, to touch that place inside her. We are all in this together, I would say, women laying down the stones of a new road one by one.

I had the answer to her question burning my lips. My spit could have lit a fire. But contrary to her opinion about me, I was no fool. "I understand completely, Nurse Stricker."

I waited for Violet and was sure that things would get easier. But her affable exuberance didn't arrive with her. She seemed to have left it at the front door. She was all business with her instructions, her gestures, a tone reserved for an underling, a neophyte, someone she had never met. Her manner was certainly detached, as if she spoke to me from behind a wall. And I watched Tom Haney, the profile of his face as Violet went through the procedures, the when and how of applying a dressing. He was on his side and seemed to be listening to every word. His eyes tried to follow her, and now and then I would catch him trying to look up at me. I always smiled. He needed more than a doctor or a nurse to patch the black cave of his wound.

"Nurse Stewart," Violet said, oddly formal, "do you see how the flesh comes away with the dried fluids? The dressing requires frequent changing. And the pillow placed just so to keep his weight away from his injury."

All at once a memory like a horrible revelation. It wasn't Tom Haney that made me remember just then. It was the foul smell of the wound and the red–brown stain of the bandage. It was the white sterility of the sheets that tried in vain to conceal coming death. And I felt him like a rush of wind. How he had followed me across the sea, never leaving me even as I had forgotten him? He had been as close as a breath as the train clacked through the barren immensity of Canada, and up the brooding shadowlands of forest and harbours to Anyox, to the end of the world. And I gasped silently to myself as I saw in a flash, an instant, Jimmy with his retribution fire-red in his dead eyes.

"Mary?"

I was jolted back, but momentarily confused. I waited for the memory to fade, waited for my reasoning to reassert itself. "I see, Violet," I said drawing a deep breath, "but I'm wondering how well Mr. Haney takes his food? I would like to ask him, if that is all right, Tom."

"I don't know what you're getting at, Mary," she said leaning to speak into my ear. She seemed a bit worried, but back in my corner, it seemed. "The matron made it very clear to me. You must listen. Please, just do what I say."

"I don't mean to frustrate you, Violet. I am here to learn. I thought it was a reasonable question."

"I don't feel like eating," Tom said all at once.

Violet seemed rather surprised that he spoke up. But why wouldn't he, as he was lying right there, in full view, in earshot? It seemed we were discussing a wound as if it existed on its own. I couldn't understand why we were ignoring the person.

"And why is that, Mr. Haney?" Violet asked.

"Don't know. I just don't."

Then at the door, some muttering, another doctor. He was much older than Dr. Trig, with white hair and a pink complexion, a heavily built man. Grandfatherly. I was aghast that he had been listening. What rule had I broken now?

"How is Mr. Haney doing today, Nurse Daly?" he asked.

"He seems to be the same, Dr. Madden. No change."

"I see," he said. Then he turned to me, appraising me, it seemed, perhaps wondering what had landed in his hospital. "See me in my office," he said.

Violet waited for the doctor to leave. "You wouldn't listen, Mary," she said to me. "I told you so. Now you're in for it. Dr.

Madden is the boss. I'll finish here. You best not keep him waiting. And watch that mouth of yours!"

I walked down the hallway decidedly doomed. And Violet's vacillation, now her shocking censure like a well-placed knife. What I had offered seemed so mild, if not benign. I wasn't trying to be anything but a good nurse. And the sign on his door was intimidating. *Medical Health Officer.* It seemed I couldn't last longer than a day as a nurse. I only hoped that whatever came out of my mouth was at least civilized.

"Have a seat," he said, leaning back in his chair and lacing his fingers across his broad chest. He regarded me rather severely.

I sat straight-backed, hands folded, a slight lifting of my chin, but not too high, just right. I was looking for noble, perhaps dignified. My mind raced, kept pace with my heart. I waited for him to speak.

"They come back with awful wounds," he said, "missing an arm and a leg, burns, disfigurement. Many end up in the cemetery here in Anyox. They're damaged in mind, too. I overheard what you said. Nurse Stricker warned me about you, that you were different, had your own ideas, and perhaps not suited to this hospital's mandate. Now the war has brought many new treatments, due to the nature of injury from heavy artillery, long-range cannons, and machine guns. The wounded would lie in the trenches and then the rapid necrosis sets in. The usual antiseptics like bichloride, carbolic, and iodine were not at all helpful. So now we use sodium hypochlorite for the wounds and nitrous oxide to put a patient to sleep during treatment. We needed to change. Now, Mr. Haney may be the next casualty. We may have received him too late. But I am willing to allow you to see to his personal care while you are on duty. It does not pose a risk. See to his bandage and see to his food intake, and if you can, see to his well-being. It doesn't sit well with me that these Anyox boys survive the horrors of the war only to die in my hospital."

"Yes, sir. I understand clearly what you mean. I have the same feeling about it."

"Very good, Nurse Stewart, I will speak to the matron. And further to that, I want you to attend the next safety meeting of Granby and their employee representatives. The Granby Safety Committee reconvenes in September. They meet once a month. They want a nurse to attend. I can't afford one of our experienced nurses. So, you will go, make notes, and return with any questions or requests that come out of the meeting. I don't expect you to be able to answer health concerns at this time. Is that something you can manage?"

"Do I need to know how a smelter operates, sir?"

"I see no need for it. You will be a presence, Miss Stewart. Leave the workings of the smelter to the men."

I would like to remind you, sir, that women have the right to vote in British Columbia now and they are as competent as men will ever be. "Yes, sir," I said with civility, and good fortune. I silently thanked my mother for her discerning qualities that magically appeared just then.

When I returned to the ward to look in on Tom Haney, Violet was waiting. She looked like her old self with a curious smirk that suggested she was pleased to see me. But I was no dafty girl. She was, in fact, happy that I was reprimanded, scolded, upbraided, put in my place.

"Oh, Violet," I said quietly, and wonderfully sarcastic, "I'm so glad to see that your good nature has returned. I was a little concerned at your manner early on. You know, you were a little terse with me with your instructions, and perhaps a wee bit condescending. But I take no offence, I want you to know."

"Well, the matron said you had trouble listening, Mary. I only wanted to help you."

"Oh, that was it?"

"Yes, of course."

"Well, it hardly matters now, I suppose."

"Why is that?"

"It seems that Dr. Madden quite approves of my unorthodox style of nursing, particularly with Tom Haney. Tom is not well, of course. He wishes me to see to Mr. Haney's well-being. Can you believe it, Violet? The Medical Health Officer himself."

Violet just stared at me, as if I were an anomaly before her sense of the world. And I wondered if she thought me a murderer *now*. I could be mean, cleverly wicked when the need arose. I had my instructions from Dr. Madden, after all.

The day wore on and I fed Tom Haney some broth from a spoon. I spoke about the bright sunny day, the favourable breeze coming in from Granby Bay. And when I asked him what he wanted, he said so clearly and effortlessly that he wanted to go to the shanties. I didn't know what to say him, so I said nothing at all. I was there to listen. I knew the others in the room were listening as well, and so I asked each one of them in turn what they needed. Most of them wanted a cigarette. One man was old, used up and oddly cheerful. Another worked in the smelter and was suffering from dizzy spells. He faded in and out of sleep. One other had died earlier in the day, and perhaps that is what he had wanted. But it was Tom's answer that stayed with me, circled my head like the plume, clung to my hair, fastened to my history.

And as I removed dirty linens from the bed of the one who had passed, I glanced casually out the window. I could see the veranda. Violet was smoking a cigarette, taking a break, I surmised. Then Dr. Trig came up the stairs. She had her back to him. He did not turn to Violet to say hello or to acknowledge her in any way. He simply and so subtly moved his hand toward her, a thinly disguised gesture, and ran his index finger up her bare arm.

CHAPTER

NINETEEN

WELL, IT WAS THE COLD SHOULDER FOR MORE THAN A WEEK. As it turned out I had committed another abominable sin. It seems that Violet was overlooked for the safety committee appointment. The glares and upturned noses from Violet and the matron, but still I did my work, tended to the ward of men, fed Tom Haney with a spoon, listened, and at times joked with them all. Some levity to comfort them. And it seemed to me that Isla's grasp of my character was proving out. The salvationist had told me quite confidently in the dark cellar of the *SS Missanabie* that I would be despised or admired in my life. And which one did I favour? The answer was not so simple or clear, not so crystalline in my mind. How could I prefer one thing over the other? I suppose I could be accommodating every moment of the day, aim to please every soul I met. But surely I wouldn't be admired for it, and perhaps even despised. *I wish to be as God made me,* as Emily Brontë once said, though my relationship with God was dubious at best. I suppose it was as simple as that. Only a fool would argue otherwise.

It rained on my first day off, and I was out in it with Violet's umbrella, hurrying to the Anglican church. It was early morning and the pastor wasn't expecting me. The rain rolled in from the sea in a succession of waterlogged sheets, relentless and silver-flung, a summer deluge the like I had never seen before. It bounced on the wooden roads, leapt a foot in the air, and underneath ran in torrents down the hill, uncontained in the treeless neighbourhoods. There was thunder in the black clouds above my ducking head, and raindrops splattering around my feet like driven nails into the slick wood. It was dark enough for the streetlights to remain lit.

One could not possibly get lost in Anyox on the wooden paths. I passed the Granby Hotel to a bend in the road and continued on, and another bend, and down an incline to where the church sat at the edge of a ruined civilization, and beyond, the shadowed underworld of the smelter. That's what it looked like to me with its foundries and mills and industrial ambitions opaque in the eerie murkiness of weather, all contained in a floodplain of meandering creeks all but razed. Still I wanted a better look. I had been appointed to the Granby Safety Committee, after all.

I might have missed it under the shroud of the umbrella, but the church's steeply pitched roof set it apart from the larger residences and their dreary redundancy. And the gothic stained-glass windows made it seem more church-like as I got a better look at it, though the colour was a sadly muted white on that gloomy day. I had a longing for colour in that colourless world. I went up to the large double doors and gave a good rap with the fat of my fist. It wasn't long before the pastor opened the door. He looked at me rather surprised, a drowned rat before him, and then let me in. I shook the rain from the umbrella and left it at the door.

"Welcome to the remote and the wet, Miss Stewart," the pastor said. "The rain is letting up, thankfully. You are the new nurse at the hospital."

"Yes, that I am, Pastor. News travels fast."

"It surely does. How can I help you?"

"Well, Pastor Burke," I said, "would you mind if we had a word?"

"Not at all. We can sit in the reception. I have made a pot of tea. I will get another cup."

"Thank you, that would be very nice indeed." He seemed rather happy to have a visitor.

I followed him down the aisle, past the pews, and looked up at the stained glass, brighter now with the Virgin Mary holding the baby Jesus, all magically aglow. Though it couldn't be compared to the churches of Edinburgh with its divine and sanctified history, a scale to fit the supernatural glory of the ages, I was moved by the glass and its presence so far away. The reception was behind the altar. There were two chairs at a table, and on the table a teapot and a cup and saucer. He held out his hand for me to sit. He left and quickly returned with another cup and saucer. I had a good look at him in his robes. A slightly greying man with soft pouches under his eyes like blue thumbprints. I wondered if he was having trouble with sleep.

We sat in that awkward interlude where talk awaits the ritual of tea and civility. I became aware of my personal tendencies sitting with him and thought that perhaps I should be at my best behaviour. I needed someone in Anyox who was on my side, who wouldn't be so quick to judge me. And I respected the church, although I had no history of church-going. I was hardly devout. Scandalous, I was sure. But there I was, starting anew.

"So, Miss Stewart, are you in need of some counsel?" he asked. He poured the tea with his unused hands.

"That is not quite correct, Pastor," I pointed out. "Since I am new to Anyox, there are certain things that I don't understand."

"Are you having a personal crisis, Miss Stewart, perhaps at the hospital?"

"Not a personal crisis in the way you would understand it, but one of place and relevance."

"That sounds rather ambiguous, if you don't mind me saying."

"Not at all. I confuse myself at times. I wonder where I am. You see, I have arrived in a wilderness, in a strange town that I had thought would be a city, but it is clearly not. I suppose what I would like to know is how all the parts of Anyox operate and relate to the others. It would be very helpful."

"I am curious to know why you came to my church."

"I suppose I believe you to be neutral. In your dealings with the people of your congregation, I mean."

"You trust the church."

"I would like to, Pastor Burke."

"Very well. What would you like to know?"

"You see, I have only been up on the hill above the harbour. I see the plume from the smelter. I see the dying trees. I have walked the wooden streets, but I haven't seen the smelter itself. Just now on my walk to the church, I glimpsed it, but all seemed dim and incomprehensible. This company town is a mystery to me. I would like only to solve it."

"So, you do not seek *spiritual* counsel?"

"Not at this time, Pastor," I said to appease him, "but there may be things revealed to me when that might change."

"Very well, Miss Stewart. I believe the rain has stopped. If you are brave enough to venture outside, I will you show you what is what. There is a good vantage point not too far from the church. How does that sound?"

"It would be much appreciated, Pastor."

We went out into the dripping morning after our tea. The sun brightened behind the clouds but did not make its presence known, only a teasing light. We hadn't walked far before the pastor turned and led me to the edge of the plank road where the sloping land gave way to what seemed to be a narrow valley bottom below. He stopped and motioned with his chin. "That hill is Smith Bluff. It blocks the smelter from the harbour, and I suppose hides the lay of the land. Now if we move along a little further it'll come into view."

He hadn't taken twenty steps before he stopped once again. But this time he raised his arm and swept dramatically with his hand. "There it is," he said, as if referring to the extraordinary — the Great Pyramids of Egypt, or perhaps Stonehenge of Wiltshire — but no, it was the gushing smelter itself in all its industrial eminence.

I looked and took in the breadth of the operation, the industrial complex of our age, a swath of ruined earth festooned with the ambitious zeal of men, building after building, rail lines and trestles, power poles with ribbons of electrical wires, so many things unknown.

"Down there is what is commonly known as *the flats*," the pastor said. "The yellow buildings are the bunkhouses, apartments for the single men and small families. There's a separate building for Chinese workers who tend the mess hall and clean the bunkhouses. There are blacksmith shops, foundries, a mill for making lumber, repair shops of every kind. A machine shop with tradesmen from Europe and England and Scotland, where you come from. And that long building is the powerhouse. It generates electricity from the harnessed flows from Falls Creek, and there's a coal-fired powerhouse to compensate for lower winter flows. It is something to behold what man can do, aided by God, of course, when he has his mind set on a vision. The smelter itself is the largest copper smelter in the Commonwealth. You cannot see its furnaces where they apply the great heat from coking coal to the crushed ore and extract the copper. The gases and slag are separated, leaving the copper behind. That black mass is the slagheap, the refuse of smelting."

"The gases?" I asked, allowing the slag to take its place momentarily in the back of my mind.

"The sulphur dioxide in the stacks. One hundred and fifty feet high."

"It's what's killing the trees." It was a panorama of obscurity, muddy apparitions, a veil of smouldering gauze settling over the man-made, tongues of woolly clouds fastened to the grey stick forests. The smell of it, nearly normal, but still a sting deep in the nose.

"Yes, I'm afraid so. They die more and more every year. Alice Arm is seeing the sickness in the trees now. There have been fires. All citizens must remain diligent to prevent them."

"It's rather a deadly plume, Pastor."

"I can make no judgements, Miss Stewart. A town needs its divine guidance, and a church answers the call. I go where I am needed. I take in a lot of information from the congregation and by observation. I don't mean to give a sermon on the smelter. But it gives life to this town. It's the price one must pay."

And I wondered about what he said, his making no judgements, and thought about the slag and what lay beyond it. There were two bridges crossing the creeks. He hadn't mentioned them in his dissertation, and one seemed to end near the slag pile. "I understand there are ladies living across the *slagheap*," I said as if it were just another Company feature.

"Yes, they live beyond the boundary of Granby's influence."

I was so curious now but managed to supress my eagerness. "Can you tell me about them?"

"I am reluctant to discuss such a great sin in our midst, Miss Stewart. We should get back." He started to turn away, but I touched his arm, held it briefly.

"I only ask, Pastor Burke, as a nurse whose duty is to care for the people in her village. This is my village, my town, and I believe I am needed as well. Does God not wish them good health? I believe I shall visit them. I thought, perhaps, you had some vital knowledge about their circumstance that may be helpful. They are just human beings, after all, trying to get by. Don't you agree, Pastor?"

His grave eyes squeezed nearly shut with dismay as he pulled away. I had annoyed him bitterly but didn't know why. My zeal leaked through, perhaps. And I may have exaggerated my motive but thought my inquiry reasonable. I followed behind him. I was confused. "Pastor Burke," I called out to him.

He turned back to me abruptly. "I have a book for you, Miss Stewart, that I think you should read before going off in a direction that you do not fully understand. You are young and perhaps a bit too naïve for the wilderness life. You are no doubt a curious girl. It seems that you arrived at the church door with that very question."

It was no time to fight the church. I needed him to understand that *morality* was a loose term, something tossed as easily as a stone. I followed back into the church. I stood in the reception as he went to fetch the book, the *good book,* I was certain. I wouldn't discourage his aims, his calling. I would be receptive to the articles of his faith and realized it wasn't the time to offer my own version of a sermon. And besides, I was sure he knew far more about the shanties than he was willing to divulge.

"Now take this, Miss Stewart," he said, handing me a black book. "Read it at home. I have marked the passages for your perusal. I would prefer you not to open it in the church. I don't want the words to spill out into the *sacred space,* as it were. I hope you understand."

"You have me at a bit of a loss, Pastor," I said. "This is surely not a bible." The cover read *Safe Counsel.*

"Take it with you. There are things in this modern life that the church cannot articulate as well as others. I am most sure you will find the information useful. It is my hope that it will shed new light on your unaffected views."

I took the book and left the church. It was a rather successful visit, I thought. But I was a bit unsure whether Pastor Burke would prove to be an ally at the end of the day. I was pleased with myself nevertheless. I hadn't ventured into the deeper and perhaps more disagreeable aspects of my nature. He didn't provoke me in the way of some others. And if I was guilty of duplicity, then a greater cause would be worthy justification. I just didn't know what that might be.

Violet was still at work at the hospital when I returned to the apartment. I hadn't seen much of her. She worked many late nights. And she gave me a wide berth on the ward, all business when we worked together. I didn't want her to resent me. I wondered what had happened to our friendship. We lived together, after all.

I sat down on the upholstered couch and turned on the lamp beside it. It seemed to be always dark in the flat. I opened the cover of the book. An illustration of the Chicago World's Fair with *Light on Dark Corners* written above it. And then I opened the book to where the pastor had placed a cloth bookmark, gold-stitched in the shape of a cross. The title of the chapter: *Sexual Proprieties and Improprieties*. A number of passages were noted in ink. I was intrigued and read on.

10. ILLICIT PLEASURES. — The indulgence of illicit pleasures, says Dr. S. Pancoast, sooner or later is sure to entail the most loathsome diseases on their votaries. Among these diseases are Gonorrhoea, Syphilis, Spermatorrhoea (waste of semen by daily and nightly involuntary emissions). Satyriasis (a species of sexual madness, or a sexual diabolism, causing men to commit rape and other beastly acts and outrages, not only on women and children, but men and animals, as sodomy, pederasty, etc.), Nymphomania (causing women to assail every man they meet, and supplicate and excite him to gratify their lustful passions, or who resort to means of sexual pollutions, which is impossible to describe without shuddering), together with spinal diseases and many disorders of the most distressing and disgusting character, filling the bones with rottenness, and eating away the flesh by gangrenous ulcers, until the patient dies, a horrible mass of putridity and corruption.

I was out of breath. I imagined them out in the street at that very moment, like a medieval slum, men lustful and evil skulking in the shadows, dogs running wildly for the hills, and women, bare breasted and mad chasing the hapless men down the plank roadway. I continued on.

11. SENSUALITY. — Sensuality is not love, but an unbridled desire which kills the soul. Sensuality will drive away the roses in the cheeks of womanhood, undermine health, and produce a brazen countenance that can be read by all men. The harlot may commit her sins in the dark, but her

countenance reveals her character and her immorality is an open secret.

Why did I feel the narrative was directed at me, a personal affront? The last passage.

12. SEXUAL TEMPERANCE. — All excesses and absurdities of every kind should be carefully avoided. Many of the female disorders which often revenge themselves in the cessation of all sexual pleasure are largely due to the excessive practice of sexual indulgence.

I closed the book. I sat staring into space while the words buzzed around inside my skull like bees. Then I had an awful realization. Pastor Burke had no empathy for the women of the shanties, thought them sinful harlots, *filling the bones with rottenness*. And he surely didn't want me to go there.

CHAPTER

TWENTY

I WAS ON MY WAY TO THE HOSPITAL AS ASH DRIFTED DOWN from the fire in the mountains. The dead trees burned as if the life in them wasn't quite done. Grey and white filaments gathered along the railings, and the ash on the plank road drifted like confusing snow. Even after the rain the summer sun bleached the hills enough to burn. The firemen from the smelter knew what to do with their hoses and fire buckets and climbed to the perimeter of the vanishing forest and dug out firebreaks with pick and shovel. There were only a few trees near the company homes, but there were water barrels and buckets with rounded bottoms at every street corner, always at the ready as such danger seemed a companionable arrangement. The boggy ground where the ancient forests once stood would occasionally erupt into fire. I heard it called *spontaneous combustion*. Not a match was needed — only the chemistry of heat and matter. One had to be heedful in a world of all things wood. And then I noticed I wasn't alone on that plank road.

Tom Haney had a visitor at the hospital now and then. He would sit with Tom in the morning and speak in a low voice, sometimes staying well into the afternoon, and when Tom was up to it, would wheel him out onto the veranda in a wheelchair to get some fresh air, if that was possible. I was told that they had served together in France and, both suffering terrible injuries, had returned home. His name was Sandy Hall, a mild-faced young man who walked with a cane. His legs had been badly broken at the Battle of the Somme, and though he recovered, his one leg never mended properly. And now that limping profile. I knew it was Sandy and soon caught up to him.

"Good morning, Sandy," I said, coming up alongside him.

"Nurse Stewart," he said, "I would return the greeting if it was in fact a good morning."

"The leg acting up?" An Irishman a few years older than Tom, Sandy had a rather unusual manner. I thought his wry impressions quite endearing. And his profusion of red hair was like a beacon under the fleeting sunshine.

"The Company is dragging its heels, I'm afraid," he said. "I should be at work. Light work, they told me, but I haven't seen much. I want to do more for them, get back to the machine shop. Now and then I push a broom in the Granby office, in shops along the harbour. It doesn't take any talent at all. I was a fine machinist, you know. I didn't leave that in the trenches of France. But the white shirts wouldn't know anything about that, would they?"

"That's not good at all, Sandy," I said, walking slowly with him.

"I shouldn't complain. Granby gave me a room above the bank. A small room with a view over Granby Bay. I get by. And when I see Tom, I do feel grateful to be out and about, thumping along these planks. And I do believe he's getting better, his spirit anyway. It's the way you are with him, Nurse Stewart."

"Perhaps it's your visits, Sandy. You are his moral support, and he surely needs it. He is so young."

"He asks me things at times, things I can't do for him. It makes me feel low that I can't. Sometimes I wonder if he thinks he's going to die. He asks me the same thing every time I see him."

"Perhaps I can help?"

"No, it's a particular matter, to be frank. I wouldn't speak of it in front of a woman."

"I'm a nurse, Sandy. I don't believe that there's much I haven't heard or seen." Sounding like a veteran of the hallowed halls of healing.

"No, I shouldn't say."

"Very well, but if you find that you can —"

"Nurse Stewart, it doesn't matter much anymore. Tom is still in a bad way in spite of your good efforts. It is certain that he has improved, but he couldn't possibly ..."

I stopped and touched his hand. He looked at me, but only briefly. His eyes turned downward, as if to the safety of his cane. We were still a few minutes from the hospital. "Sandy, please just say it. I won't be alarmed or shocked. I promise."

"It's a thing particular to a man, Nurse Stewart. We were taught to never talk about it."

"Yes, I think I understand."

He looked up now. He waited for several men on their way to work to pass. "If I can be so bold, it seems young Tom Haney hasn't been with a woman. Please don't think ill of Tom for saying. He's afraid he'll die a virgin. There, I said the words. Now it's an awful weight on his mind. You might think it a foolish thing to dwell upon, but I can tell you that it's a common fear among the boys serving in the war. Those young men in the slaughtering grounds with gruesome deaths of their fellows all around them. Most wouldn't talk about it, but we all knew. We were of one mind. There's no soothing young men facing death who haven't done it. There's a drive in them they can't stop. It seems to consume them. Tom thinks there's nothing to live for. I sit with him, but what can I tell him?"

I had a memory of Allan Rose just then. Was he still alive? He had his own worry sitting on the bed next to me in Josie's flat. War, with its masculine predilection where men were the meat of battle, the sacrificial, reduced to the mechanized instruments of dictators and bureaucrats. Give them a hero's mission but forget that they're imperfectly human. And then bring back the damaged survivors and give them a broom. I had a soft spot for Tom, and I was duly impressed with Sandy, a loyal friend, but perhaps more than that, something deeper in them both. They had endured the unshakable experience of horror.

"Tom mentioned something similar to that, Sandy," I said as we continued on to the hospital, "but it was more of a last request. It was sad, really. He said very clearly that he wanted to visit the shanties."

"I'm not surprised, Nurse Stewart. At times he goes on about it. He's not insane. I'd take him if I could, wheel him across the footbridge. He'd die in peace."

"I've seen the footbridge," I said. "Pastor Burke showed me one day. I had asked him to show me the smelter and how it all works. It seems the shanties and the ladies who live there are a reviled part of Anyox. The pastor certainly did not hide his resentment."

"They say the pastor keeps a book of every man who crosses the bridge to the slagheap. He knows where they're going. I don't know his purpose. Perhaps he shames them into repentance. It's just what they say."

Interesting, I thought, as I helped Sandy up the stairs and into the hospital. As he shuffled along to the men's ward, I quickly realized that Nurse Stricker was waiting for me. She stood in the hallway with one hand on her hip, the other holding a cup of tea. The essence of lavender once again.

"What have you done now?" she said. She had the pursed lips of displeasure.

"Well, I am not late for my shift today, so whatever it is, it cannot be that bad."

"Dr. Madden wants to see you right away."

"Thank you, Nurse Stricker," I said. "I will go at once." The smirk on her old chin, I had seen more than once, and it was most nasty. It seemed the matron wanted me to fail, trip up, something to ensure I didn't pass my probation. How unfair that I be measured by her degrees of resentment.

I went quickly to Dr. Madden's office, peeked in. He waved me inside.

"Sit down, Nurse Stewart."

I sat in a chair opposite him. He was looking down at his desk, notes scribbled on a page. I waited patiently, thinking of the things I had said and to whom. Perhaps it was the matron, impatient to let me go.

He looked up. "I have received word," he began, "that you are going to visit *the shanties*, the brothel as it were, and that you believe that it is your responsibility as a nurse, a responsibility to the citizens of Anyox, or something similar to that affect. Can this be right, Nurse Stewart?"

I couldn't deny it outright. "And who has made such a claim, Dr. Madden, if I may ask?"

"Pastor Burke. He tells me that you made such a statement during your recent visit to his church. He was quite agitated for a clergyman. Can you explain yourself?"

I couldn't conjure up a reasonable fabrication of the truth just then, one that would baffle the good Dr. Madden. I would speak the truth, what suited me at least. I was learning that truth had certain flexibility.

"You see, sir," I said, "I have been studying the sexually transmitted diseases in the library, in the books. The hospital has a fine collection of educational medical books and periodicals. The matron, Nurse Stricker, recommended that I do so. I'm eager to learn, Dr. Madden, I really am. Now about the ladies in the shanties, well, I most certainly will visit them, sir, to see how they're getting on. I'm concerned about their health. Of course I intend to go on my own time, on my day off, sir. I thought it a prudent thing to do. It seems the town shuns them. I do believe that they shouldn't be treated as sinners or transgressors, or as evil, for that matter. They are citizens of our world, and to maintain their health would be maintaining the health of the so-called customers. There seems to be no shortage of single men in Anyox. I believe it an act of compassion, and fundamental to health care. It's not a moral question at all. I also believe that the Granby Hospital has a role to play, Dr. Madden, if you don't mind me saying. Regular visits by a nurse, I would suggest. Venereal disease is a ghastly affair, and we can help prevent it."

He held his mouth with a hand, a finger nearly touching his eyes as if astounded. It was neither good nor bad, as far as I could tell. He hadn't lost his temper. And perhaps he had no temper to lose, as all at once he became very relaxed and leaned over his desk.

"I must be candid with you, Nurse Stewart," he said. "I have had similar concerns since their arrival. One's health can't be reduced to a moral question. I wasn't quite sure how they could be approached, how the hospital best ensures the health of the ... customers. I don't believe that sticking our heads in the sand will make them go away. The provincial police have been ineffectual in that regard. Constable Cobb doesn't seem to have the time. You seem far more prepared, quite educated on the matter."

Well, I could have claimed Scottish Enlightenment once again, perhaps, but I had the appropriate response. "We go where we are needed, sir," I said, to use the decree of the pastor.

"Prostitution is certainly not new to this day and age."

"No, it is not, sir. And do you ever wonder why we put all our attention on the prostitutes and not the johns?" Oh, my, I couldn't shut my mouth in time.

His blank face. I didn't quite know when to stop, always pushing a little too far. "No," he said, "but I thank you for your suggestion. I will endeavour to have the matron arrange scheduled visits. She will undoubtedly need your input. Don't judge her harshly, Nurse Stewart. She has lost a son in the war and, sadly, her husband left her. She grieves, but you seldom see it."

"Yes, sir, and thank you. I wasn't aware of that."

"Carry on, then."

"One more thing, sir, if you don't mind."

"What is it, Nurse Stewart?"

"What will you tell Pastor Burke?"

"I attend the Presbyterian church with my wife. And I do believe, although I listen to concerns from our churches, I do not answer to them. As you seem to have chosen the Anglican faith, you will respond accordingly. The pastor may be more willing to hear from one from his own congregation, one from his own flock, if you will."

"Yes, sir," I said. It was more of a duty. I felt no communion with the Anglican church, or any church, for that matter. And I felt no rapture for having been unceremoniously ordained into the assembly of the devotional. I heard the word *prudence* quite loudly in my head. I suppose I needed to listen.

Later I was folding linens and placing them on the shelves in the supply room. The matron had been noticeable in the hallway, even as I spoke to Dr. Madden. For some time, I had the suspicion that she thought I was up to something, perhaps trying to undermine her position. When she finally stepped into the supply room, I knew by the look on her thin blanched face that Dr. Madden had spoken to her.

"Nurse Stewart," she said, "it seems that you have been a very busy girl."

She stood blocking the way out, hands on hips, elbows out in fortification. A siege, no doubt. But a strange sweet smell on her breath.

"Well, Nurse Stricker," I said, "you know what they say about idle hands." I continued stocking the shelves.

"I was referring to your temerarious mouth."

"Please speak plain, Nurse Stricker."

"This self-possessed will of yours is disruptive, if not intolerable. I am the matron of Granby Hospital, and I do *not* appreciate having to be spoken to by Dr. Madden pertaining to some scheme you have. In the future, I would appreciate it if you would come and see me before you act. Do you understand?"

How strange that Violet was suddenly standing in the doorway. Oh, their little plot. "Come in, Nurse Daly," I said.

"I have concerns myself," she said. Her flimsy reinforcement.

I could see it all just then, the little hurts, the bruises they must have felt. But I never tossed a single stone. Still, I had the good sense to weigh the circumstance, to recognize the unfolding nature of life in Anyox, the web of it all. There was nowhere to go, nowhere to run. Yes, there was the wilderness, but it was burning. And I could see, perhaps for the first time, that the lines crowding the matron's eyes were her grief.

"I thank you for being so candid with me," I said, so very pleasantly. "How is one to learn without a little criticism? I take your concerns to heart and will do my best to uphold the spirit of this hospital. The next time Dr. Madden calls me into his office, I will inform you, Nurse Stricker."

"There's no need for that," she said. She had lost some steam.

I smiled politely, and to Violet as well as Dr. Trig passed behind her with his slowed-down stride, the slightest turning of his head, then hers. It was their language, I had discovered over the past weeks, but the grieving matron was as oblivious as a stone.

CHAPTER

TWENTY-ONE

I DIDN'T CARE TO STOP AT THE CHURCH ON THE WAY PAST it, walking with my nurse's bag filled with things particular to my assignment. Nurse Stricker never uttered a word when she handed it to me, only one more chilled squint. I knew the pastor would see me, see my urgent and defiant strides. I wondered if he would suddenly burst from the double doors and chase me down, take hold of my arm and urge me not to go *where the harlots commit their sins in the dark*. I wasn't too worried about Pastor Burke, as I had Dr. Madden on my side, though I had difficulty understanding why. I sincerely didn't want him to regret it. And I was sure the pastor would be waiting for me upon my return.

As I came down the hill onto the flats, the plume from the smelter lay over the industrial lots like Edinburgh fog. It was difficult to gauge the weather when all about was the unbroken smelter clouds. It could rain, I thought, and perhaps the sun might shine. It was all confusing in the haze and gloom, the mills and foundries, but still the plank road kept going and I kept following, under the electric train trestle and power lines, and soon the first bridge over Hidden Creek. The water moved slowly under the bridge. It smelled of oil and grease, not like the organic smell of the River Forth. But on I went, feeling quite smart in my nurse's uniform, Mary Stewart on a mission. And I began to wonder what my motive was, why I felt compelled to go to the shanties. It was both fear and curiosity, I suppose. At some level it seemed I was returning to something I had left behind, perhaps out of some absurd sense of kinship that I couldn't explain.

The plank road made its way past company houses and three-storey bunkhouses. I noticed men gathering on the porches — to watch me, I surmised, a spectacle unknown to them. I heard a cheer rise up and hurried on. And then at last the footbridge over Falls Creek. I hesitated, then began to walk out over it, careful steps as the water below me roiled and foamed where pipes discharged uncertain water into the stream, a seething caldron, an insidious stew. The smelter loomed above me like a steel-clad dragon and I could hear its hot breath, the murmuring of furnaces, and the chaos of copper-making clapping like thunder. A noise of such clamour, and always the shrill of the electric train sliding over the steel rails, something that lifted the hair on my arms. The ore spilled down the embankment like rusty vomit. I felt so small, so insignificant. I was in the centre of the maelstrom, the eye of the storm where it wasn't calm at all but a riot of machinery and industry. And then all at once a wind rushed down from the nearby gorge of Falls Creek and threatened to remove my cap, and I turned to face it, holding myself together lest I be lifted from the footbridge and pitched into the foul waters.

I held onto the railings and finally I was across.

The plank road now continued, but upstream to the power-house and smelter. But that was not my destination. I looked to the water, to the bay and the slagheap that spilled from the smelter and into the sea. It was black as a shadow, but I could see a footpath rutted into the slag and followed it. The path was well worn and the slag crunched underfoot. I was now entering that forbidden territory beyond the reach of Granby. I could see through the thin sulphur mists that there was a cluster of cabins above a spit of land and a rough-made dock and a boat. The land was ruined here as it was everywhere, without shrubbery, only the stark dead trees. The hills and mountains were grey with them, many felled, and some, as above the hospital, smouldered as if land clearing were an endless preoccupation.

The cabins lacked the well-made composition of the company houses, small and shabby and tilting. I went up to the first cabin. I decided that I would call out before I knocked on the door, though I was certain they had watched me come across the slag in my white uniform as if I were a holy messenger, or perhaps an uninvited nuisance. I will admit to have felt a tremor of nerves standing there. I wondered if they would simply ignore me.

"Nurse Stewart," I announced, "from the Granby Hospital. A friendly visit." Then I knocked. I could hear the murmuring, the rustling, the drag of chairs on the floor. I waited, holding my bag in both my hands before me, all duty and appearance. I suddenly realized who I could be to them, a servant of the Company with agendas, pronouncements, and ultimatums. Then a crack in the door.

"What do you want?" came a sifting and rather husky voice.

"The hospital would like to make regular visits if you don't mind. If you could let me in, then I can explain. It's all a matter of good health."

"Is it?"

"Yes, of course. I will not ask you to do anything you don't want to do. I promise."

"You promise?"

"Yes, I do." And then I heard a sudden grunting from the rooftop of the cabin next door. I looked up and there getting to his feet, and now standing precariously, was an old man, bearded and skinny, a strange creature hatched from the shingles.

"For Christ sakes, let her in, Sass, she's not going to bite you!"

"Shut up, Goose, and mind your own business!" she barked, her head popping out the door then craning to look up at him. "We're paying you to shingle over the leaks, not to flap your gums. If you fall and break your neck you'll be of little use!"

"She's bossy, that one, Nurse," the old man said.

"Well, come in," the woman said. "Don't listen to the old *Viking*. Nobody does. And don't ask him a question if you know what's good for you." More obscure advice. She opened the door all the way and let me in.

Inside, the cavernous dark. I couldn't see a thing right off and was a little disoriented. The curtains on the windows were drawn and I couldn't tell if I was alone with her. A kerosene lamp flickered, and then another, and soon I could see the room and what filled it. I was surprised to see two other women. They sat in their petticoats and stockings on couches covered with burgundy draperies and red velvet pillows with tassels. On the walls paintings of ladies in similar poses, all very posh and daring, and garnished with a rich absurdity compared to what was outside the door. And how different from Dumbiedykes, from Josie's flat. My mind went there in a flash, but I couldn't linger. It seemed a trap somehow, something I could fall into if I wasn't careful.

"Well, sit if you wish, Nurse," the one called Sass said. She remained standing.

I noticed the robe she was wearing, deep green like the sea, and patterned with fronds of some kind, perhaps palm leaves. She seemed to be the oldest of the three, and full in the face and body, *amply endowed* some would say. I guessed that Sass was the *Madam* of the shanties. They all wore paint on their lips and around their eyes, theatrical, dramatic, and hair coiffed for a ball.

"Thank you," I said and sat on a soft chair that matched the couches.

"You can call me Sass, and those two lovelies, in order, Melody and Dolly." They each flicked a wrist languidly, their unhinged hands hardly a greeting at all.

"Pleased to meet you all," I said. And then I just sat a moment, absorbing the room that was filled with a sweet unrecognizable odour, a perfume unfamiliar but exotic. And the fineries that seemed so out of place against the slagheap just a few short steps away. Shopkeepers setting out their wares.

"Nurse," Sass said, "do you have a name?"

"Mary," I said without hesitation, my designation falling away like a leaf. I quickly corrected myself. "Nurse Stewart." Then something on the shelf in the bookcase behind Sass drew my attention. I stared at it. I wanted to know what it was. It was sitting on a shelf in plain view. I looked hard, so familiar and so recent, like a word on the tip of my tongue.

"Get on with it, Mary," Sass said, turning to see what had distracted me. "We've heard it all before. You seem like a nice girl but we don't have all day, you know."

But I was momentarily preoccupied and could not speak, so taken with the object.

Sass turned all at once and went to the bookcase. "Do you like books, Mary?" she asked. Then she picked it up, a cloth bookmark with a gold-stitched cross.

"I have one just like that," I said.

Sass looked to the other girls. "Don't start, girls," she said, a mild warning.

"You're no fun, Sass," Melody said. She moved on the couch, stretched as if awaking from a long slumber. Dolly did the same.

"Then you had a visit from Pastor Burke," Sass said.

"I went to see him," I said.

"He gave you a copy of the book, didn't he?"

"Yes." How unsettling to see the pastor's bookmark. I couldn't make sense of it.

"Not *the book?*" Dolly lampooned.

"*The book!*" Melody chortled. She went to the bookcase and removed a book. And there in her hands, the black companion of human pitfalls and censure. *Safe Counsel.*

"There's no stopping her now," Sass forewarned and took a seat.

Melody opened it and moved to the centre of the room. Then strangely, she stood before me and, as if an actor in a play, made a dramatic proclamation.

"I am guilty of a sin, my dear Mary," she intoned, "and not the one you so wholesomely assume. No, it is not my vice, but the precedent of my vocation, the root cause, as it were. Had I known? Had I known? So please bear with me and my crimes so evident."

I was mesmerized and confused, forgetting even why I was there at all as she leafed through the pages. And then she found the right passage and began a most astonishing and theatrical reading.

5. READING NOVELS — How often have I seen girls not twelve years old, as hungry for a story or novel as they should be for their dinners! A sickly sentimentalism is thus formed, and their minds are sullied with impure desires. Every fashionable young lady must of course read every new novel, though nearly all of them contain exceptionable allusions, perhaps delicately covered over with a thin gauze of fashionable refinement; yet, on that very account, the more objectionable. If this work contained one improper allusion to their ten, many of those fastidious ladies who now eagerly devour the vulgarities of Dumas, and the double-entendres of Bulwer, and even converse with gentlemen about their contents, would discountenance or condemn it as improper. Shame on novel-reading women; for they cannot have pure minds or unsullied feelings, but Cupid and the beaux, and waking of dreams of love, are fast consuming their health and virtue.

Melody bowed, and Sass and Dolly clapped enthusiastically. It was an outstanding performance and I wanted to join them, but I could only sit dumbly in my uniform. A part of me understood and I wanted to say so. And then I said something after the enthusiasm subsided, perhaps too revealing, something to appease them after all.

"And yet Edward Bulwer-Lytton gave us the ever memorable *It was a dark and stormy night ...*," I said artfully. But there was only a look of disappointment on Melody's made-up face. It seemed I had deflated her masterful moment of self-mockery. It was careless;

I had to be more mindful. I couldn't show them another crack in my illusion.

"I must apologize for the theatrics, Mary," Sass said, "but I'm afraid Melody is what some would call a *helpless romantic*. She reads incessantly, devours the romantic plots fervently. Have the modern fictions corrupted her? No, *I* must take some credit for that."

Melody went back to the couch and took up her place, a kind of lazy repose. She teased her hair and stared at me, then Dolly too, watching me with their illustrated eyes. They seemed dreadfully bored, lounging like two well-fed cats.

"I found these two waifs," Sass went on, "wandering the streets of Anchorage. They were roughed up some, penniless and desperate. Imagine taking a steamer from Seattle with nothing but their visions of chivalry, looking for their White Knight in Alaska. Well, they needed a mother more than a hero. I saw it straight away. Now look at them."

They tossed up their hands and nodded their heavy heads warily as if the story had been told too many times. And the ensuing lull after the entertainment reminded me why I was there. "I suppose there's not much I can tell you, Sass," I said. I heard my words, my tone like an old friend.

"No sores, no rashes," she said.

"But you will take prophylactics as surely they will be of some use to you."

"Not me, exactly, but I will take what you offer."

I opened my bag and removed a packet. She took it without hesitation. I got up to leave. The dark vault of the brothel was pressing in on me. It stifled the breath in a way, although the drama I had witnessed was most unusual, and I'll admit, most entertaining. It was a show. But there was also a pervading sense of despair, waiting the way they did, ready and willing. I wasn't so troubled by the way they lived, the three of them, but more so by the men who made the crossing from the flats to the shanties. It was all very secretive, one of the many sins of that black harbour, an underworld of earthly needs. I thought of Tom Haney and how obsessed he was.

Sass opened the door for me. "At least I left you with something," I said to her affably.

"And Pastor Burke," she quipped, "left Dolly with a little something, too."

I turned to her with the bright light of an overcast day pouring in through the door. Her eyes, blue now with blunt honesty, wandered my face like a memory. But I quickly turned away before she could read the book of me.

CHAPTER

TWENTY-TWO

OUTSIDE I STOOD DAZED IN THE LIGHT, THE FOREST TO THE north in its death throes, its grief. I couldn't return over the slag-heap, across the bridges under the scrutiny of Pastor Burke. And I didn't want to confront him with what certainly was an outrage, the appalling and the unthinkable. Lifting his black book in a display of contempt. Damn you, I thought, and damn your complaint to Dr. Madden. But the damning gave me an idea, and now I was emboldened more than ever.

I noticed the old man on the dock with the sea behind him that rippled and disappeared in a ghostly haze of dead islands. Always the sulphide veil settling on a windless day. He seemed about to leave. I thought I would have a word with him and called out. He simply looked up, then stood slackly as he waited for me. I had a question, but I couldn't understand why Sass would caution me. He seemed a harmless sort, as thin and tall as the stiff trees that loomed above the shanties.

"Hello, Goose, isn't it?" I said, coming onto the dock.

"Well, *ja*, my name is Gustav, if you must know," he said. "Gus for short." His lips were concealed behind a tangle of silver-tinged beard. Peering grey eyes and an accent much like Marta's. "But Goose stuck to me like a burr," he went on. "I don't mind much. The ladies have fun with it. *Goose this. Goose that.* I'm flattered, to tell you the truth. An old man flirting with the likes of them. Don't they know I'm not in good working condition anymore? Of course they know, but they like to tease. So, what can I help you with? I do most anything. The boat here, the *Hecate Queen*, I keep in town, all thirty-six feet of her — live right on board. The Company don't mind. I take the visiting shareholders on trips up to Alice Arm to see the grizzly bears, and occasionally to Prince Rupert on an errand. They pay me well. I keep it in top shape. A new diesel engine. A rough sound, you know, smokes a bit, but dependable. I'll take folks wherever they want to go. Some on fishing trips.

"But I like to get away from the dead wood, back down Observatory Inlet to the strait. Not much life here anymore. I saw a grouse the other day and nearly fell over, and an orchid, a little pink flower in the forest. Just over there. You see, the plume never touches those woods as the westerly winds blow the other way. All in all, it's a good life. Had a wife once, and a boy, brought them from Norway. I was a fisherman, you know. But she didn't like the wild sea and went back to Oslo. Took the boy. It was a tearful parting for me, but not for her. Did I ask you what you needed?"

I was exhausted. I couldn't breathe, listening to him. It seemed he would go on forever. I thought that I would have to slap him, but thank God, he stopped in time.

"So, Goose," I said, "if I were in need of a boat, say from the harbour to this very dock, what would you say?"

"I do it all the time. Some of the young men don't want to be seen crossing the footbridge and the slagheap."

"Is that a fact?"

"*Ja*, a good foggy day and there's no telling where I've gone. Climb aboard and I'll take you back. It's a short trip. A pretty nurse shouldn't be walking across that black slag. That's an awful trek and some watching and making their judgements. Not a place I'd ever be. A boy fell into the creek not a year ago. He didn't drown. They say the cyanide killed him. It's a hell of a way to go for the youngster. And no barnacles or mussels attached to the piers on the dock, no starfish among the rocks, no life to see when the tide goes out. It's the creek, you know. Did you tell me your name?"

There I was standing on that rickety dock at the end of the world, and if I was scheming, it must have been for a good cause, for I hesitated before I gave Goose my name, but I did.

"Mary, and you may call me Nurse, if you don't mind," I said. It occurred to me standing there with the garrulous old man that when Melody addressed me as Mary before her wordy frolic, I fell out of my role as a nurse, though luckily I recovered.

I climbed aboard the *Hecate Queen* and wondered about Hecate, the goddess of sorcery and witchcraft. It all seemed rather fitting in an inexplicable way. Goose untied stern and bow and soon we were away. Not far at all, it was true, a short cruise beyond the estuary of Falls Creek and Hidden Creek that was silted and spilled in a broad fan. Steamships coming and going. I stood with Goose in the wheelhouse, the harbour always in view and Anyox like it was the first time I had seen it, blurred beyond definition, but now I knew a few of its secrets, its sins, and I was certain Goose knew a few of them as he yammered on about one and the other as if he couldn't settle on a topic. He seemed a man heaped with local knowledge.

And when the dark man in the long boat, whom I assumed was one of the natives, appeared once again sitting in the harbour as we approached, I asked Goose about him.

"That man in the boat, Goose," I said, "I've seen him before, sitting in his boat and not moving at all. On the prairie I saw from the train young boys watching in much the same way, just watching with their burnished blank faces. It seemed to me they had a question."

"*Ja*, the boys on the prairies were likely Cree or Blackfoot," he said. "Some starved, you know, when the government gave them ploughs and such, wanted to make them farmers, keep them in one place. They'd be easier to manage that way. I'm sure the boys wanted to know what was happening to their land. That fellow here is Tsimshian. He comes from a village down the inlet. He has a different question."

"And what would that be?"

"When are we leaving?"

"Seriously?"

"These creeks were full of salmon at one time, not too long ago. Great trees filled the flats and uplands and all the mountains. The Tsimshian would come here in the fall of the year to harvest fish for the winter. Other times they would take refuge up Hidden Creek from the raiding Haida, taking their canoes up among the shelter of trees where they would remain hidden. *Ja*, we only see the smelter and all the money and commerce it can produce. Most mining operations don't last. The ore peters out, or the gold plays out. It's the story of corporations like Granby, backers and businessmen chasing the next gold rush. But you know, Granby just might last a while. *Ja*, they seem to have the golden touch. There was an island in Granby Bay over there. It was called Goose Bay back then. They needed to remove it to make way for a new harbour before Anyox was a town. Wouldn't you know it, when they blasted the island they found gold in the granite, three million dollars' worth, enough gold to finance the town and everything else. I can't complain, Nurse, and I won't, as I've moved up and down the coast myself chasing one thing or another. I'd still be fishing out on the trackless sea if Granby wasn't so generous.

"And as for the natives, *savages* they're not. It was fifty years ago when the missionary William Duncan thought he would civilize them. Few have cared to consider that fellow, Nurse. Now they wear the European dress, trousers and suspenders, and with their Christian God seem to be in a kind of shock. If there is a God looking after these matters, well, I haven't seen him."

We passed him and the waves from the *Hecate Queen* rocked the little boat, but he remained as the boat itself, up and down in a gentle roll until the waves moved on. He did not look our way. It seemed that he did not exist at all, but an apparition, perhaps appealing for the past to return.

Goose tied up to a dock in the harbour with the smaller craft, apart from the steamships and barges. "If you're in need of passage," he said, "then you know where to find me." He held his hand out and helped me up the stairs and onto the wharf.

"And what is the fee today, Goose?" I reached into the bag where I kept a few dollars.

"Fifty cents, if you don't mind."

"Not at all," I said. "You spared me from the slagheap." I reached into my bag for the correct change and gave it to him. He looked happy to have assisted as the day bustled around us, and it seemed, as always, that the entire town was strolling the harbour on business and pleasure. It was the only place in Anyox that resembled a seaside town at all. We stood and watched the crowds. Boys chasing boys, running this way and that, past the girls, who watched as if they had never seen such a sight in their short lives, or perhaps had only discovered the boundless energy of boys.

"It's a lively place to be, on the harbour, Nurse," Goose went on, "but you'll need to get away from town now and then before you lose your mind. I'll take you up Alice Arm where the trees are green and the streams are clear right down to the pebbles. I've taken a nurse up there a time or two when someone took ill, or a baby was coming."

"I'll keep that in mind, Goose."

As I enjoyed that pleasurable interlude on the wharf, I was conscious of how rare that was for me since I had arrived in Anyox. Half were Scots, my uncle had said, an exaggeration perhaps, but still there was a sense of kinship just then, although I hardly knew anyone on the harbour. There was the postmaster and librarian, of course, simple acquaintances really, but the man with the broom in front of the Granby offices, I knew. It was Sandy Hall. Oh, providence, blessed co-conspirator. How many times had I looked up hoping to see him in the window of his room?

"There is someone I would like you to meet, Goose," I said. "He may need a boat. I can't say when at the moment, but I'll know when I fetch him."

"I like an optimist, Nurse. I surely do."

I hurried down the wharf through the crowd as Sandy limped about with his broom, leaning on it now and then as he tired.

I called out to him without much restraint on my enthusiasm. "Sandy," I shouted, waving madly. There was much commotion on the wharf and I was certain that I was hardly noticed. He stopped sweeping and turned to me. He smiled, and I knew that he was glad to see me as we had good talks those many mornings walking together to the hospital.

"Nurse Stewart, I thought that was you," he said. "I saw you talking to old Goose."

"So, you know him, then?" I shouldn't have been surprised.

"Everyone knows Goose."

"Well, as it turns out, I have just come into his acquaintance. I have made my scheduled visit to the shanties, a nurse's inspection, you might say. All is well, of course. And I discovered that Goose travels up and down the harbour quite regularly. I was thinking that he might be of some interest to you." All discretion now.

"Some interest to me?"

"Yes, a certain interest. It has to do with a certain pickle."

"Pickle?"

"This certain pickle is the subject of your attention."

"Is it now?"

"A certain friend in the hospital."

Sandy regarded me as if I had just lost my mind. A look of such bewilderment. The astonishment of witless blather. Then all at once his face lit up, so pleasing with his ginger hair.

"That certain friend has made a last request," he said, eager to his part now.

"I believe he has."

"And that certain friend would like ...?"

"A boat ride, I'm sure."

"Would he, now?"

"I suppose he would."

"And how does this certain friend get about?"

"I suppose this certain friend would like very much to be brought out in his wheelchair now and then. It would be good for his spirits. Get some sunshine and fresh air — if you can find it, of course. He could be shown the harbour and the ships, and perhaps a small boat."

"So, this certain friend would need an hour or two away from the hospital. Would that about do it?"

"I suppose he wouldn't be missed at all."

"I can see the old Viking looking this way. He's expecting me. Have you arranged ...?"

"I haven't done a thing, Sandy," I said, reaching into my bag for the fee, "and I haven't had a word with you today. There is only an old man with a boat." I handed Sandy a dollar but he wouldn't take it.

"No, it's my pleasure to do something that matters. I am a proud man and I push a broom, Nurse Stewart. It's a hard thing to find your self-respect sweeping through the day. And besides, you have done enough."

I watched them carry out their business from across the wharf, Sandy's gestures, how they turned as one and looked up toward the hospital, and then down the bay. All that for one young man's obsession, to relieve him of something that was difficult for me to comprehend, a fire born in him, something raging that he was unable to extinguish. But was it not a human thing to reproduce, some urgency stirring in a man? There seemed to be no fervour of appetites in the town that I could see. But still it existed, in me as well, that had been all but extinguished. And yet I had felt its rise within me standing next to Sandy Hall, how at times his eyes drifted over me. It came as a gentle pull, perhaps a vague persuasion, as if he brushed the hair from my cheek with a finger. I wondered about the subtleties of its flowering, and as much as Tom Haney longed for it for himself, Violet, too, was bewitched in a dangerous way. And Pastor Burke, what of him?

CHAPTER

TWENTY-THREE

SEPTEMBER CAME AS A RESPITE, THE END OF THE SLOW BURN of summer, but endings come in many ways, some clothed in mercy. Tom Haney passed away. Sandy Hall said that Tom had died a happy man. I was certain that Tom wanted to live, but I suppose he had been resigned to his condition for quite some time. After his palliation at the shanties, I became aware of the absence of a certain angst, which was perhaps his surrender to what he knew was coming. I suppose saying that he had died a happy man served only to appease those left behind, mollified the griever and the grief.

His mother and father travelled from Toronto for his service, a glum affair for those who would not have appreciated the details of his happy ending, knew not the tenderness of Melody toward a dying man. However, they did appreciate the Company's offer for his gravestone, a soldier's helmet cast in concrete that accompanied so many in the cemetery now. And the line of teary veterans standing tall and proud and vulnerable as dust. But it was the image of Nurse Stricker that stuck with me, altered my view of her innate bitterness, and transformed it, if you will. In her unflattering grey dress, the matron, a mother, stood regally behind the mourners like a statue bearing witness, and yet her mind was not present at all but somewhere in the wreckage of France where her own son's unrecovered body lay. I knew then what she sipped all day long, a teacup with the only medicine she could keep from Granby.

I had errands at the harbour and was on my way down the plank road. I had a book to return to the library, Conan Doyle's *The Lost World*, an exciting escape from the plume that reared up in front of me beyond Smith Bluff and dominated existence there in the north wilds. I was quite smitten with E.D. Malone. *Madman that I was to linger so long before I fled!* But the smelter had no "huge projecting eyes" or "row of enormous teeth in his open mouth, and the gleaming fringe of claws." It seemed that if it stopped, the world would cease to be, so dependent the town, the people. And yet it all seemed to work and was as constant as the days. There was no such standard of living in Old Town, in Dumbiedykes, nothing like that self-contained town of Anyox and the paradox of giving life as it was taking it away. Was I coming into a certain tolerance, I wondered, or was I simply experiencing the comforts of affluence?

There was a cool breeze coming in from the bay, and the sun poked its brilliant head out from the clouds now and then. The day had possibilities. It felt that way, at least, to experience autumn in my new home, and then the coming winter. Even the children felt it thumping up the plank road to school, what a herd of buffalo must once have sounded like on the hard prairies. A rush of excited feet.

Mrs. Moffatt, as it turned out, liked me. How strange when so many others thought I was evil or, at best, conniving and wicked. But Mrs. Moffatt, who would be leaving the library soon as her replacement was due to arrive from Boston, was still quite pleasant with me whenever I came in to study the medical texts and manuals.

"Good morning, Miss Stewart," she said, never abandoning the formal. I suppose a librarian had a certain station in life, keeper of knowledge, a rank above. She cradled a teacup.

"And the same to you, Mrs. Moffatt," I said. I placed my book on the counter and she duly recorded its return. I took a moment to look around the library, to the spaces on the shelves that seemed to have grown over the summer. "It seems that Anyox has some avid readers," I commented.

"Oh, yes," she said, "and some, you know, never return their books. I have to order new ones all the time. A real problem. What can I do? I suppose I could knock on doors. That might do it. But alas, the Company's pockets are deep."

I thought that was quite generous of her. "Aren't I the dutiful one?"

"A rarity in this town."

"And you said that you'll be staying with your sister."

"Yes, in Victoria. She has a tea shop on Government Street. She'll put me right to work. We'll do quite well. It has a literary ambience. You know, catering to the well-heeled of the capital. Smoking rooms and ..."

A word missing at the end of her sentence. The ladies of Anyox and their tea. "You seemed to have adjusted to the fact of your leaving. I'm so pleased to see it, recalling how distressed you were."

"Yes, very distressed. But chin up now."

"Well, then, I must be off. I bid you a good day, Mrs. Moffatt."

"And I bid you a good day, Miss Stewart."

I left the library, my little head full of one's changeable nature. There was hope for me, I mused lightheartedly, but as I entered the post office, I was both hopeful and guarded. There were several ladies and a gentleman in front of me. I waited patiently. On the counter I noticed a stack of parcels nearly a foot high wrapped tightly in brown paper and bound with string. I was killing time with my mind unable to still itself. Finally, I was at the head of the line.

"Good morning, Mr. Curly," I said.

"Good morning," he returned blandly.

"Miss Stewart," I reminded him. He had the look of an old ram, peering over his eyeglasses, his head slumped as if he were about to charge me with his unseen horns.

"Oh, yes, Miss Stewart. How can I help you?"

I had the same question whenever I came into the post office, two questions really, one before the other. I would have hoped that he could spare me the agony of the first one and get right to the second one. "So, Mr. Curly, have there been any inquiries?" I asked.

"No, Miss Stewart," he said, remembering the ritual now, "no person has asked about you. Are you expecting a visitor, family perhaps?"

"And that is my second question." But he only stared back at me, oblivious. Perhaps you should retire, Mr. Curly, I silently suggested. "I am expecting a letter from my sister."

"Such a letter arrived this morning," he said, his words rushing out of his mouth as if to prove me wrong. He turned away to retrieve it.

I was excited now. I had been waiting for it, so desperate to hear from Lizzy. It was then when my attention returned to the stack of parcels momentarily. The one on top was quite interesting, its destination Victoria, British Columbia. And then Mr. Curly returned with the letter. Lizzy's cursive hand was unmistakable.

"Thank you, Mr. Curly," I said. I took the letter, but before leaving I hesitated out of growing curiosity. "Now that's a stack of something going to Victoria," I commented. At once I realized that it was an inappropriate comment to make to the Anyox postmaster. But Mr. Curly was most obliging.

"Oh, the librarian is always sending such parcels to her sister."

"Interesting." I looked closely at the shape of the parcels. She made no attempt to conceal them, how the slightly curved spine of a book differs from the hard edge that shields the pages.

"Is that all, Miss Stewart?" Mr. Curly asked, quickly removing the parcel of books.

"Oh, yes, and good day to you, Mr. Curly." A fine arrangement, it seemed to me, co-conspirators. A few coins for his retirement. Oh, I was devilishly suspicious. I left the post office and walked out on the wharf with Lizzy's letter in my hand, so happy to have it at last, but the residual of what I had discovered flopped about in my head. The librarian's revenge, a most creative sin. How clever, Mrs. Moffatt, how insidiously clever.

There was one more stop I needed to make. The Granby General Store kept everything one needed, and how brilliant of the Company to pay you one day and get it back the next. There was, however, a fine selection of women's sweaters, something to warm me from the chill that was noticeable now. But first the letter. There was a bench on the wharf and I sat under a pearl sun that gave a tolerable warmth. I was wearing my Stewart shawl and snuggled it under my chin. I took a breath of tolerable air and looked out to the steamer leaving the harbour, to the gulls and crows following behind, or perhaps hurrying away. I opened the letter.

August 19th, 1917

Dear Mary,

I hold your letters like a treasure. They had come from so far away. I cannot comprehend the distance, nor can I imagine what you have seen. I will need to see it for myself in the coming year. Still, I imagine us together again, and that's what keeps my spirits up. There is only this small space where I tend to Father, who, I must tell you, listened with pride as I read your letters to him.

There is less trouble in Dumbiedykes since Jimmy McDuff has been gone. The speculation of his end was rampant in the street after you left. The Edinburgh Police were asking questions but did not come to our tenement. Uncle Calvin reassured me not to worry. All is peaceful now, except for the usual hollering in the hallways and lanes. Sometimes I wonder if I can get used to another life. This is the only one I've ever known. I worry that I will not have enough strength to leave. A year is so far away. When I'm down, I read your letters for the hundredth time. They're a godsend. Write another when you get this. Tell me more about Anyox. Tell me your favourite thing. Tell me about the people, your new friends. That way I'll already know them when I arrive. Silly me, Mary, but thinking of you is how I get through the days. Why does time seem to slow when you want it to hurry?

And yes, Uncle Calvin looks after us. He visits with Father often now. The local newspaper said that Solicitor Calvin Stewart is running for office and is champion of the poor. Now that is all beyond me, Mary, and none of my concern. I only know that he is a good uncle and brother now.

I will leave you now and eagerly wait for your next letter. That morning on Arthur's Seat seems like a dream now. Tell me about the "silver darlings," Mary, one more time as I haven't heard from Mother in a while. Is she with you?

All my love,
Lizzy
Edinburgh, Scotland

I stared at the letter. I had to read it once again. Lizzy seemed to be telling me something, but without words, perhaps a riddle. No, I was afraid that it revealed a crack in her sweet little mind. So much responsibility. It was if she was having difficulty holding the frangible parts of herself together. The letter was rather distressing. Seeing the name of Jimmy McDuff written so casually, a name heavy with an immutable dread, exposed now to the air of Anyox, as if were not fouled enough. Oh, it wasn't her fault, my reaction. She needed a mother. I would tell her the story of the *silver darlings* once again and pray to my *unfound* mother to go to Lizzy and comfort her. It made little difference whether I believed in such things or not. Lizzy did, and that's all that mattered.

And it seemed to me that our good Uncle Calvin was taking advantage of a certain circumstance not occasioned by him, purging Dumbiedykes of prostitution and coming to the aid of the poor, all to further his aims. I had only considered that he wanted to rid himself of a potential embarrassment, rid Edinburgh of an unholy niece. And what if his political aspirations fell to nought? Would he abandon his brother once again?

I looked up and there was Violet entering the general store. She looked so young in her gay dress and curls, much like Lizzy. Then it struck me like a blow to the heart that Lizzy couldn't wait another year. She wouldn't last. She had to come now. I had to write to Uncle Calvin, the politician in waiting, and take advantage of a certain circumstance. I believed they called it leverage.

I went into the store, not so much wanting to chat with Violet, as she most often avoided me, even in our apartment where she couldn't escape from my presence. She worked late so often that I thought it was her way of avoidance. But now we were in the same store. I wanted to make things right again. I truly did, but every day at the hospital seemed like a strike against me, something in my manner, or perhaps she tired of my wit-cracking ways. I considered the general store to be neutral, safe for both of us.

She was browsing the bolts of fabric, taking each one from the shelf and turning it in her hand. It seemed she was planning to make a garment, perhaps a dress for winter or, for all I knew, it may have been for draperies. Yes, like the shanties. But of course, I wouldn't make such a comparison as she resented my appointment, my monthly brothel visits. I made a mental note not to let that slip between my teeth if we did in fact strike up a conversation, which I was most certain we would, given she was only a few feet away from me. And I certainly wanted to. Violet would be a good friend for Lizzy.

I removed a sweater from a rack, a Norfolk knitted coat, they called it. I liked the rolled collar, the big wooden buttons, and the lovely belt. It was the colour of oatmeal with hazel stitching that gave it an appealing warmth. I held it up to see how it might fit and turned as I did so, a bit of clever manoeuvring that would catch Violet before she could flee.

"Violet," I said happily, "it's so good to see you out and about. Mostly I see you at the hospital, you know, between bedpans and bedlam."

"Mary," she said, not too enthusiastically. "What brings you here?"

"Well, to be honest, Violet, it was my feet."

"That's very funny, Mary," she said blandly. There was a time when that would have set her to laughter. But now only her dull eyes.

"Are you well, Violet?" I asked. I sensed that there was something troubling her that didn't include me.

"Perhaps I am not, but I cannot say. A mood is all it is. Everyone has them."

"That's true enough, Violet. If I can be of some help, please ..."

"No, Mary, I will be fine." Still that abrupt manner that cast me outside her favour.

I sensed that she wanted to conclude our conversation. It was the way her eyes looked down, never into mine. A nervousness. And then a family came into the store. It was Dr. Trig with his wife and young daughter. Now, that was not so remarkable, as the store was often busy with people coming and going. I thought I might warn Violet, knowing what I did. But surely she didn't know that I knew. She had her back to them. I suppose I could have done nothing, let whatever happened happen. It was none of my concern. There could be a dramatic exchange, at least an awkward moment that I just might revel in. A game for me, a bit of my own revenge for her castigation, for her resentment. But, I thought, what if that was the very reason for her melancholy? Should I not spare her from the certain heart-pounding of their triangulation? Then of course she would know that I knew.

I whispered for no other reason than to give her an option. "Look at that," I said, "Dr. Trig with his wife and daughter."

"Please don't say anything, Mary," she whispered back.

The old cat out of the bag, as it were. "He hasn't seen us, Violet," I counselled. "When they move to the far end of the store, then take my arm and we'll be off."

"I had seen them outside on the wharf, Mary. There are things I cannot tell you, but please get me away safe."

"Then you're hiding, Violet?"

"Yes."

"Take my arm now. They're distracted with children's toys. That's the way. Look straight ahead. Come now."

Outside we hurried up the plank road, up the hill, and away from the harbour. Violet was in tears. Something awful had happened. "Your heart has been broken, Violet," I said. The secret was out.

"You knew all along, didn't you, Mary?"

"I cannot say that I didn't. I was warned about Dr. Trig, you see. The matron knew a part of him that was not so professional, you might say. I had seen the way he looked at you, and you at him. There's a certain look that is not common among workmates unless ..."

"You never said a thing about it."

"No. I will make no judgements about someone's decisions. People act poorly all the time."

"I acted poorly, Mary. It's an awful sin."

"No, Violet, Dr. Trig acted poorly and the sin belongs to him. You're still a child."

"Someone had seen us and told his wife. He called it off. What was I thinking, Mary?"

"I suppose you weren't thinking, Violet. When someone gives you attention, it feels good, and he certainly would have known that. So, one thing leads to another. Then you're hooked, and when you're hooked, there's no telling how it will end."

"I see, Mary. I think I do. But I feel awful, miserable really."

"It won't last forever."

CHAPTER TWENTY-THREE

"Will you tell the matron?"

"No, I won't, Violet. What would be the point in that?"

"I haven't been good to you."

"We all haven't been good at one time or the other. Lucky for us, and the smelter willing, the sun will rise again tomorrow morning."

I put my arm around her shoulder as I remembered, with such brutal clarity, how Jimmy paid attention to me, groomed me like a queen. Oh, it felt good at the beginning, attention, gifts, and money for a poor girl. And then I was hooked. He was impaled himself when I realized how it was going to end for me. Oh, the sins of Mary Stewart that could not be told.

CHAPTER

TWENTY-FOUR

THE LONG NIGHTS OF JANUARY WERE REVEALING THEIR intimate pleasures as the babies at the hospital kept coming. An astonishing event for me to see the many swaddled lives beginning in Anyox, the wards throbbing with the incessant shrill of their primal declarations. There was a certain joy at the hospital now. Violet no longer had anything to hide, nothing to conceal from the matron. And Dr. Trig seemed to be better for it, attentive now to the new lives and nothing else, no sexual tension between him and Violet that I swear had left them panting in the hallways more than once. I wasn't one to judge, of course, but I had certain knowledge, you see, and I was starting over. Anyox was a brand-new day, you could say.

And the matron, I suppose, was deep in her grief and such things just didn't enter her sphere of sensibilities unless it was a brash young lassie, full of her untold story. But when the meeting with the Granby Safety Committee approached, she placed her hand on my arm, something she never did, and reassured me.

"Now, Mary," she said, "you're there to listen. See what the concerns are. You will be outnumbered. And there will be two types of men, those with clean hands and those with a permanent glaze of grime. They're the ones who'll have complaints. We've always seen our share of the Granby injured, and of late more with a peculiar symptom. Keep good notes, and we'll see what will come of it."

"Yes, Nurse Stricker," I said, "I'll do my very best." We stood on the hospital veranda for a moment and looked out at the plume as if to receive our daily message. *Get to work. Make us money.* How strange that my resentment toward her had somewhat diminished. And I couldn't smell the sulphur just then. Had I been converted into one of its devotees, a disciple of its money-making ways, its grandiose hunger for the ore of the earth? Had Anyox accepted me as well, at last?

The meeting was to be held in the Granby offices down at the harbour. A boardroom, I was told. I suppose it was safe ground for the Company, as relationships with the workers were still a bit strained from an uprising the year before. Of course, I knew nothing of this, who was right and who was wrong. I was there only to take notes. I had no predilections one way or the other. But before I went into the Granby office, I had a letter to post.

It was a rather simple note to Uncle Calvin in a small sealed envelope. It was tucked into the letter to Lizzy: *put Lizzy on the next ship out of Liverpool before we lose her to despair. And bring your brother to your home where he will be looked after until the end of his days* — which I knew was not too far away. Of course, my language was bold and to the point, especially the reference to a certain letter to the *Edinburgh Times: Confessions of an Old Town Prostitute*. Oh, he hated that word, the vulgarity of it. And yes, it was all bluff. I would never do such a thing, bring more shame to my father. But I was certain that Uncle Calvin knew what I was capable of, and a vainglorious man would leave nothing to chance.

And to Lizzy along with a few dollars:

Sllivery blobs like dauds of jeely,
aa come oot the fishie's belly
Hack its heid aff an its tail,
guttin on throw snaw and hail
Cuts and cracks makk fingers reid,
satty clooties sype wi bluid
Fa wad be a fisher quine,
guttin herrin frae the brine?

Postmaster Curly received the letter and postage with the shake of his head. Now, it seemed, we were of one mind with regards to the nature of my constant query. It left me in an undisturbed state of mind, and knowing that the wheels of my insistence were in motion, I felt a certain contentment with my present circumstances.

"You're in a fine mood," the postmaster said.

"Well, I suppose I am." I was rather pleased that it showed. It seemed that the world was more encouraging, more tolerating of me now. It was my nineteenth birthday, and Chief Constable Ross in Edinburgh would be most pleased, I was sure, that I had made it that far. "Thank you, Mr. Curly, I'll take that as a compliment. But I must be off to the Granby offices. Meeting with the Granby Safety Committee — can't be late."

I was beginning to believe that I just might be someone, perhaps someone like Elsie Inglis, who made a difference to so many lives. I went into the Granby offices with a modest but assured swagger, and at once a secretary pointed upstairs to the boardroom. It wasn't lost to me how I looked around the office for Sandy Hall as I climbed the stairs. No red-haired man with a broom on that day. I felt a measure of disappointment, and it surprised me.

I could smell cigarette smoke wafting from the open door, and then the stronger stink of a cigar. There was the murmur of voices and, oddly, laughter. Oh, what a gay old time they seemed to be having. And when I stepped into the boardroom a sudden silence, as if sound had unexpectedly been stricken from the world. A long table of men with their fading bright faces, suits on one side and the working men on the other, at odds it seemed now. But the laughter belied a certain comradery. What had they been laughing at? I wondered.

Then one of the working men said, "We were hoping for barley scones and tea. I see you've come empty-handed." All laughter like the gulls in the harbour.

"I would take a muffin," said another. Such laughter from the vulgar fool, and the others nearly hysterical, all at my expense.

I stood rather awkwardly, humiliated, until the gentleman at the head of the table with the cigar smoking from his fingers introduced himself.

"My name is Robert Steele," he said. "Mine Manager of the operation here in Anyox, and committee chair. And you must be Nurse Stewart."

"That I am, Mr. Steele," I said. "I suppose it was the white uniform that gave me away."

His jaw dropped slightly. The others made queer nasal sounds — like starting engines. "Take a seat, Nurse Stewart," he said tersely.

I sat at the end of the table and felt their eyes upon me, like fingers touching, searching. Men full of their speculation. I placed my notepad on the table. I could do nothing else but manage a glance to the brutes, their odd smirks, still enjoying my joke, or perhaps still full of themselves. They surely wanted to intimidate me, and for their own pleasure it would seem, but I wouldn't give them the satisfaction on that day.

"I would like to make note of those in attendance, Mr. Steele," I said.

"Very well, Nurse Stewart," he said, "but first I must say that you are here at the committee's request. I have the support of the Granby Medical Officer. I suppose you could call it a token of our goodwill that we take safety matters seriously. But saying that, you will observe, nothing more."

"A token, sir?" I said. "So, it was the workers who requested a nurse?"

"Yes, you could say that."

"Well, they gave me a rather strange welcome, Mr. Steele. I certainly hope that I can be more than a token. And I don't bake at all." At that the throaty chuckles from the workers, but from Mr. Steele only his blanched face. I wanted to win them over. I didn't want to be a token of anything. I was there to be of some good or not at all. I was no joke, and it galled me that I was subjected to a kind of belittling from people who didn't know me from Adam.

Mr. Steele began to point around the table, cigar ash falling in a filthy arc as he named the men. "Mine Superintendent Mr. Marshall. Mining Engineer Mr. O'Brien. Machinist Gallagher, Blacksmith Bruno, and Brick Mason Palmer."

They simply nodded as their names were spoken. I quickly jotted them down. It seemed the workers didn't deserve the same formality. "Thank you, Mr. Steele."

"Now, then, Nurse Stewart, can we begin?"

"Yes, of course," I said. I made a mental note of the men in the room. The Granby men in their suits and their soft pink hands folded on the table. The others were as the matron said they would be, a thickness to them in their coveralls, hands like blackened hooks, sallow pock-marked faces, elbows up on the table and hands propping jutting chins. Hard labourers all. It made me remember the photograph of my mother and the *silver darlings*, physiques like men, broad shouldered and thick in the forearm and leg. A merry crew, unlike the mocking group before me.

The meeting was rather uneventful, nothing that would require a nurse, I thought, as most incidents were of a careless nature, slips on greasy floors, a trip over a mislaid broom, a banged head on a beam, a burn here and there. All was heat and steel in a cauldron of copper-making, after all. Mr. Steele was addressed as Mr. Chairman by the committee, and noted that such minor injuries were quickly remedied at the first aid station. No action was required. I made my notes and nothing came to mind that I could impart to the committee. I was there only to observe. All at once my presence and my position felt a bit impotent. I suppose I could have said, *Well, it is my opinion that absent-mindedness in a smelter could be fatal. You best be telling the boys to pay attention or they'll be sleeping in the cemetery. Mr. Steele, a smelter is no place for a mutton head.* But how odd that most of the injuries were near the furnaces. A man wouldn't dare doze next to a volcano, the bubbling conglomerate, now would he?

As the meeting seemed to be coming to an end, I thought it quite appropriate to say something at last, perhaps express a certain observation. "Mr. Chairman," I said, to be consistent with meeting protocol, "it seems to me that the majority of the accidents took place in the vicinity of the furnaces, in the smelter. Does the committee have an explanation why that might be?"

"Nurse Stewart, may I remind you ..."

"Yes, Mr. Chairman, I understand my role as observer. It is my observation that there may be more to understand."

"The men feel light-headed," Brick Mason Palmer said all at once. All heads turned to him. He had the look of the betrayer, perhaps the bravest of the lot.

"Palmer, there is no evidence of this," Mr. Steele rebutted — the betrayed.

"I've heard it from the others," Blacksmith Bruno said, "and I've personally experienced it. I couldn't finish my shift on one occasion."

The men seemed to be suddenly empowered to speak, thereby empowering me. "I've been sitting here for nearly two hours, Mr. Chairman," I said, "and I cannot recall that light-headedness was raised by the committee. Perhaps it was the very reason the men asked for a nurse. I find this most unusual as it would seem the more serious of the incidents. I believe that committee members should feel comfortable in speaking candidly, Mr. Steele."

"It's the gas," Palmer said, "the long exposure."

"Rubbish," Mr. Steele said. It seemed he was no longer the chair.

"Men passing out hardly seems like rubbish," I added. "Perhaps you can shorten the men's exposure. Perhaps two-hour shifts would be the sensible thing."

"I will not listen to another word, Nurse Stewart. You are not here to make suggestions!"

"Oh, I understand, Mr. Chairman. I am a token of your good-will toward the workers. But the men are suffering from sulphur gas exposure, and it is unclear how much they can tolerate. There may be serious consequences. There are men in the Granby Hospital at this very moment with an unspecified illness. It is surely the gas. I believe the sulphur gas affects the children as well. There have been nosebleeds reported, particularly when the plume settles low over the town. There must be a connection. And as for the men, it seems only prudent to reduce the hours of exposure to maintain their health."

"I will not have you interrupt this meeting, Nurse Stewart, with unqualified statements!" The slam of his fist.

There was a temporary lull, a kind of unsettling realization that the committee knew about the gas in the smelter. And for some reason the men were afraid to speak up. Perhaps another workers' revolt would do it. But I didn't need to enter such provocation as Mr. Palmer got to his feet. In fact, all the men, the thick working men, stood up.

"Hold on there, Mr. Chairman," Palmer said. "I believe the nurse has made a sound case on behalf of the affected men, and I am prepared to bring it to a vote in this committee, or among the men if needed. They will support me in this matter, I can assure you."

"I will not agree to this at a safety meeting!"

"Then what is a safety committee for, sir?" I posited. "Is it not to ensure a safe working environment for your employees?"

"Enough, please!"

"Hear her out," the men said, a chorus, a delegation now.

"Who would bear the cost? Not you!"

"The mine in Phoenix is closing," the blacksmith said. "There are miners coming from the Grand Forks smelter, some expected on this very day. There'll be no shortage of men. That means you're expanding operations. More ore coming out of the mountain. More copper. More money to be made."

"She's here to observe!" His anger rising like the plume, straining over the table, the polished and brilliant table, his last defiant roar. He looked to his managers, who had remained silent, who, it seemed, knew better than he. He sat back in his chair all at once with a thump. The cigar gripped in his fingers, smokeless.

"And I will take my observations, Mr. Chairman," I said, "and my suggestion to the matron of the Granby Hospital, and to the Medical Health Officer. It's a matter of public interest, I would say. I would further suggest that many of the families are unaware of the gas hazard. Perhaps they should know. A young boy or girl shouldn't fear for their father's safety at your mine, sir. Where would you be without your workers?"

I cannot say that the workmen cheered, for they all had good jobs and recognized that such victories had to be tempered with a certain measure of discretion. But as the meeting let out, they took my hand in turn with their thick and lovely but grimy mitts.

Outside I was swelling with pride, a certain satisfaction that was strange for me. The day had turned grey; thick clouds rolled in over the harbour and fused with the smelter plume as if out of kindness. The rain would dampen the stink, and soon it would be spattering over the plank roads like liquid thunder. I needed to hurry back to the hospital, but I noticed the postmaster outside the post office. He was looking my way as if he had been waiting for me. Then he held up his hand. I hurried over to him.

"Yes, Mr. Curly, what is it?" I wasn't expecting a parcel or letter.

"That first question, Miss Stewart."

"Go on, Mr. Curly." I felt my heart lurch in my chest all at once.

"Well, there's been a query not an hour ago."

"Someone asked about me?"

"Yes, that's what I'm telling you, Miss Stewart."

"And what did you tell this person, Mr. Curly?"

"I could only say that one man couldn't possibly know all the residents of Anyox, the way they come and go. That's the truth of it."

"Who was it?" My short breaths.

"He wouldn't leave a name, but he said you'd know him. He came in on that steamship." He turned to the steamer and the great milling of activity. "Most of the passengers were miners. Granby brought in a bunch from their Phoenix operation. I wanted to tell you about it. I hope it's not bad news."

All of a sudden everything began to spin, the wharf and cranes and steamship funnels, all a dizzying confusion, a nightmare that I never thought possible, that I had put away lest I lived my life in fear. I felt weak, my knees sinking into the wharf, into the sea.

"Miss Stewart, are you all right?"

His question brought me back from the brink of dissolution. I had to think. I managed to steady myself. I hadn't the time to be indisposed. "Mr. Curly, sir, can you tell me who keeps the passenger manifest?"

"The Canadian Pacific office will have it, I'm sure. There, beside the general store."

"Thank you, sir, I'm in your debt."

I didn't hurry, even in the rain, nothing to stand out, nothing to draw attention to myself. I mingled with the shoppers and passengers, walked abreast with them, and ducked under a stranger's umbrella. And inside the steamship office I hesitated. If he was in Anyox, he wouldn't be far. At the desk, I asked to see the passenger list from the steamship that had just arrived. I looked over my shoulder, out through the windows to the wharf, to the movement of bodies hunched in the rain, the familiar and questionable. The clerk returned with a ledger.

"Anyone in specific that I can help you locate, Miss?" she said.

I ran my finger down the list before answering her, my eyes looking for that foul name, the one who had threatened to find me, who had beaten it out the businessman on the *SS Missanabie*, who it seemed *had* found me. I flipped the page.

"Miss?"

And all at once my legs gave way, and my heart tripped with the unthinkable shock. There it was in cursive ink, the curse of his black soul etched into every letter, and more than that. It all became clear. *Quinn McDuff.* The note that fell from my hands into the sea in Vancouver. *I'm not evil like you think.* Oh, yes, you are, I said silently to myself. Yes, you are, stalking me to avenge a black-hearted son's death. A man and his son who had made claims to my body. A nightmare that knew my culpability, that would not let me rest. How could I not have known?

"Miss, an acquaintance, perhaps a fiancé?"

"Where did they take the miners?" I asked her. I heard the desperation in my words.

"I believe the single men, if I'm understanding you correctly, are taken to the bunkhouse down on the flats."

"And they're gone now?"

"Yes, on the electric locomotive, not long ago at all. If you hurry, you may catch up to him. You'll find him. Don't you worry."

I backed away from her. She had it all wrong, as if something lewd emerged from a twisted translation. And behind me, I could hear the rain on the wharf, the falling of the blackened sky. How it roared on the north coast, how it punished, my birthday horror.

CHAPTER
TWENTY-FIVE

IT WAS TIME FOR MY VISIT TO THE SHANTIES, AND NOT A week since the arrival of the miners from Phoenix. There would be new customers, I was sure, and good business for the girls, but I cared less about their financial gain than who would likely be among them. Quinn had a singular mind, driven in the way an animal would be when the season came. But for Quinn the season was as regular as his rages. On a winter night in Dumbiedykes he had left me in a naked heap for refusing his vile wants. A closed hand and all went black. And Jimmy had cared less and scalded me for my suffering and would not spare me from him. I had feared Jimmy, that was true enough, but now I feared Quinn, his father, like the devil incarnate. He had the visage of a depraved man, shadowy, and possessed a sexual hunger that swiftly mutated into violence. I didn't wish to remember those nights, and I abhorred the musky smell of him like rotting cabbage, but I needed every bit of knowledge now, every bit of remembering.

I was trapped in that isolated and godforsaken town, some promise that I had only recently enjoyed now sullied by an unassailable affliction. Not even the plume could surmount it. How was I going to protect the ladies, and more narrowly and immediate, how was I going to protect myself? I could leave Anyox, of course, I considered, board the next steamship and leave him no trace. I would run until he would never find me. But my dear Lizzy was on her way. I couldn't leave. I had to survive Quinn once again, but now it had to be once and for all. I had to know where he was, where he'd go, and when his madness would come for me. Revenge drove him to pursue me to the ends of the Earth, and he had found me.

Goose was waiting for me on the dock beside the *Hecate Queen*. I sensed he looked forward to our short journeys along the harbour. He had a lot to say, most of it an accurate account of Anyox life. The old Norwegian kept an eye on the comings and goings on the water and would know who was new in town — and unapologetically what they were up to. "News in Anyox," he was apt to say, "travels on the plume, touching one and all without discretion."

He tossed the lines and we hopped aboard. "Now you can see, Nurse Stewart," he said, "the snow on the mountain peaks, the new snow. It's come down in the night, lower all the time. Soon you will see snow the likes you've never witnessed. I'll say you've seen a bit of it in Scotland, but nothing like the suffocating snow of the north coast. You'll always see the mountains from Granby Bay, from the sea. There's only one view from the town, all plume and stumps. A never-ending sulphur fog. That's why I take to the water. It suits my temperament. It's far sweeter air."

"It's true," I said, "most days we breathe an uncharitable air."

"*Ja*, now to the shanties."

We moved out into the bay, calm waters and a clear sky to the west. Always Anyox with its own weather, its own clouds and wind. I understood why Goose sought refuge on the water. It possessed a tranquility, a sense of freedom from the cramp of the town. I had considered a question for him, not a question that would incite his lengthy narrative, but one that would require my trust.

"Goose," I said, "it seems Granby is expanding operations. A shipload of miners arrived earlier in the week. And a few of the single men will surely visit Sass and the girls. There might be a rough one in the lot. You would tell me if you came across a man with his anger, a man wanting passage to the shanties?"

"I will deliver no scoundrel, Nurse Stewart. But you must know, if there were scoundrels, they'd come across the footbridges and over the slag."

"Yes, of course."

"No man has harmed the girls. This I know."

"If there were a violent man in town, Goose, who is it that would protect the girls from harm?"

"I don't know the answer, Nurse Stewart. It's a precarious occupation, you must know. There's not many who give a damn about what goes on in the shacks. If one was hurt, people might say they had it coming. I would stand up to a scoundrel who would mistreat them, I surely would."

An old man full of words and gallantry, but one who would surely be wounded in a scrape. "You're a brave man, Goose. I can see that plain."

"Is there some scoundrel you have in mind, a miner, perhaps?"

I led Goose right to the question that I didn't want to answer so quickly. I wouldn't put him in harm's way. "Aren't they all miners?"

"Most of the bunch that came in this week are back in the mine blasting the ore from the glory hole. Not so much in the smelter. Newcomers do the grunt work. They are strong men, and some not to be fooled with. But they know they've got good steady jobs with Granby. They tend to be a civilized lot, but liquor is a short fuse for some. Some like the hotel a bit too much, like flies on a dead thing. The provincial policeman, Cobb, knows paydays and Saturday nights, he surely does, but he defers mostly to Granby on matters of law in Anyox. He sits outside his office most days, smoking his pipe and watching the business of the harbour."

"I had that man for a loafer. And how will he protect the women?"

"Cobb sought a peaceful life in Anyox. But I suppose he wouldn't tolerate a beating."

I let it rest there as we tied up to the dock below the shanties. What I knew pressed against my judgement, made me evaluate the danger Quinn posed. He wanted me, and our meeting was only a matter of time. I could avoid him as much as possible, but still he would find me. I felt a moral responsibility to warn the ladies. More a duty: an allegiance to an uncommon sisterhood. And I remembered Josie's knife under the mattress, my searching hand. I had done it once, killed a man, Quinn's son, as it turned out, his hot blood on my hands. But not again. I was no match for Quinn and his animal strength. The thought of it brought on a strange sensation, a feeling of such visceral dread. I felt a fullness inside my skull. My fingers tingled, prickled, and my face was chilled as the snowy peaks. I closed my eyes praying that whatever it was would leave me, but I was seized by a weakness as if stricken with boneless limbs. I began to wilt like an autumn rose.

"Nurse Stewart," I heard Goose say more than once, but muted and distant.

I didn't answer him. And then I opened my eyes. I was holding my bag and standing with him on the dock. His craggy hands upon my shoulders and then his old worried face. I turned away and looked up to the shacks. Sass was out on the stoop watching, a hand up to shield her eyes from the rickety sun. And then Goose, with his hand under the crook of my arm, guided me up the grade.

"Come now," Goose said, "the girls will look after you."

"What is it, Goose?" Sass asked, concern in her voice to see a nurse in distress.

"Likely the diesel fumes," he speculated. "They can be trouble for some."

"I'll be fine," I said.

Goose left me with Sass at the door. The other girls came out and helped me inside. And then the dark warmth, the sweet perfume of the parlour. They sat me on the floral couch. Outside Goose was yammering through the door.

"I'll be up on the roof fixing it proper," he said.

"It's what we paid you to do in the first place," Sass called back to him.

"*Ja, ja,* I'm not partial to a terrestrial life, you know."

226

"I'll make a pot of tea," Sass said. "Rest up now. It was probably just the old fool with his runaway mouth." She laughed.

The girls sat with me, all attentive and motherly, Melody and Dolly, as pale as sheets as if they never ventured from their burrow. I hadn't seen them in town. Perhaps Goose took them on excursions to Alice Arm, or perhaps down the inlet to the strait. And now they were quiet, just sitting in a kind of floating stillness, the dim lamplight enfolding them like rarified cloth. I lost all sense of my priorities, and when Sass returned with the tea and sat with us, I wasted no time.

"I have word of a dangerous man," I said, barely able to contain what I wanted to say. "He's come in on a steamer. A miner, he is. A brute of a man. I felt I needed to warn you, the way you're isolated from the town. There's no telling when he might show up but ..."

"Slow down, Mary," Sass said. "This is a mining town, after all. Even though we may not be part of it, we *are* part of it. We handle a good amount of roughness. At times it's just playfulness, but there are times when they cross the line. We show them the door, you see. They understand what *no* means, as all I need to do is threaten to notify Granby. That puts the fear in them."

It was clear that Sass was an experienced *madam*, knew the bad and the good, and seemed to have survived well enough. Melody and Dolly were safe under her care. But it didn't quell my fears altogether, as a man like Quinn was not a normal man, not a single working man with a need to lay with a woman. There was something in him that couldn't be denied or controlled, a trait common to the most dangerous of men. I had to press on. Perhaps Sass had known of such a man.

"This man, Sass," I continued, "is a fixated man. Drunkenness gives him a murderous courage. He has no boundaries and pursues what he wants with extraordinary effort. There is no stopping this man. If he wants a particular girl, he will have her. He lives in the shadows. No one knows he is there or that he exists. How can such a man be stopped? He wants dominion over the girl. He wants to own her. Perhaps it is only death that can end it."

"Are you telling us a tale," Melody said, "perhaps a novel you have read?"

"Quite alarming," Dolly said. They both made frightful gasps in jest.

Sass raised her hand. "No, my sweet ladies, Mary is most serious." Then she turned back to me. "Is it pleasure that he wants, or is it the violence that he seeks?"

"I'm afraid his pleasure soon becomes a rage."

"Then, Mary, you said that perhaps only death can end it. And whose death might that be?"

"I'm not so sure, Sass. I don't want to get to such a place. I surely ..."

"*You* don't want to get to such a place?"

I stared at her in the mist of lamplight. She knew as surely as I knew. Just then I realized that my very life was more important than a position, an identity, or what the town thought of me. I had been nothing before. "I don't wish to die in this town."

"Then tell it all now. You can't trust a town, but you're safe with us. There's something more about Mary Stewart. It's all over your pretty face."

"A man has pursued me from Edinburgh. He has arrived in Anyox."

"That's far too short a story, Mary. Is he a husband, or perhaps a jilted lover?"

"None of those."

"Then what is he?"

The silence waited for me. I could feel their holding breaths. "He occasioned the brothels of Edinburgh. It was in Dumbiedykes, a poor ward in Old Town. He was often drunk on liquor and was known to beat the prostitutes when he was finished his business. And no one cared enough to stop him."

"He hurt you?"

"Yes."

"And you have come so far to get away from him. But now he has found you."

"He knows I'm here. It's just a matter of time."

"What's his name?"

"Quinn."

"There are men such as him who have an illness of their passions. Such a hunger may be satisfied for a time, but it will rise once again like the moon, and the wolf will slake its thirst for blood. It cannot be stopped. I've known such men in the gold rushes of the north, Skagway and Dawson, men sick with liquor and lust. Most ended up dead. A bullet from the police, or a knife well hid and then tucked up under the ribs. They have a kind of sickness that can harm without conscience."

"What can I do?"

"I suppose you could leave, Mary," Melody said.

"Yes, that is a possibility," Sass said, "but *you* may have to run for the rest of your life. And I cannot see how that would suit you."

"My young sister Lizzy will arrive in a month's time. I have to wait for her. She is not yet fifteen years old. Perhaps we will leave then, leave without a trace. I will tell no one."

"Until then?"

"I don't know."

"You could stay with us," Sass said. "We will protect you. There are times when evil has possessed a man, and he will die of certain causes. You see, not many know where he's gone. The body is weighted down with a chain. He is taken beyond the tides where he is sunk. Soon there will be nothing but bones and his eternal anchorage. No more worries."

"That sounds so very awful and final. Savage, too, perhaps. But I understand very well why it must be so. You are very considerate, all of you, and I thank you for your concern and kindness, but I cannot bring trouble to the shanties. It is not your fight. There must be another way. I'll find it. I have little choice."

"But Mary, you have already warned us that trouble is on the way. This I must heed and take measures to protect us if he arrives at the shanties. Perhaps someone you trust must be apprised of this."

"Can I chance that a woman's word will be believed? I've been told that it is a man's world in Anyox, and I would be a fool not to believe it. And yes, there is one man that I trust, but I would not expose him to the perils of Quinn. I just couldn't. And the policeman, Cobb, I do not know, but it would be certain that word of my past would come out, and the details ripe for gossip. Granby would surely deport me from their town. Lizzy is a child still, you see."

"You are a strong woman, Mary Stewart. But you know there is no telling when Quinn might appear. He will exploit the moment to his benefit. Perhaps the moon will not rise as soon as you think, or perhaps it is rising as we speak. An animal is both savage and cunning."

"Then I must match him on both accounts, and best him, shan't I?"

I couldn't deny the fact of how comfortable I felt with Sass and her girls. There was something honest and decent about them, in spite of their vocation. They were not sinners. One day I wanted to know more about them, what their lives had been like when they were just little girls and what circumstance steered them to the working life. Still, I could not tell them that I had killed Quinn's son. I so wanted that to remain in Edinburgh. And as Goose manoeuvred the *Hecate Queen* away from the dock, I looked back through the wheelhouse window. They were all outside watching us leave, their hearts full of prayers, and perhaps unsettled by what I had brought to them. I had the sad realization that my employment as a nurse was over, that all my hard work had been for nought. Had I brought it on myself? Every decision that I had ever made in my life was with me in that boat, and every consequence was drifting, drifting, looking for home.

CHAPTER

TWENTY-SIX

I FOUND MYSELF SITTING IN DR. MADDEN'S OFFICE ONCE again, but now Nurse Stricker was with me. I couldn't think what the reason was, what I had done, which could have been any number of things. Perhaps it was concerning my probation. I felt a little anxious, you see — more than that, really. I was in an awful state. I had seen him. I had seen him in the street outside my window. It was the same way that I had noticed Dr. Trig with Violet, a figure just beyond the streetlight, a shadow, a trace of a man. And now and then cigarette smoke would emerge from the darkness and into the light. A plume from a wretched mouth. Had it been carelessness, or had he wanted me to know that he was there? It had been going on for many nights. What was Quinn waiting for? What game was at play?

"Well, now," Dr. Madden said, addressing me in particular, "you seem to attract controversy wherever you go. Why is that, Nurse Stewart?"

He sat back in his chair and laced his fingers, a habit of his that I had found rather intimidating. That serious regard. I had to answer him, of course, but my enthusiasm was waning to say the least. "I suppose I can see where change is needed, sir," I said. "And there will always be those who are threatened by it. I observe and then offer some practical suggestions on any given matter. I don't believe I'm wrong in doing so, Dr. Madden. I'm intelligent and willing to get things done. That is all." The great strain of my composure.

"When did you get so creative?"

"I've said it before, sir, that I'm certain that the Scottish Enlightenment had an influence on me. It was a period of great creativity in our history. I don't strive to be creative or set out to prove one thing or the other. I look at what's presented or asked of me. I'm a common girl who's had to outsmart the others. A woman finds herself disadvantaged at every turn, it seems to me, overpowered by men. Now, take no offence, but I would like to change that."

"Hmm."

"Does that answer your question, sir?"

"Perhaps the matron can enlighten you on why we are here this morning."

"I took your notes from the safety meeting," the matron said, "and made our recommendations. We received an official letter from the Granby Mine Manager in response —"

"I must say, Nurse Stricker," I interjected, "that Mr. Steele was not too pleased with my point of view. He more than once tried to silence me. Well, that seems to have an opposite effect with me, I'm sorry to tell you. Perhaps you know this by now. And Mr. Steele was a bit condescending, a boorish man, really. The workers, though, seemed to appreciate my effort a great deal. I was only —"

The matron interrupted me. "Allow me to finish, Nurse Stewart."

"Yes, of course."

"Mr. Steele, although reluctant at first, agreed to restrict the shifts in the smelter to two hours for each man, to reduce gas exposure. He went on to say that this change has greatly improved relations with the workers. He was duly impressed with your grasp of the matter, to use his words, and your tenacity."

"Oh, my goodness, it's what I had hoped for. Can it be true?"

"He didn't stop there," Dr. Madden said. "Mr. Steele has made available to you, and your sister, who I believe will arrive in Anyox shortly, a new bungalow near the elementary school. He believes that you have earned it. And so do I, as a matter of fact. Now, it seems to me that you would make a rather productive administrator

— with proper training, of course. I am willing to recommend that you attend the University of British Columbia. You have a quality that is not so easy to define. Your suggestion that the schools should take measures to prevent sulphur gas from entering the schools on 'weather inversion days,' as you called them, and therefore eliminating the ensuing nosebleeds, headaches, and such, has been well received by the Anyox School Superintendent. I would like you to be a liaison with the school district as it relates to the children's health in general, as well as the mine. As for the brothel, just continue on with your inspections, as there has been a noted decline of a certain condition. Of course, you must keep up with your nursing duties."

"I don't know what to say, sir," I said. I truly didn't. Everything was falling into place, and yet falling apart at the same time. How could that be? It felt both satisfying and cruel.

"I must say, Nurse Stewart," the matron said, "I had my doubts about you. I confess that I don't understand your ways at times, how you are with the patients. But I have seen the results. Even Nurse Daly seems to be benefitting from your ethic of late. The hospital is a kinder place now."

"Thank you, Nurse Stricker." I couldn't say another word.

I should have been joyful, *over the top with happiness,* as they say. I was at the cusp of a dream coming true, but I had been afraid to dream in a dreamless world. I had only wanted dreams for Lizzy, for her good heart. There had always been something snapping at my heels, the fangs of poverty, and the sorrow of our motherless flat in Dumbiedykes that gnawed at my bones. And now the dogs of doom were close and would soon be knocking at my door.

All through the following days I thought about my good fortune, but couldn't enjoy the thrill of it, or my future possibilities. They had always been luxuries unavailable to me. I slowly began to realize that none of it would come to be with Quinn stalking me. How could I manage the expectations Dr. Madden and the matron had for me when each night I could feel the loom of him outside my window? It was all very traumatic, a constant tension that wore me down, that had me up most nights. Finally, I could no longer bear the waiting, the never-ending alarm of his presence. I could feel the very real unravelling of my mind and wits. I had to go to him before Lizzy arrived. She would be exhausted and in a fragile state. I had to meet the tormentor, and on my terms. His mad vengeance had to die. But I needed a plan, something decisive and absolute.

One night he never came, never coalesced with the vapours of the liquid dark. Something had changed. In the morning before my shift, the time had come. I would go down to the harbour. I felt an urgency now. I had seen knives at the general store and had stopped to look at them, how they would fit my hand, how I could conceal them. I had looked, but the thought was terrifying. I had used a knife on Jimmy out of desperation, for my survival, to save my very life. It wasn't planned at all, although in my mind I had thought it. So different it was now, more a plan of murder than self-defence.

The day was cool and without a breeze, as if the world were holding its breath. I wore my green coat over my uniform, my tam, and my Stewart shawl. A man approached, coming unhurriedly up the hill. I was diligent, alert to my surroundings, and rightly suspicious, but the man had the floating robes about his feet. It was Pastor Burke. Now I didn't wish so much to speak with him, but my present circumstance was rather unpredictable. His appearance was serendipitous. I had a request to pose to him, but he would need a certain persuasion.

"Miss Stewart," he said, "how good to see you about."

We stopped on the plank road overlooking the harbour. A moment of awkwardness between us. "And you, Pastor Burke."

"I haven't seen you at our Sunday service. I would be most happy for you to attend."

"At our meeting on that rainy summer day, we were a bit at odds regarding a certain matter."

"That is true, Miss Stewart. I remember quite well our discussion. You felt a need to visit the ladies of *the shanties*. I must say that I was disappointed."

"They are lovely girls, Pastor Burke. Perhaps one day you can see them as such."

He turned on his feet, taking in the breadth of the town, as if conjuring up some wisdom. Then he turned back to me. "The sexual act must be reserved for procreation purposes in a civilized world, Miss Stewart."

"That must explain why men are so driven to make babies. They want a baby all the time, it seems."

"Your humour is annoying."

"You wish the world to be as *you* wish it to be, Pastor. A contradiction, don't you think?"

"How do you mean?"

"You presented the ladies with your emphatic moral wishes and, as it turned out, a bookmark. And in return you gladly submitted to what they could offer you. Perhaps you are trying to be someone you are not. You're a human being, after all. You cannot will a dog to purr. And I'm wondering, Pastor Burke, why you keep a book of young men who frequent the shanties? Is it a card you keep up your sleeve?"

He stood nodding his head in agreement, all slack in his shoulders. "I try, if you can believe that," he said. "And I'm sorry to say that it's not just young men who cross the footbridge. You would be shocked to know who they are. I deeply regret my intrusion now. You caught me at a fool's game, Miss Stewart. Please forgive me."

"I have not repeated my observations to anyone," I said, "and I will not say another word about this topic. However, Pastor Burke, there is one thing you could do for me."

"Yes."

"If something were to happen to me, I would like your assurance that you and your congregation will see to the well-being of my young sister Lizzy. She will soon arrive from Edinburgh. She will need a certain guidance, and always a gentle hand. She's far more God-fearing than I will ever be."

"That is a strange request, Miss Stewart, but I will do as you wish."

"Thank you, Pastor."

We parted on a better footing that day, something undeniable between us now. I forgave him for something that did not need forgiving. But I hadn't asked for his forgiveness for my guile, for my ruse. I kept the truth just out of reach — like I had done with everyone. All the sins of Anyox, and what I planned to do was the greatest sin of all.

The harbour as usual was a busy place to be. At the far end of the wharf a barge took on the copper slabs, what the smelter made of the earth and what made a prosperous life. I stopped near the Granby offices. I had something urgent on my mind, a frightening proposition. But still I looked up at the room above the bank. It always made me feel hopeful, and for what, I didn't quite know. Then his voice.

"So, what has your interest up there, Mary?"

I turned to him, and if I hadn't been so dreadfully distracted, I might have blushed. "I'm always seeing how the weather will be," I said.

"Plume today," Sandy Hall said, "and plume tomorrow." He stood with his cane, no broom on that day.

"That is so true," I said. "And no *Nurse Stewart* today?"

"Excuse my lack of formality, but *Nurse* is a title and not who you are."

"Yes, please do call me Mary."

"I must admit that I've been trying to muster the courage to ask you to tea at the café. A friendly chat with a friend."

"A friend?"

"I hope so."

A man with a gentle disposition, looking down at me with such kind regard. I had hardly considered that characteristic, only that it suited me. He was much like Allan Rose, perhaps not as bashful. They were both decent young men. Decency. It seemed to be such an overlooked word. "Why is it that you need the courage, Sandy?"

"I worry that my bad leg would offend you. Just now, speaking of it makes me feel self-conscious. I hope you don't mind my candour."

"My father lost a leg in a terrible accident in Leith. He hobbles about with difficulty, complains at times, unable to work. I suppose that's why I'm here. He is more than a man with a missing leg. He is a whole man, nothing less. And you can see that I have all my limbs, and that I walk about without trouble. But, Sandy, you must know that I have the same trepidation."

"You?"

I wanted to remain in his presence all of that day, but I couldn't continue any longer. There was no life to dream of, no other to share it with. He knew nothing of my crippled past, a disability that he couldn't see with his own eyes. And he couldn't know the plan that I had to carry through. We stood rather restlessly, as something that couldn't be said whisked away the goodness of the moment. Then all at once he looked beyond me, shifted his body, and tilted his head, as if to understand better what he was looking at. Curiously, I turned and was suddenly aghast. The malignant Quinn, and not an arm's length away.

"Can I help you, my dear fellow?" Sandy said.

"You're awful chummy with the lady here," Quinn growled.

"Excuse me, sir?" Sandy said, a reasonable response that I knew would only incite misfortune.

I stepped toward Quinn, who stood solidly before us. A part of me wanted to protect Sandy Hall, his innocence, his good nature. "You leave him be, Quinn," I said. "You have no quarrel with him."

I was emboldened by the presence of the crowd on the wharf and my grave circumstance.

"I only want another chance," he said. "I have a proper job now. I'm a changed man, and you must see it."

"I told you before to leave me alone. I want no part of you. Do you understand?"

"It's your thinking on the matter. We're not done. Don't you see?"

"Mary," Sandy said, "do you know this man?" Such disappointment and disbelief in his voice.

"Yes, I know him." I hardly recognized Quinn in the light of day, his cap pushed back to expose his rough, menacing features. But there was another look to him, a crushed aspect, as if a mirror of his inner mind — all broken glass, shards of thoughts, deeds, and intentions. He seemed pathetic now, even pitiable, but his puny pig eyes regarded Sandy Hall the way one would greet an enemy. His nature unpredictable like an unlit fuse.

"You could be my wife, you see. This town is fit for us both."

I had to find a way through, some measure to send him away forever. I had no knife, and if I did, the blade would have to find its way through his coveralls and coat and the armour of his chest. And the witnesses would certainly favour him. So the truth that had followed me around the world was sure to come out now, but I no longer cared.

"I hate you, Quinn," I said looking straight into his black eyes. "I always have and always will. There is no you and me, or us, and never will be. What you think and what has happened in the past is rubbish. The errors I have made in my life haunt me still, but you will not be a part of another breath. You have a sickness of mind, a predator hunting me like meat. So be gone with you!"

Quinn began to tremble, a volcanic shuddering. He stood, his mouth parting to speak but his words wouldn't come. I moved back. I wanted to get Sandy away. The crowd on the wharf had all turned to us, hands to their mouths, a spectacle of uncertain outcome before them. And then Quinn turned to Sandy and raised a stabbing finger, his glare like firebrands.

"This one you fancy is an Edinburgh whore," he said, "nothing more. She didn't tell you? She's bedded a hundred men for lust and shillings. I've had my share of her flesh. And you will not have her. No man will ever have her again, I swear. She's a killer! She murdered my —"

A body lunged past me, Sandy Hall with his hands clutching and reaching for Quinn's throat, but he stumbled on his weak leg and fell heavily onto the wharf. And like an animal Quinn was upon him, pummelling away with his meaty fists. And then out of the crowd, a voice called out, a warning directed at Quinn. It was Mine Superintendent Marshall. He was with the policeman, Cobb. They rushed up and the superintendent pulled Quinn away.

"You, get back to work," he said. "Go on, or you'll collect your pay and be shipped out. The Company will not tolerate such a public display. Do you hear me now? Back to work!" The superintendent helped Sandy to his feet, dusted him off, as Quinn sulked away.

The crowd moved haltingly, then returned to their business as if nothing had happened at all. But the look on Sandy's face showed something far different. It seemed that something had been stolen from him, and he didn't understand what or why. Was it a future, our future that he had kept in the sanctuary of his mind? And as his hopes and dreams fell through his fingers like sand, I couldn't bear to look at his awful sorrow.

CHAPTER
TWENTY-SEVEN

IT SEEMED THAT MY LIFE COULDN'T TOLERATE A MOMENT'S respite, as old Goose rushed toward me, his waving arms and jabbering. Such commotion at noon stopped the citizens of Anyox once again to see what calamity had visited their harbour sanctum for a second time in minutes.

"Melody is in a bad way, Nurse Stewart," he said breathlessly. "You must come to the shanties!"

"Slow down, Goose, and tell me what has happened."

"She can't draw a proper breath. Something in the lungs. Coughing herself blue. The *Hecate Queen* is waiting. Please come at once!"

I was jolted out of a kind of torpor, of fear and dismay, the very worst of moments when there was only the suffering truth. And Quinn watching as he loaded supplies onto a railcar, never quite done, never finished, and Sandy Hall retreating with a devastating silence, wanting to get away from me. And now such urgency, perhaps what I needed lest I fall down and die another sad death.

"All right then, Goose," I said. "I'll need to run to the hospital for my bag."

I hurried up the plank road with the *clop clop* of my feet not unlike my rampaging heart that I feared would stop at any moment, no longer able to endure my torments. But by some miracle I endured the uphill grade and then to the hospital and up the stairs. I called out to Nurse Stricker as I burst through the door, and she met me at once, always her demeanour alert and prepared for anything.

"Get it out now, Nurse Stewart: what is it?" she said waiting for whatever disaster had visited Anyox.

"It's Melody," I said, trying to catch my breath. "She lives in the shanties, as you may know. She can't breathe. Goose said there's something terrible in her lungs. A bad cough. He was quite frantic. I would say she needs to be brought into the hospital, but I need to attend her at once. Goose is waiting at his boat."

"Stay calm, Mary. It is likely a respiratory ailment, congestion in the lungs. She will not be coming here, I'm afraid, infecting the population and such. So take your provisions, sheets and towels, pine oil. Surely they will have a kettle. Get the steam going. You've seen it before."

"Yes, Nurse Stricker. I know the treatment."

"Go, then, and advise me accordingly when you return."

I went right to the supply room and stuffed my nurse's bag with the necessary supplies. And as I looked around the room to make sure I hadn't forgotten anything, I spotted a tray of surgical scissors of various sizes, and one with long, sharply pointed blades. Without thinking, I took it. I wrapped it in a cloth and slipped it into my coat pocket.

And then back down the hill to the harbour with my mind occupied with duty and usefulness. I wanted to help Melody. I quite liked her, her humour, and what she did for Tom Haney. But more than that, it was clear that the ladies were on their own on the edge of town, not so much outcasts, as they were tolerated, but inescapably deplored. There were a few, however, who thought them human beings. Goose was one of them. He took my bag and helped me aboard the *Hecate Queen*. Soon we were off on the short jaunt to the shanties. He said not a word, so fond of the women who teased him and made him feel worthy and not a caricature of some other's making. Sass met me at the dock.

"Hurry now," she said, "there's something awfully foul and alive in her chest."

"She must be treated here," I said.

"I guessed as much."

"I'll be back to fetch you, then, Nurse Stewart," Goose said. "Granby shareholders want to see a bit of Alice Arm. Shoot a bear or drink their expensive whiskey. Melody is in good hands; that I know."

Inside the vault of the brothel I could hear Melody at once. A cough like the seals in Granby Bay, and then the wheezing and gurgle of her congestion. I removed my coat and tam and set them on a chair, fleetingly aware of the scissors hidden there and why they were there at all.

"Put a kettle to boil, Sass," I said, "a full kettle now. I'll need a basin of hot water."

I went into Melody's room, the warm amber of lamplight. Dolly stood beside her with a damp cloth and patted her brow, speaking softly to her. She turned to me with a conceding smile. Melody was as pale as the dead-bleached trees, her hair wet with perspiration, and she tossed and turned as her breath laboured, and then stopped all at once. I set my bag down on her bed. She looked up at me, expressionless, her mouth open as if the life inside her had stalled. I waited, alarmed. And thankfully a fit of coughing drew bits of blood and phlegm. Then the great heave of her chest and strings of mucus ejected like green vomit. Her face, wet-hot and pink with the painful effort, but only for a moment. She quickly paled as if her blood had drained away.

"We'll get that out of your lungs," I said calmly as I could, "but not all at once. We'll draw it out a bit at a time. You'll breathe easier in no time at all."

Sass soon brought in the basin of hot water and set it on a table. I took a cloth and soaked it, then wrung it out. I wiped the percolation of dribble from Melody's chin and neck. At times it seemed her breath wouldn't come, and she struggled and fought for it, and then as her body knew what to do, she would cough and hack until the hard stones of mucus were borne from her mouth. A fetor of sickness. Then I helped her to the edge of her bed so that she was sitting. The table was moved before her. More hot water was added to the basin, and drops of pine oil. I placed a towel over head, and she leaned over the basin and slowly drew the rising steam into her clogged lungs. Little by little her lungs loosened and her cough urged it out, expelled the long, ropy infection.

We continued for the remainder of the day, adding more steaming hot water, and silent in our ministrations, for in silence, I had learned, things were healed and forgiven. Words seemed to get in the way and were strangely unnecessary. It seemed that the worst was over. Melody rested as I stood and watched her, watched Dolly lovingly hold her hand. They were all in that life together, I thought to myself, so committed to each other. I wanted the town to know them, that they weren't bad, that they weren't unlovable creatures. There were reasons for the circumstances that brought them there. Destiny, perhaps, and not immoral and iniquitous ambition. There was nothing more for me to do. I would leave towels and pine oil. Then Sass returned from outside.

"It's nearly dark," she said, "and Goose should have been back a while ago. Perhaps Granby is not done with him. They're mostly drinking excursions, he'll tell you. But if you must go across the slagheap, Mary, you must go now before darkness falls ever deeper like a funeral. I'll take you as far as the other side with a lantern. The smelter lights will guide you to the footbridge."

"Then I should go at once."

Sass held the lantern ahead of me as we set out across the trail. Darkness arrived like a shutter in the mountains and it soon swarmed about us. But the track was well worn with foot traffic, and broken bottles littered the way — sea-green shards of glass catching the lantern light like beacons for sinners and skulkers. Sass turned to me.

"That fellow hasn't showed up," she said.

"I pray he never will," I said simply. There was nothing else to say.

"Anyway, we're closed for business until Melody mends. If you come across a boy with an itch, turn him around."

"Yes, of course," I said, "and Melody's a sweet girl. She should see a proper doctor. Every ailment comes your way."

"That's the chance you take when the town has no use for you, other than satisfying a young man's desires. A secret society, they are. But we're a public service and no different than the post office." She laughed.

We came to the edge of the slagheap where the lights from the smelter showed the trail well enough, and the footbridge beyond.

"You'll be fine now," Sass said. "And thank you for caring for Melody. I believe we have a friend in you, Mary. Now that rarely happens. Most people shun us like lepers."

"We have something truly in common, Sass."

"We must talk more about that."

"Yes, one day we will."

As I began to walk past her, I hesitated and reached out with my hand. She took it and we embraced momentarily. It was a loving gesture, but sadly it felt more like a farewell. I watched her walk away, back along the track toward the shanties, the lantern swinging in her hand. The light faded and then she was gone.

The plume above me was close and flared in pulsing clouds, illumined in the smelter lights. And the burn of it in my throat with each breath. I looked out from the edge of the slagheap to the streetlights that dotted the town like a necklace, a string of pearls in the ink of night now. I started down the grade toward the footbridge. The grind of the smelter and the engines of the powerhouse occupied all sounds. Falls Creek flowed silently in a ribbon of molten silver, its sheen broken only by the piers of the footbridge.

I was startled briefly by the sudden appearance of someone on the bridge just as I stepped onto it, bookends of humanity out on a chilly autumn night. It was a man, broad shouldered, a miner no doubt, and as he walked toward me, I knew that I would have to break the news. The shanties were closed due to an unfortunate illness to one of the ladies. It would disappoint him, but the circumstance would surely be understandable. He wasn't walking very fast, an unhurried look to him, all black silhouette. But as I neared him, I noticed something in his hand. I stopped in the middle of the footbridge all at once and took hold of the wood railing to steady myself. I was seized by the realization of my fatal error. The man was no ordinary john, not a customer at all. He had been waiting for me. It was Quinn, and he was holding a length of pipe.

I reached into my coat pocket but couldn't loosen the scissors from the cloth I had wrapped them in. He was only a few steps away now. His breath smoked in the cold air.

"I knew you'd be here," he said, his words slurred. He was surely drunk. "That old fish-eater could take a licking, but he won't be piloting a boat for a while. Perhaps in heaven. All bone and mouth, that one."

"No, not Goose! You're a coward, Quinn, and you will surely burn in hell!"

"Wouldn't you know it," he said in a calm, chilling tone, "the mines in Montana knew Granby. You'll get on in Phoenix, they said. And then my luck really changed. Granby brought me here. That's where I was going all along. And you, Mary, knew that. You knew I was coming. A change of heart is what I wanted. Don't you see, Mary? It would have been easier to kill you that way. And now it seems you have a fella, a cripple no less. I've come too far to burn in hell."

"Why can't you just leave me alone? It's a reasonable thing to ask, Quinn. Leave me be and no one gets hurt."

"I know pain. I'm not afraid of it. You killed my only child. You killed young Jimmy. You thought you got away with it. But that's not true. Are you afraid, Mary?"

"There's a sickness in you, Quinn. You're not in your right mind."

"My mind is voices. The priests might liken them to God."

"Then you're surely sick."

"The miners think you some kind of heroine. But no, I had to set them right on the matter. The whole town will know who you really were. It'll be no loss."

"But you have a good job. Why ruin it?"

"There will only be your bones. That bad water will surely wash them clean. Who could say how you came to the water — killed yourself for your shame, they'll think."

There was no reasoning with him. All talk was futile, always a fruitless endeavour. I needed to get back to the shanties, to the safety of numbers. Sass would have a remedy for a raving drunkard. I turned to run back, but he lunged and seized my arm and pulled me back to him. I screamed but all was mute and lost. And then his hideous grunt as the pipe came around. I turned away, but it struck me a glancing blow to my head. I toppled to the bridge deck. I was stunned, unable to move. Warm blood trickled down my cheek and into my mouth. The metal taste of it. I could feel him lifting me, his big awful hands. And he began to speak, a guttural string of curses and condemnation affixed to his liquored reek.

"You're damned now," he said. "The cyanide waters will be your tomb. No man will have you. No man will look upon you ever again. The death of a whore and murderess will not be grieved!"

My arm swung uselessly as I fought for my pocket. He was going to pitch me over the railing into the roiling water. I managed to kick at the railing as he tried to push me over, braced myself against it. I raged but it seemed all in vain, drowned by the deafening smelter. I managed to find my pocket at last and took hold of the scissors, but I still couldn't loosen them from the cloth. But I was desperate and as I pulled them out, the cloth fell away. I stabbed at his arm repeatedly, hacked through his thick coat. He let go with a terrible howl and I fell heavily onto the bridge deck. I tried to scramble away, but he caught my arm and dragged me back.

"You terrible bitch woman, you cut me!" he snarled, then drove his boot into my ribs.

The wind was knocked from me, but still I looked up at him. "I'll fight you to my death, Quinn!" I swore. I still had the scissors gripped in my hand, and with all my might I drove them into his leather boot, into the top of his foot.

He roared and reared back against the railing, a man slow and staggering. And in an instant, I spotted the pipe on the bridge deck. I took it and swung at his legs. It made a sound like cracking bone. He leaned over clutching his knees, crazed and wailing and momentarily incapacitated. I regained my feet and stepped back. I held the metal pipe in both my hands, swung it with all the life I had left in me, and struck him on the side of his head. He fell back against the railing, and then the sound of cracking. It was not the bone of his skull, but the splintering wood. The railing gave way and Quinn fell backwards, his brainsick eyes fixed upon me in disbelief, shocked and doomed. He hit the water without a sound.

He went under the footbridge and I turned to find him, to make certain he was gone. But he appeared on the downstream side, his arms flailing wildly. Then I could hear him, the feral bawl of his struggle as the toxic water poured like mercury into his gaping mouth. A violent retching, frenzied gulps for air. He fought for his own life now, fought for a foothold. A man who couldn't be killed, it seemed. In the light of the smelter I watched him crawl toward the creek bank. I watched and I waited. I feared the waters weren't going to kill him. I willed him to die. He staggered and reared up like some beast spawned from the fouled waters. But he wouldn't go down. He slowly turned back to me as if to inform me of his immortality, that he was coming back to finish me once and for all. I fell to the bridge deck, my legs failing, my body broken. I held my burning ribs and watched through the railing. And then I screamed at him from the farthest depths of my suffering.

"No one will look upon *you* ever again. The death of the wretched will not be grieved!"

That distance between us still, that unfinished business, that ungodly moment as he looked up at me from the poison water. He held that pose for an eternity, it seemed, and then he turned and looked toward the creek bank. His head slumped down over his chest. He seemed to teeter, his footing uncertain. And then he heaved himself upon a rock and moved no more.

CHAPTER

TWENTY-EIGHT

I COULD SENSE THE MORNING LIGHT THROUGH MY EYELIDS. The cold of my back. There was a moment when I didn't know where I was, perhaps still in the awful dream, and perhaps even dead. I became aware of the sound, the pulse of the town, the heartbeat of Anyox. I opened my eyes to the smelter above me. It wasn't a god at all, but rather a heartless creation, for I remembered now. I touched the side of my head, the crusted blood. And then people around me, some kneeling, some speaking, but I couldn't understand them. A blanket draped over my shoulders. Perhaps they were praying. And I wondered through my fog who or what they prayed for. Did they pray for the sinners, the copper, the dead trees, or for the earth to continue to give of itself? Did they pray for the gone salmon, or the Tsimshian man and his people? Did they ask him for forgiveness? Did ...?

They helped me to my feet, men in their work clothes — hard hats and carbide lamps. One handed me my tam that he had picked up from the bridge deck. He asked me if I was all right. I wasn't sure.

"That's a nasty gash," another said.

I touched the wound to show them that I was aware of my condition at least. I was cold and felt a steady throb in my head and ribs, but I had survived. I was alive. I painfully placed my tam back on my head, over my blood-matted hair, and then slowly turned to look downstream, below the footbridge to the creek bank. Quinn was still humped on the rock, his legs flagging slightly in the white-frothed current. Men were assessing the situation, how to remove him. One of them I recognized as the policeman, Cobb. He was instructing two men with a gurney. I watched in a rather detached way. It took four of them to lay him out, as Quinn was a large man, imposing even in death.

Then Cobb looked up. He regarded me from that distance for a moment, then proceeded along the creek bank. A labouring man, Cobb gained the path to the footbridge, his pipe smoking in blue puffs. I could smell it, its sweetness against the stink of the plume. As he approached, he looked at me, not aghast but appalled somehow.

"You seem to be fit enough, Miss Stewart," he said. "You'll need to come with me. Murders are a rarity here. The first one that I have attended."

"Murder?" I said. Such a strange word to hear.

"That bloke's head is caved in, punctures in his arm, and a pair of scissors stuck in his foot. Yours, I surmise."

"I don't think you should surmise anything, sir." I looked for the iron pipe, but it was gone, perhaps had fallen with Quinn. There was only the broken railing and drops of dried-black blood on the bridge deck. But Cobb didn't seem interested. It seemed he had made up his mind.

"Well, I'll sort that out at the police station. A man's dead and the cause will require a thorough investigation."

"I'm innocent of whatever you think I've done."

The workmen crowded in to listen. Cobb waved them away. "Back to your duties," he said. "Nothing more here."

"There's a reason for all this, Mr. Cobb. Please listen to ..."

"You'll have your say, Miss Stewart."

"Yes, sir." I thought it best to be civil, even to the incompetent.

"Now, please hold your hands out in front of you. I require you to be in restraints under the circumstances. It's a matter of public safety."

"Handcuffs, sir? I don't believe that's necessary."

He didn't answer and removed a pair of handcuffs from his belt. He placed them over my wrists and locked them with a key. Something wasn't right. I felt like a criminal, a true *murderess*. But that wasn't so. I was overcome with a sudden impotence, an inability to mount any kind of defence of myself. Cobb led me off of the footbridge and on to the next bridge. We crossed Hidden Creek under a dark brooding sky and onto the plank road where some of the men stood along the verge of stumps and industry. Some drifted away, back to the smelter, back to the shops and the mine. A Chinese family watched, the mother pulling her children back. Cobb walked in front of me, the constable in his uniform, drawing on his pipe. He seemed to have grown taller. Perhaps he was elevated by my apprehension, my capture, and perhaps my guilt. He seemed to have taken great pride in leading me up the plank road, a certain air to the man. But I wouldn't have it.

"Mr. Cobb," I called out to him. "I should go to the hospital, sir. There's no need to take me to the police station. I took a blow from a pipe to my head. Please reconsider your presumptions."

"Don't waste your breath, Miss," he said half-turning to me.

I raised my clasped hands to straighten my tam, my shawl and bloodied coat, the same green coat I had worn since I had left Edinburgh. I remembered how lovely Uncle Calvin thought I looked that day. My father was proud, Lizzy too. How grown up I had felt, how fearful but resolute. And now I must have been a dreadful sight marching up the road, perhaps how one would imagine a killer. All things in bitter disintegration. The whole town would surely know now, as spontaneous as the summer fires, as if they were of one mind, appendages to the Granby will. What would they do with me? It began to penetrate my consciousness, the circumstance I had found myself in. Would I go to the jail, imprisoned like Mary, Queen of Scots? But it wasn't for long, as she was sentenced to death at Fotheringhay Castle, her scaffold draped in black cloth, a cushion for her bended knees. And before the executioner's axe came down to sever her head, she whispered a prayer: *Into thy hands, O Lord, I commend my spirit.*

I had a way to frighten myself, but I couldn't allow such thoughts to vanquish me. Lizzy needed a sister, and I would make no prayer to an unknown God. And then, the sound of footfall, the unmistakable feet on the plank road. I turned, and how strange to see Brick Mason Palmer with the other men from the safety committee walking behind me, workmen abreast. Perhaps they were ensuring my incarceration, a duty to a fallen mate. But that wasn't so at all. And on we went through the flats and up the hill, marching slowly behind the unaffected Cobb, who was occupied with his singular duty. And townsfolk began to appear along the side of the road, coming out of their houses as if a parade were passing by, holding their children in their arms, but not a waving hand among them. Of course, they all wanted to see me, what evil had been routed from the flats, condemned me at every lot.

Some began to call out. "Shame," one said. "Whore!" said another as she covered the ears of her child. Even the pastor was standing outside his church. What was on his lips, castigation or perhaps a call for leniency? It was then when I remembered the Stewart motto: *Courage grows strong at a wound.* I had been wounded over and over, and now fought for the courage to look into his eyes, a solicitation, a plea. But I could not. I looked straight ahead and passed the Anglican church, and then I noticed Pastor Burke starting back down the hill. He never looked my way. I suppose he couldn't tolerate what I had done. I turned to watch him with my own burning intolerance. But much to my utter disbelief, he fell in line behind the workers to join a growing number of marchers. That's when the pipe-smoking Cobb turned to see what the commotion was behind him. Oh, he knew at once what it was and picked up the pace. Get it over with. Well, that's just what I needed, the footed-thunder of dissent. Bring the thousands to the streets.

The plank road was a unified concussion of sound now — like the thumping shields before battle, the collective tattoo of the ancients I felt new strength in my stride, encouragement rising in my heart. Up ahead at the crossroads that led down to the harbour, a crowd had gathered. They were waiting for the procession, it seemed, not wanting to miss the spectacle of a lifetime. Those who admired me or despised me, I wasn't sure. Violet Daly lifted her hand, tentatively, but a gesture nevertheless. And Mrs. Moffatt and Mr. Curly, partners in crime, nodded in support. I had hope that all wasn't ravaged, that my life still had a chance. I turned to them not with a look of self-pity or humiliation, but one of clarity and sovereignty. It was if the sinners of Anyox had come to make reparations.

Then the last stretch of the plank road was coming to an end, down the hill to the harbour, to the police station. I didn't want it to be over. It began to rain and the road was at once slick and silent. I turned and the marchers had stopped. It was if they had done all that they could have done, all that was possible. There was no rallying speech, no furthering the cause, no call for a mutiny or a strike. And as I looked at them standing in the cold rain and nodded my appreciation, I was reminded of who was absent. Sandy Hall was nowhere to be seen. I had let him down, that kind man, too conditioned, perhaps, to know what price the powerless pay.

At the harbour, the shaming examination from shop doorways like astounded sheep. The bloodied and rumpled nurse. A divided town, it seemed they believed what they had heard. It was a mercy to be ushered into the police station — and out the window a rising wind and driving rain. The marchers dispersed like melting snow. I hadn't the chance to acknowledge each one of them, thank them personally for their very public affirmation. They had taken a risk, and I only hoped that there would be no repercussions for their courage.

Mr. Cobb took me to the rear of the building, down a dark and narrow hallway to a holding cell. A steel door ajar. He removed the handcuffs and then motioned with his head, saying nothing. And after I went in, he closed the door behind me. But after he locked it, he did manage a few words.

"I suggest you think about what you've done," he said. "A good explanation is better than a bad one. And if you need to speak about the matter, a solicitor would be in order."

I walked up to the door and spoke through the narrow, barred window. "Dear sir, what have you charged me with?"

"You know very well."

"And I suggest you think about what is proper police work, Mr. Cobb. A copper who has made up his mind is a bad copper. I wish to make a statement. That should be your first order of business, should it not? It seems my wrists have been bruised for your convenience, or to enhance your own self-regard."

"That's enough of your snide remarks, Miss," he said. "That kind of talk will only make matters worse for you. There's a prison for women like you in Vancouver. They call it the Oakalla Prison Farm. So, watch yourself."

"There's nothing malicious in my words, Mr. Cobb. I speak only for your benefit. You think of yourself as a fine policeman, a great capture for the crown on this day. But it'll be your bane if you're careless, sir. You'll be remembered one way or the other."

He stood outside the barred door, considering what I had said. He took the time to light his pipe. It was a device of reflection for old men. He drew until there was a good burn in the bowl and then left.

I sat on a hard cot in a cold cell, the meagre light from a window too small to crawl through. It was a grey world in and out, and such dullness made my filthy green coat seem like a flare of hope. A fiction, of course. I was in trouble once again, a policeman holding my fate in his compromised hands. Just as Chief Constable Ross in Edinburgh consulted with Uncle Calvin, I knew Cobb would be speaking to Granby on matters of my containment. I couldn't say arrest, technically speaking, but it surely was just that.

I sat in the stillness of the cell, the only sound the wind blowing against the shiplap outside. And the rain dripped and smeared the window until the world disappeared. Tears would not come, as if life wouldn't allow me even that, only a narrow place to be, a role to play in a dream of some other's making. Who decides now? I wondered fitfully. The cause of my present crisis ran back to Edinburgh and Dumbiedykes — perhaps to my unfound mother. But how could I blame circumstance when I chose every bit of it?

The longer I sat, the more I thought on the matter. Another man dead by my hands. It was utter agony to defend one's actions in one's head, to recount it all. The deaths of Quinn and Jimmy McDuff, father and son, were not the result of my desire to kill or harm another human being. They had removed the *humanness* from our relationship, the conventions of decency. I may have been culpable as a willing party, as I supplied my body as it were, but I had not envisaged being stalked or killed as part of the bargain. All the seemly details would surely come out now, but would it be my defence or my admission?

My fingers were white as candles, chilled and bloodless, and trembled like aspen leaves. I shoved them in my coat pockets to stave off the creeping damp. The ache in my ribs eased now, my breath in longer measures. I waited well into the afternoon before anyone came. It was Cobb, and with him, a visitor.

"Just a few minutes," he said.

I walked up to the steel door. Sandy Hall was looking back at me through the barred window. His mouth opened slightly but said nothing, as if he had withdrawn his words. Then he cast his eyes downward and tried once again.

"Is it true?" he managed.

"Which part?" I said.

He looked up, braver now. "Did you kill that man?"

"It's true that he's dead. But I suppose it was the cyanide in the water that killed him. I'm no killer, if that's what you're thinking."

"They say —"

CHAPTER TWENTY-EIGHT

"I don't want to hear what *they* say, Sandy."

He stood rather uncertain now. "You've been hurt, Mary," he said, coming back to himself.

"Yes, a scratch."

"It's no scratch. You need to go to the hospital."

"I suppose I have bigger problems."

"I saw you coming down the hill and how the miners had followed in behind. The Anglican pastor, too. I was afraid, you see, of losing my job. I was a coward. It's a hard thing to swallow for a man who fought in the trenches of war. That's something to be afraid of, and we all were."

"You have come to appease your guilt?"

"I won't deny that fact. But one can come to his errors by the sickness writhing in his belly. You told me you weren't offended by my sorry leg. That's something. I don't believe what they say, Mary."

"Some of it may be true, Sandy."

"I've done things in war, things I can't speak about, inhuman things to be sure. War gives a man a good defence. He'll die if he's not prepared to kill the enemy first. And he's not particular how it's done. No one asks."

"But I'm a woman."

"I know, but ..."

Cobb appeared at the door just then. "That's all the time, Mr. Hall." He waited for Sandy to leave, and then he pushed his face up against the bars. "The Granby men have gathered. They've made their decision. I'll bring you hot water and a cloth. You can clean yourself up."

CHAPTER
TWENTY-NINE

OUTSIDE THE WIND HOWLED, AN AUTUMN STORM HURLING itself against the puny structures of Anyox as if insulted that they were there at all. The gall of men, the gall of Granby. They weren't the type to be manoeuvred, and I without a string-pulling uncle. Cobb escorted me into the Granby offices knowing that fact was not in my favour. There was a lady who stopped her work to stare, hands still poised over her typewriter. I lifted my chin for her. I had nothing left but my self-worth, which was an uncertain value, I must admit, but when Cobb opened the door to the committee room, I remembered the laughter, the derision. I wasn't done yet.

Cobb sat me at the end of the long table, and immediately all the heads of the managers and shareholders turned to me, regarded me as an arrival from another planet. Cobb sat beside me. He looked toward Mr. Steele, deferring to him, I assumed. Now, I was on good terms with Mr. Steele, impressed him enough to earn a bungalow for myself and Lizzy. Sadly, it seemed I had earned its rescission. There was a murmur of discussion that Mr. Steele interrupted. He raised his unlit cigar.

"As Mine Manager," he began, addressing the table of snowy-haired men, "I have a duty to ensure the efficient operation of the mine. That being said, I would be remiss in not considering the human element of our town. All types live here, from all over the world. It is a town of immigrants as much as Canada is a country of immigrants. We have good workers and not-so-good workers, but we manage good profits nevertheless. One must include a contingency for the unknown that at times someone will go afoul of the law. Mr. Cobb sees that the punishment meets the crime. We have a peaceful town. Anyox is a model community. Labour relations are always a challenge for any enterprise, and work stoppages must be avoided for the good of the company." He paused to light his cigar.

"Excuse me, Mr. Steele," I said, making good use of his hesitation, "but I'm confused. You don't seem to be speaking to me. And I don't understand these proceedings at all. I was placed in handcuffs and paraded along the plank road for all to see. This does not seem to be an impartial assembly. It seems more like a convention of aristocrats, Mr. Cobb excluded, of course." I regretted the sudden ascension of snickers just then.

"I'm speaking to you now, Miss Stewart," he continued. "I will get right to it and spare you further discomfort."

"Discomfort, sir?"

"Hear me out. A man has been killed, and one of our fine nurses was involved somehow. There seems to be a history between you and the deceased. And further —"

"Would you blame a rat for biting the nose of the cat that cornered it?"

"Miss Stewart, if you would allow me to finish."

"Yes, sir."

"The deceased was, let me say, an intolerable disruption in the bunkhouses during his short stay. He incited rumours, and I must say without reservation that Granby will not tolerate drunkenness or rumours. Everyone comes here with a story. And every man in this room has at one time erred in his conduct, and it remains in him as a reminder to uphold a greater vision of himself. Fortunate is the man that the incidents of one's life are not committed to hearsay. Your value to this town will not be expunged by hearsay, Miss Stewart. That's all it is. We are a town set apart from the mainstream society of the south. We will manage our own affairs. I regret your treatment. The working men, from whom you have gained great favour, regret your treatment."

"Thank you, Mr. Steele," I said, "for your judiciousness in this matter. It is heartfelt, sir, as it has not come often in my life. But I must say, if you haven't already noticed, there's a provincial policeman sitting right next to me. He seems to have no regrets at all. Mr. Cobb was more interested in keeping his pipe lit than seeing to my injuries."

A near riot of laughter ensued, but quickly Mr. Steele raised his hand once again and the room self-collected, a rather impressive power he had. He turned his attention to the constable.

"Constable Cobb," he said, "I did not wish to embarrass you, but I believe that you have something to say. One of your clerks brought something to your attention earlier this afternoon."

The constable chewed on his pipe stem. It was all very strange how he had seemed to be the authority, the overseer of law and order, a representative of governance. Something troubled him now. And as the Granby men regarded him expectantly, it was clear that he best answer.

"It was an oversight," he said, then cleared his throat of some guilt, it seemed. "A certain telegraph was received a number of weeks ago from the government wireless station here in Anyox. It described a man wanted for a murder aboard a passenger liner bound for Saint John in June of this year. A notable businessman bound for Montreal was killed. It seems that our Mr. Quinn McDuff was the perpetrator. The provincial police regret this omission and regret the treatment of Miss Stewart."

All that had happened that day, all my pain and outrage, somehow dissolved in my mind as I listened to Mr. Cobb, not due to justice or the reclamation of my honour, but simply because I sadly remembered the businessman, on the train bound for Liverpool and on the SS *Missanabie*. And I didn't know his name.

"Now, if you have nothing further to add, Miss Stewart," Mr. Steele said, "I will end this unfortunate meeting."

I simply shook my head and sat a moment before leaving the Granby offices with the others. There were such terrible things happening in the world, so much suffering. I wondered if it would all end one day, or perhaps suffering was a need in us all that we didn't understand. But something had ended for me. It seemed all a horrid dream now, but it was over. I said a silent prayer for the innocent. And I would go to the hospital before anything else, to sit with the harmless and the blameless.

I looked down at the old man asleep with his swollen eye like a squashed plum, all raw and purple, a rainbow of colour that spread down his cheek and disappeared under his thatch of beard. "Oh, Goose," I whispered, "what did he do to you?" I spoke softly, words that might find that peaceful place inside him, words to his own unseen God. But he opened his good eye.

"I never knew until I woke up," he said.

"But are you all right?"

"A few days in bed, Nurse Violet told me."

"I'm so sorry. I feel responsible. He wanted to get to me, Goose."

"*Ja*, not to worry. They say you got the best of him."

"I suppose I was fortunate. I got a banged head, but I have a thick skull."

"*Ja*, Nurse Violet said that too."

"Did she now?" Then his one eye looked past me. Nurse Stricker was at the door.

"I think Goose should rest now, Nurse Stewart."

"Yes, of course." And then the matron motioned with her head that she wanted to see me in private. I kissed Goose on the forehead, then followed her.

I took my usual seat in her office while she sat looking at me from across her desk, a certain scrutiny now, and a hand on her teacup.

"Are you done, Mary?"

"Excuse me, Nurse Stricker?"

"Do you have any more surprises?" She got up from her desk and moved to my side. She bent to inspect my wound.

"Not that I'm aware of."

"You don't sound so sure."

"Life is full of surprises, Nurse Stricker. Isn't that what they say?"

"I suppose."

"You suppose?" I looked up at her. She had such a look of bewilderment.

"It's a bad abrasion," she said, "but it should heal nicely." She returned to her chair and took up her cup of tea, then sat looking at me once again, her fingers tapping the sides of the cup. She wanted to tell me something, but seemed reluctant for some reason, perhaps afraid.

"I would like a cup of tea," I said.

"I suppose."

"You suppose a lot, Nurse Stricker."

"You are a very insolent girl, aren't you?"

"I suppose I am, Nurse Stricker, but at this moment I would like what you're having. You seem very partial to the lavender, or perhaps it is something stronger. You're never without your cup of tea."

"Nothing gets by you. I should have known."

"Well, then, do I get my tea?"

She smiled. It was such a rare moment. I broke through her defences, her grief, however briefly. It seemed that I hadn't taken the time to know her. She parcelled out the rare bits of herself for my speculation. I had learned that much in Anyox. There was always more to know about people, their stories and their secrets. And I was an open book, more or less, though the chapter on Jimmy McDuff would never be read.

CHAPTER

THIRTY

THE SKY OVER THE HARBOUR WAS LIKE A SHEET OF IRON, hard and cold, and held a darkness that would surely unburden itself over Anyox. The SS *Camosun* was moving slowly down the inlet, through a fog of smelter gas that had settled inconveniently over the water. I finally had a good winter coat, but stood with others shivering in November's mood, but it was not so cantankerous on that day. No frigid squalls to batter Granby Bay. Of course, nothing could keep me away. I only prayed that Lizzy had an open mind when she walked off the steamer, and that perhaps she would forgive me for my omissions, the things I did not tell her about her new home. In time, she would grow to accept the faculty of Anyox, the entity that breathed life into the hearts of a willing people. The sense of family, though strange, and at one time, inconceivable, had unexpectedly worked its way into my affections.

I was beginning to consider my gratitude and what I could do with it. I had never experienced the sense that I was all right, that nothing pursued me, be it poverty, a man, or my past. Perhaps it was only possible in that north land where Granby men thought me worthy as a citizen. It was the Wild West where laws were malleable at times, given the remoteness of the coastal inlets. Robert Steele was a kingly man, perhaps a descendent of monarchs. It seemed at times that I belonged to a country, not to Canada so much, but the tiny dominion of Anyox. Its longevity was in the hands of such men as Mr. Steele, its future seemingly limitless. I knew that commodities ran out sooner or later, market prices changed, and the summer fires, though accepted as part of our lives, threatened it all. But we were all in it together, in our dirty town, however long it lasted.

The *SS Camosun* found the harbour and settled along the docks. Soon it was tied aft and stern by the harbour men and the gangway was lowered and passengers began to disembark. The excitement I felt was tinged with worry. I knew the astonishing breadth of the country and how intimidating it was to an immigrant overwhelmed with fear, uncertainty, and the weight of personal responsibility. There was no one but oneself seeing to one's affairs. And Lizzy was so young. How had she managed? I was about to find out as she appeared at the top of the gangway holding her suitcase.

I hesitated before I called out to her. I wanted to see her for just a moment, know her through and through, just by the way she stood, her hair falling to her shoulders in ringlets and that pout of her own worry as she tried to find me in the crowd. I waved madly to her. And she searched and searched and at last found me. She ran down the gangway, nearly knocking people over, impatient to end her journey, impatient to bury her head into the protected sanctuary of her sister.

She cried and cried and I just held her. And at last she was able to speak.

"Mary, I thought I had come to the wrong city," she sobbed. "The ship went further and further away. But this is it, is it not? This is Anyox."

"Oh, Lizzy, it is."

"And the smell?"

"Ah, yes, the smell. You'll get used to it."

"I'm a bit cold, Mary."

"I have a fire going in the stove. Our house will be nice and warm. A pot of stew simmering all day long."

"A house?"

"You'll see." I took her suitcase. "Come now, Lizzy, up the plank road. You've never seen a town such as this."

I pointed things out to her, the general store, the post office, the library with the new young American librarian, and where the Granby men designed our futures. I stopped momentarily and pointed to the bank. I knew it wasn't much interest to a young girl, but I was looking at the room above it. And he came to the window for I knew he had been watching me. It was a game we played while I wondered if I could belong to a man and Sandy wondered if he could belong to me. Perhaps we could belong to each other. I smiled as I knew that he smiled. One day.

And up the plank road to the crossroads and past the Granby Hotel and finally our street. Lizzy was so taken by the houses, their sameness, the brown cottages with white trim. She spun around and around to see where she had ended up in her life. We stopped in front of our bungalow. Wood smoke rose in a singular thread and then curled away. She wasn't so much looking at her new home as she was looking at the stumps and torn earth, the tortured ground on which every house had been built. And her gaze lifted to the dead hills and mountains, to the smelter across the flats gushing its foggy breath over Anyox.

"I didn't know the world was so big," she said.

"Yes, it's too big to be imagined. But you will know this place, Lizzy. You surely will."

"Mary, there's not a horse and carriage or a motor car anywhere to be seen."

"There's no need, Lizzy. Everything is right here. We need only our feet." I remembered my first day in Anyox, looking out over the demolition of forest and ground. I had the same thoughts. And now I realized that it was best not to describe Anyox with any detail. One had to experience it. And then a peculiar fragrance arrived on the cold air like a messenger, the smell of coming snow.

The snow came like a blessing on that day, flake by flake, smothering the brokenness with such purity. We watched it from inside the house, from its warm-sweater interior. I felt as our mother must have felt, her children safe and home. The snow fell heavily all day long. There was nearly two feet of it when the streetlights came on. It was magical in the illuminated gyre of light. And by the next morning under a blue dome of sky, three feet of snow lay in the yards and covered the plank road in a seamless white ribbon, unbroken and perfect.

AUTHOR'S AFTERWORD

THE FOLLOWING PROVIDES THE HISTORICAL FOUNDATION of people and places that inform Mary Stewart's story.

ANYOX: Anyox was a company town, a copper-mining town built by Granby Consolidated Mining, Smelting and Power Company Ltd., deep down Observatory Inlet near the British Columbia and Alaska border. It operated from 1914 to 1935 and boasted a population of nearly three thousand people. It had the amenities of a modern city: a hotel, a hospital, churches, schools, a cinema, and even a brothel, although it was certainly modest compared to Edinburgh. Granby provided electricity and indoor plumbing to all its company houses, an unheard-of luxury at the time. The town prospered for years until copper prices fell in 1935 and Granby discontinued copper production. Anyox was finished. People left. And in 1943, the final death blow. Always under threat from forest fires, what was once the largest smelter in the Commonwealth was razed by fire that summer.

My grandfather, Herbert Hedley Neil, was born in Prince Edward Island in 1887. He came to British Columbia in 1907 to work in the mines and to play for the very active hockey teams of the day in the Kootenay District. He worked in the historical mining town of Phoenix as a diamond driller for Granby and was eventually sent to Anyox. My father had only a few stories of my grandfather's years in Anyox, which had remained with me mostly as a vague mystery. There was one story, however, that I found in one of the many archives during my research. There was a labour dispute in Anyox in 1916. My father once told me that my grandfather took an injured miner into his company house. The man had been hurt in a skirmish with company sympathizers. It is not much, but still it provides a connection to past and present.

Before my father passed away at the age of ninety-two in July 2019, I visited him in his long-term care facility in Abbotsford, BC. Due to his failing cognition, my brother and sister had set up an improvised method of communication. We wrote questions on a board with a felt pen. Strangely, he could read and understand the questions. I asked him if his mother had joined his father in Anyox. It was something I wanted to know. I wrote the question on the board and, as clear as a bell, he said that she had. I can only imagine my grandfather and grandmother in 1916, travelling from Phoenix, BC, on the Kettle Valley Railway, making their way to the Union Steamship dock in Vancouver's Coal Harbour, then ocean bound for Prince Rupert, and finally to Anyox.

THE SCOTTISH ENLIGHTENMENT: In the eighteenth century there was a period of intellectual and scientific advancement in Scotland that had overflowed from Europe. A culture developed that espoused the virtue of human reasoning; it was humanistic in its endeavours, which included book readings and gatherings of like minds. The movement advanced the fields of philosophy, engineering, medicine, literature, law, sociology, and many other disciplines. One product of the passions of the Enlightenment was the development of the *Encyclopedia Britannica* in Edinburgh between 1768 and 1771. It is the oldest English-language encyclopedia still in print.

JOANNA BAILLIE: A Scottish poet and playwright born in 1762, Joanna Baillie was one of the most highly acclaimed literary figures of her time. She was celebrated as a Scottish woman of letters. She was admired for her lyric poems, which often took the form of meditations on life. The daughter of intellectuals, Baillie was influenced by the Scottish Enlightenment movement. The excerpt that forms the epigraph to this book is drawn from her poem "Life."

ELSIE INGLIS: Elsie Inglis (1864–1917) was a pioneering surgeon in Scotland and, as the headstrong founder of the Scottish women's suffrage movement, advanced issues relating to women's poverty and health. She established a small maternity hospital for Edinburgh's poor on High Street; this later became the Elsie Maud Inglis Memorial Hospital. When war broke out in 1914, she established medical units staffed entirely by women to provide medical aid to some of the most horrific battle zones of the First World War. She served in France, Serbia, and Russia.

SS MISSANABIE: The *SS Missanabie* was a Canadian Pacific ocean liner pressed into service to transport Canadian troops and munitions across the Atlantic during the First World War. The voyage home from Liverpool to Montreal and Saint John included returning troops, immigrants, and orphans accompanied by the Salvation Army. In September 1918, the *SS Missanabie* was torpedoed off the Irish Coast by a German U-boat and quickly sank, with a loss of forty-five lives.

SAINT JOHN, NEW BRUNSWICK: Saint John was the first incorporated city in British North America. In the early nineteenth century, the port experienced a significant increase in shipping demand with Great Britain. It grew to become a strategic point of entry into Canada. A national harbour, it's the site of Partridge Island, a quarantine station built to manage the steady arrival of immigrants. It processed nearly three million immigrants before its closure in 1941. Some two thousand immigrants are buried there, having fallen to typhoid fever, smallpox, and cholera, many of these casualties of the Irish Potato Famine of 1847.

CAPE SCOTT: Danish settlers arrived on the northern tip of Vancouver Island between 1898 and 1907 to establish a Danish community. They planned to live from fishing until such time as a road was built by the provincial government. The government did not build the road as it had agreed to do, and the community could not bring its beef and dairy products to market. Due to the harsh climate and the lack of government support, the community failed and most settlers left Cape Scott.

PRINCESS MAY and SS CAMOSUN: The expansion of coastal communities in British Columbia in the early twentieth century required an efficient shipping and passenger service. The Union Steamship Company, along with CPR Coast Service, served the coast from Vancouver to Skagway, Alaska, often in treacherous weather in waters where groundings and wrecks were not uncommon. Both of these ships made regular stops in Anyox, deep down Observatory Inlet. The *Princess May* was sent to the Caribbean in 1919 and in the early 1930s was deliberately sunk. The *SS Camosun* was sold for scrap in 1935.

SPANISH FLU EPIDEMIC: The epidemic began in Spain in the spring of 1918 and arrived in Canada on returning troop ships. The first outbreak occurred in Quebec in September 1918; the disease quickly spread across Canada as soldiers headed home to their communities; trains carried it with devastating speed. The medical community was powerless to stop it. The first case in Vancouver appeared in early October 1918. Public health officials urged people to avoid contact with others, to stay indoors, and to keep away from crowds. Schools closed, and a ban was imposed on public meetings and sporting events. BC chronicler Daniel Francis observes, "Every place of assembly closed, every meeting stopped, all public amusement curtailed." The infection spread to the BC interior along rail lines and then up the coast on steamships. First Nations communities were hit brutally hard, with a death rate of 46 per 1000 people. (The death rate among the wider public was 6.21 per 1000 people.) In BC the death toll reached approximately four thousand by the time the epidemic ended in 1919. The death toll in Canada reached fifty thousand. Anyox was not spared. Steamships brought the flu to the remote mining town, and dozens died from the epidemic. Ultimately, the Spanish Flu killed twenty-one million people worldwide.

ACKNOWLEDGEMENTS

IT IS IMPORTANT TO RECOGNIZE THAT THE STORY OF ANYOX, its history and ambition, was carried out on the unceded traditional territory of the Nisga'a people. The name *Anyox* is the anglicized version of Nisga'a language for "hidden water." Though I created a story of fictionalized characters and events, the town of Anyox did exist with a kind of audacity that defined a time in our history, when wealthy men, coupled with the brawn of labour, could build an industrial complex and city in the wilderness. Anyox had a short life, and nothing remains except old concrete foundations in an emerging forest and the tall stack from the original smelter. I used the factual name of the mining company that built Anyox, Granby Consolidated Mining, Smelting and Power Company Ltd., to help make the reading experience as real as possible.

The book *The Town That Got Lost* by Pete Loudon, published by Gray's Publishing, provided an invaluable glimpse into life in Anyox. Various online sources of reference and archival material were required in the creation of this book, including the British Columbia Provincial Archives; Regional District of Kitimat–Stikine Archives; Prince Rupert Regional Archives; City of Vancouver Archives; Dent Family History pages; Geoscience Canada Journal — "The History of the Geology of the Anyox Copper Camp, British Columbia"; Union Steamship maps; topographical maps; countless historical photos; and the photos of Leonard Frank from the Vancouver Public Library.

"The Fish Gutter's Song" was a Scottish folksong from the herring boom of the late nineteenth century. The passage quoted from *Safe Counsel* was drawn from my personal copy of the book.

ACKNOWLEDGEMENTS

The book, by Jefferis and Nichols, was published in 1894 and offered at the time as *Light on Dark Corners: Complete Sexual Science and a Guide to Purity and Physical Manhood*.

I would like to thank my editor, Leslie Vermeer, for her precise editing and her careful attention in maintaining the triumphant voice of Mary Stewart on every page; and Matt Bowes, Claire Kelly, and all the staff at NeWest Press, who exceeded my expectations. It was a pleasure working with such a dedicated and professional team.

And I would like to thank my good friends and readers of the original manuscript, Victor Seder and Rick Tough, for their encouragement and always thoughtful review of my work. I would also like to thank Rod Neil, Kathy Parrish, Rick Hansen, Mitch McLellan, Scott Neil, Mark Neil, and Kathy Jameson for their unshakable support. And finally I wish to thank Pamela at Starbucks at Main and Indy in Penticton, Medici's Gelateria and Coffee House in Oliver, and Jojo's Cafe in Osoyoos for getting me out of the house and kindly allowing me writing space.

DANIAL NEIL WAS BORN IN NEW WESTMINSTER, BRITISH
Columbia. He began writing in his teens, journaling and writing poetry. He took his first creative writing course in 1986 and
worked steadily at his craft. His short story "Grace" was published
in the 2003 Federation of BC Writers' anthology. He went on to
participate in the Write-Stretch Program with the Federation
of BC Writers, teaching free verse poetry to children. He won
the poetry prize at the Surrey International Writers' Conference
four times and studied Creative Writing at UBC. His first published novel was *The Killing Jars* in 2006, and then *Flight of the
Dragonfly* in 2009, *my June* in 2014, and *The Trees of Calan Gray* in
2015. *Dominion of Mercy* is his fifth published novel. Danial has
completed twenty novels since beginning his writing journey. He
lives in Oliver in the south Okanagan of British Columbia.